SHOOT FIRST
(THINK LATER)

BOOKS BY STUART WOODS

FICTION

Shoot First[†]

Unbound[†]

Quick & Dirty[†]

Indecent Exposure[†]

Fast & Loose[†]

Below the Belt[†]

Sex, Lies & Serious Money[†]

Dishonorable Intentions[†]

Family Jewels[†]

Scandalous Behavior[†]

Foreign Affairs[†]

Naked Greed[†]

Hot Pursuit[†]

Insatiable Appetites[†]

Paris Match[†]

Cut and Thrust[†]

Carnal Curiosity[†]

Standup Guy[†]

Doing Hard Time[†]

Unintended Consequences[†]

Collateral Damage[†]

Severe Clear[†]

Unnatural Acts[†]

D.C. Dead[†]

Son of Stone[†]

Bel-Air Dead[†]

Strategic Moves[†]

Santa Fe Edge[§]

Lucid Intervals[†]

Kisser[†]

Hothouse Orchid[*]

Loitering with Intent[†]

Mounting Fears[‡]

Hot Mahogany[†]

Santa Fe Dead[§]

Beverly Hills Dead

Shoot Him If He Runs[†]

Fresh Disasters[†]

Short Straw[§]

Dark Harbor[†]

Iron Orchid[*]

Two-Dollar Bill[†]

The Prince of Beverly Hills

Reckless Abandon[†]

Capital Crimes[‡]

Dirty Work[†]

Blood Orchid[*]

The Short Forever[†]

Orchid Blues[*]

Cold Paradise[†]

L.A. Dead[†]

The Run[‡]

Worst Fears Realized[†]

Orchid Beach[*]

Swimming to Catalina[†]

Dead in the Water[†]

COAUTHORED BOOKS

TRAVEL

MEMOIR

[*]*A Holly Barker Novel* [§]*An Ed Eagle Novel*
[†]*A Stone Barrington Novel* [**]*A Teddy Fay Novel*
[‡]*A Will Lee Novel* [††]*A Herbie Fisher Novel*

SHOOT FIRST
(THINK LATER)

A STONE BARRINGTON NOVEL

Stuart Woods

G. P. PUTNAM'S SONS | NEW YORK

PUTNAM

G. P. PUTNAM'S SONS
Publishers Since 1838
An imprint of Penguin Random House LLC
375 Hudson Street
New York, New York 10014

Library of Congress Cataloging-in-Publication Data

Names: Woods, Stuart, author.
Title: Shoot first: (think later) / Stuart Woods.
Description: New York : G. P. Putnam's Sons, 2018. | Series: A Stone Barrington novel ; 45
Identifiers: LCCN 2017050288| ISBN 9780735217201
(hardback) | ISBN 9780735217225 (ebook)
Subjects: LCSH: Barrington, Stone (Fictitious character)—Fiction. | Private
investigators—Fiction. | BISAC: FICTION / Action & Adventure. | FICTION /
Suspense. | FICTION / Thrillers. | GSAFD: Suspense fiction. | Adventure fiction.
Classification: LCC PS3573.O642 S54 2018 | DDC 813/.54—dc23
LC record available at https://lccn.loc.gov/2017050288
p.   cm.

Printed in the United States of America
3   5   7   9   10   8   6   4   2

BOOK DESIGN BY NICOLE LAROCHE

SHOOT FIRST
(THINK LATER)

1

Stone Barrington and his friends Dino and Vivian Bacchetti had just finished a dinner of Caesar salad and Dover sole at Patroon, a favorite restaurant of theirs in the East Forties of New York.

"Oh, by the way," Stone said, "there's a Steele Group board meeting this weekend, and I wondered if you two would like to come?"

"Let me get this straight," Dino said. "You want us to come to a corporate board meeting?"

"Did I mention that it's in Key West?" Stone asked.

"Love to," Dino said.

"Same here," Viv echoed.

"Joan has found a rental house for me, and I'm told it's

comfortable, and she's stocked it with food and drink. Why don't we all stay a few days?"

"I can get some time off," Viv said.

"I'll ask my boss," Dino said. Dino was the police commissioner of New York City.

"The mayor?"

"No, me. I asked, and I said, 'Sure, it's okay, stay as long as you like.'"

"You're a very generous boss," Stone said.

"Thank you. I try to cultivate good employee relations."

"I can back him up on that," Viv said. "When I was his employee, he cultivated relations with me."

"I hope he's not that generous with all his employees," Stone said.

"I hope so, too," Viv replied.

"You can both hope," Dino said. "When do we leap off?"

"Saturday morning. Pick me up at ten. We'll be in Key West by four. The board meeting isn't until Friday, but most of us will be playing in a golf tournament on Sunday and Monday."

"Arthur Steele is getting very generous with his directors, isn't he?"

"Oh, once in a while he'll spring for a jaunt. They're all staying at the Casa Marina, the old hotel built by Henry Flagler, the railroad guy who built the Breakers in Palm Beach and others in the early part of the last century."

"So why aren't we staying there?" Dino asked.

"You want to rub elbows with a lot of suits this weekend?"

"We'll stay with you," Dino said. "Should I go armed?"

"I'm not anticipating bandits in the Keys, but suit yourself."
Dino always went armed.

THEY WERE wheels-up before noon on Saturday, and Stone's Citation 3 Plus made the flight easily in one leg, no refueling along the way.

At Key West International there was an envelope waiting for Stone at the FBO's front desk, containing house keys and a car key and instructions for operating the house, as well as some history of it. The car turned out to be a metallic white Mercedes S-Class convertible with twenty-eight miles on the odometer. They stowed their luggage in the trunk, and Stone put the top down.

"I hope you like freckles on a girl," Viv said. She was a redhead. "Dino will turn the color of mahogany in about an hour, and I try to keep up."

Stone followed the directions in the envelope; their landmark was a strip club called Bare Assets.

"Sounds like a nice neighborhood," Viv said.

"Can we have drinks there tonight?" Dino asked.

"If we do, it will be the only sex you'll get on this trip," Viv replied.

"They don't have sex there, just looking," Dino protested.

"I'm aware of that, and it's all you'll get. How many bedrooms are there, Stone?"

"Four, I'm told."

"Then you'll have two to choose from, Dino."

"Here's a thought," Dino said, "let's stay home and grill some steaks."

"Good idea," Viv replied.

The house was on a narrow lane between Truman Avenue and the island's cemetery. It had a bricked driveway and a garage and a carport, housing a golf cart, and Stone pulled into the garage. They got out and toured the house.

There was a book-lined study, next to an outdoor courtyard, followed by a dining room, a living room, and another, larger courtyard bordered by a koi pond, and beyond that there was a spa and a sunken swimming pool, all of it surrounded by jungle-like vegetation and flowers.

"Stone," Viv said, "this is spectacular!"

"We haven't seen the guest rooms and the kitchen," Stone said, consulting the note, "and there's a bar/video room. Oh, and that little house over there is the master suite, and we have an outdoor kitchen, bar, dining room, and living room, as well as the indoor ones." He pointed out everything. "From what it says here, I think you two will want the first guest room." They looked at it and approved. The kitchen was next. "Laundry room off the kitchen, in case Dino wants to rinse out his underthings." The next room contained a fully stocked bar and a very large flat-screen TV. They went back to the car, got their luggage, and settled in. "Drinks in half an hour," Stone said. "Outdoor bar."

STONE CHECKED OUT the master suite and found a bedroom, dressing room, and a bath with a large tub. He found a TV remote control on the bedside table, but no set. He pressed the on button and a flat-screen TV rose from a cabinet and filled the facing wall. He could watch the Sunday political shows from there.

EVERYBODY MET in the outdoor living room, which was covered with an awning, in case of showers. There was no rain, and Stone tended bar, also making a couple of bottles of vodka gimlets and putting them in the freezer. In the process he found steaks and groceries in the outdoor kitchen fridge.

"I could live here," Viv said, settling into a sofa with a gimlet.

"If only it were in New York City," Dino responded, "on top of a tall building, maybe."

"Oh," Stone said, "there's a little house next to the back door that used to be free-standing, but a previous owner moved it over, bolted it to the main house, and made room for the driveway. A caretaker lives there. He keeps the place running and feeds the koi."

As if on cue a large, well-built man appeared and introduced himself as George. "Let me know if you need help with the electronics or anything else," he said, then he declined a drink, excused himself, and returned to his little house.

"There'll be a housekeeper, too, tomorrow morning." Stone looked at another sheet of paper. "The property was originally three small houses on three lots. Somebody bought them all and made them into the property you see now."

"Smart move," Dino said. "And you're playing golf tomorrow?"

"Arthur hustled me into playing in his tournament, and I haven't touched a club for more than a year."

"Then you'll lose," Dino pointed out.

"I think that's what Arthur has in mind," Stone replied.

"Oh," Viv said suddenly, putting a hand to a cheek.

"What?" Stone asked.

"I just had a premonition."

"A premonition of what?"

"I don't know, but something bad."

Dino waved an arm. "Bad? What bad could happen here?"

"As Fats Waller used to say, 'One never knows, do one?'"

2

tone was up early and found a housekeeper cleaning up their dishes and the grill from the night before. She introduced herself as Anna, then went back to work.

When she was done with the kitchen, Stone scrambled himself some eggs, microwaved some bacon, and toasted a Wolferman's English muffin, the sourdough flavor he liked. Joan, his secretary, had briefed somebody well.

He left Dino and Viv to sleep as late as they liked, then he recorded the Sunday political shows on the DVR, got the golf invitation from his briefcase, and followed the directions to the golf club. Somebody took his clubs from the trunk and carried them to the practice tee, and Arthur Steele greeted him there, his nose already sunburned.

"You'll be in my foursome with Arthur Junior and Meg Harmon, both new board members," Arthur said.

"I'd better hit a few to find out if I still can," Stone said.

He teed up a ball and made a big swing with his driver, then watched it slice fifty yards into a swamp. "Nothing's changed," he muttered, and he hit a bucket of balls, working on his swing until it began to straighten out a little.

Arthur Jr. was a clone of his old man, and Meg Harmon was a thirty-five-ish blonde, slim and fit-looking. She, Stone knew, had started a Silicon Valley software company in her early twenties and had recently sold it to a syndicate, with the Steele Group as a partner, for $1.5 billion. She teed up, and her drive went straight for better than two hundred yards. Arthur Jr. was next, and he drove about the same distance, but hooked it into the rough, muttering under his breath. Big Arthur hit one straight for two hundred and fifty yards.

"You've been practicing, Arthur," Stone said. "That's cheating." He teed up and sliced into the rough, but he was long and he still had a shot to the green, if his lie was good.

They were walking back to their carts when Stone heard a single *crack*, and he immediately thought: rifle! A man in the next foursome, waiting to tee off, made a loud noise and was knocked down.

"Everybody on the ground!" Stone shouted as he ran to the man, who had a bleeding shoulder wound. Stone looked around him and from the way the man had fallen, thought the shot had come from a swampy area to his right. He heard a vehicle door slam and gravel spraying beyond the trees. "From over there," he said, getting to his feet.

A club employee came running up. "Call nine-one-one," Stone said, "and tell them a man's down with a gunshot wound. Ask for an ambulance and the police."

Arthur walked over, dusting himself off. "That's Al Harris," he said, nodding at the man on the ground. He knelt. "How are you feeling, Al?" He got a grunt for an answer. "Hang on, help is on the way."

Stone looked around him at everyone's position. From where people had been standing when he heard the shot, he calculated that the shooter could have been aiming at Meg or Arthur, and with a miss, Al Harris had caught the stray bullet. It could, Stone thought, also have been aimed at himself.

THE AMBULANCE arrived first, the hospital being nearby, and two detectives were next by a couple of minutes. Stone greeted them and introduced himself, then he told them his theory of where the shot had come from and where it had been aimed.

"Are you a police officer?" the older of the two men asked.

"Retired detective," Stone replied. "I worked homicide."

"I'm Harry Kaufelt," the man replied. "This is my partner, Moe Cramer. We work anything that comes up. Did you see the shooter or his vehicle?"

"No, but from the sound of the door slamming and the engine, I think it could have been a pickup truck."

Harry got on his radio and reported. "Look for a pickup with a rifle rack. Yeah, yeah, I know, lots of those around. He could be headed north on U.S. 1. Let the sheriff know."

The EMTs were loading Al Harris into their vehicle, and one of them came over to Harry. "He's in shock," the man said.

"Get him taken care of," Harry said. "We'll talk to him later." Then he spoke to Stone again. "And you figure either you or the lady or the gentleman there could have been the target?"

"He only needed a gust of breeze or a jiggle of something to miss one of us and hit Mr. Harris."

"Well, Mr. Barrington . . ."

"Stone, please."

"Well, Stone, we're going to follow your lead on this, because we don't have one ourselves. Moe, you go talk to the other two, and I'll grill Stone, here."

"What would you like to know?" Stone asked.

"You all look as though you're out-of-towners," Harry said. "Where you from?"

"Mr. Steele and I are New Yorkers. The lady is from the West Coast, south of San Francisco somewhere."

"And what brought you all down here?"

"All the people playing are directors of the Steele Group, an insurance company. Mr. Steele is the chairman and CEO. The fellow next to the cart is Arthur Steele Junior."

"You have any reason to think that somebody down here might hold a grudge against any of you?"

"I've visited Key West a few times, but I don't know a lot of people. I've done some business with an attorney named Jack Spottswood."

"Him, we know, and his family. You haven't screwed any of them on some business deal, have you, Stone?"

"No, and if I had, I don't think the Spottswoods would react this way. They're nice people to do business with. And, for what it's worth, I don't think this is local."

"Oh? You think a professional is involved?"

"Are you aware of any contract killers living on your turf?"

"Nope. Our killers are usually drunk or mad at an ex-wife or girlfriend."

"Then that leaves a pro, doesn't it?"

"You may have a point."

"And a pro is going to be a lot harder to catch," Stone said. "He'll have an escape route all planned. You've already covered U.S. 1—that leaves the airport, doesn't it?"

"First call I made, when we got here," Harry said.

"Look for a couple," Stone suggested.

"Why's that?"

"Because the shooter would want to blend in, and he knows you'll be looking for a man traveling alone."

"'Scuse me." Harry got on the radio. "Thanks, Stone, that's a nice insight. Not that I wouldn't have thought of it my-self, a couple of hours after they flew out of here. Any other thoughts?"

"I'd check the car rental agencies at the airport, too. I doubt if he took a cab out here."

"I doubt if he rented a pickup truck, too," Harry said, "since nobody rents pickups. A van, maybe."

"He's not getting on a plane with a rifle," Stone said. "Maybe he left it in whatever he rented."

"I think he would think it would take us longer to find it in that swamp," Harry said.

"You have a good point, Harry."

Moe rejoined them. "I got exactly nothing from those folks," he said to Harry.

"Stone, how well do you know those two?"

"I've known Arthur for at least ten years. I met the lady about half an hour ago. I can tell you that she recently sold her software company for one and a half billion dollars."

"Well, that opens up a whole new field of suspects for us, doesn't it?" Harry said. "Ex-partners who feel cheated, ex-lovers or husbands, or anybody who might profit from her death. What town is she from?"

"You'll have to ask her," Stone said. "I don't know that territory."

They both shook Stone's hand and wandered off in the direction of Meg Harmon.

Arthur walked over. "I've canceled play for today," he said. "We'll play tomorrow, if Al isn't too badly hurt. I'll call you."

"Arthur," Stone said, "do you know anybody who might want you dead?"

"Everybody who wasn't happy with his insurance settlement, I guess. That's why we try to err on the side of generosity." He walked off toward the parking lot.

Meg Harmon was walking that way, too.

"Can I give you a lift to the hotel?" Stone asked. "Or even better, join us for lunch at my house."

3

Dino and Viv were up and dressed when Stone and Meg walked in, and he made the introductions. They had a glass of iced tea while Viv made lunch, with the reluctant assistance of Dino.

"How come you're back so early?" Dino asked.

Stone told him what had happened, then Viv put him back to work.

Stone and Meg sat down on a sofa. "The detectives asked me what city you live in, and I didn't know," he said to her.

"I lived in San Mateo until I sold the company, then I bought a place in San Francisco. I'm thinking of buying an apartment or a house in New York, as well, since I get there on business a lot. Arthur tells me you're an attorney."

"That's right."

"And you serve on some boards?"

"Beats working," Stone said.

"I'm doing some of that, too, though I'm not sure why they think a software geek would be qualified."

"Congratulations on the sale of your company," Stone said. "I voted for the Steele participation in the buyout. We were impressed with both your achievement and your bargaining skills."

"I think that's why Arthur brought me onto the board."

"That and the fact that he wants to acquire other tech companies, and he knows little about them." Stone's cell rang. "Excuse me, it's the cops. Hello, Harry."

"Stone, can I come see you for a few minutes?"

"Sure. I gave you the address—it's the first driveway on the right."

"Got it. Be there in five."

HE GAVE HARRY and Moe iced tea and sat them down.

"Your instincts were good," Harry said. "A dozen flights have left Key West International since the events of this morning, and we satisfied ourselves that most of their occupants were straight-up tourists. There was one couple, though, who didn't quite ring true, but we couldn't hold them without more evidence. He was carrying a credit card receipt from a local B&B, and we had a look around there and came up with a single .223 round. He was careless. His name is Anthony Carew, and he and his wife are on a plane to LaGuardia. I thought you might know somebody on the NYPD that I could call and have meet them."

"As a matter of fact, I do," Stone said. "He's over there making a sandwich." He nodded toward the kitchen. "Dino, have you got a minute?"

Dino wiped his hands, came over, and sat down.

"These are Detectives Harry Kaufelt and Moe Cramer, KWPD. They need your help. Gentlemen, this is Dino Bacchetti, who is the police commissioner of New York City. I think he's the guy you want to speak to."

"What's up?" Dino asked.

"We have suspects on an airplane right now, due at LaGuardia in about an hour. Could you have them picked up and held until we get there?"

"Sure," Dino said. "Descriptions?"

"Male, mid-forties, six feet, two hundred pounds, bald, wearing a flowered shirt over a potbelly, and Bermuda shorts. Female, mid-thirties, five-five, and a hundred and twenty pounds. Names—Anthony and Sheila Carew, both carrying backpacks for luggage. Suspicion of attempted murder. We can get there on a flight leaving in an hour."

Dino made the call and gave the orders. "What time will they arrive in New York?"

"Three o'clock, Jet Blue flight."

"And you?"

"Six o'clock."

"I'll have you met and driven. You're going to need an extradition warrant."

"That's in the works. Somebody will meet us at the Key West airport with the warrant."

"Anything else I can do for you?"

"I can't think of a thing, Commissioner. Thanks very much for your help."

"Anytime," Dino said. Everybody shook hands and they left.

"Well," Meg said, "that's more policemen than I've ever seen in one day."

"By the way," Stone said, "I've told the cops I think they were aiming at one of us—you, me, or Arthur—and shot Al Harris by accident. Can you think of anybody who harbors hard feelings toward you? Hard enough to hire a killer to go after you?"

To Stone's surprise, she didn't dismiss the idea out of hand, but thought about it. Finally, she said, "I had a partner who owned ten percent of the business. He wasn't happy with ten percent of the sale price, figured I owed him more, in spite of an airtight contract that covered just such a sale."

"What were his grounds for believing that?"

"He seemed to think that I'd planned the whole thing from the start—suck him dry of his tech knowledge, then stiff him in the deal."

"Did you do that?"

"I can see how he might believe it, but that wasn't the way it was. He was important to the effort for a while, spent six years working on the product line but faded as a factor the last couple of years. He walked away with a hundred and fifty million for his trouble. He was also paid nearly a million dollars a year for his work. I felt he was very well compensated in the sale and didn't deserve more, but he filed a patent suit anyway, which got thrown out of court. He has a paranoid side to him, and he wasn't easy to get along with."

"What does he look like?"

"A lot like the description that the detective gave Dino," she said. "Wife, too. And he's a gun nut, had a big collection."

"Why didn't you mention him to the detectives this morning?"

"It crossed my mind, but I dismissed it, until I heard what Harry had to say to Dino."

"What are the couple's names?"

"Gino and Veronica Bellini."

"You have an address for them?"

"They left town after I sold the company. I don't know where they went."

Stone picked up his phone, checked Harry Kaufelt's number on his card, and dialed the number. "Harry," he said, "Carew and his wife may be traveling under the names of Gino and Veronica Bellini. Bellini was a partner in Ms. Harmon's business who was disgruntled with his share of the sale. Get this— he only got a hundred and fifty million dollars." They talked for another minute, and Stone hung up.

"Sounds like a good suspect," Dino said.

"He does, doesn't he?" Stone replied. "Meg, I'm glad you told us about Bellini."

"So am I," she said.

Viv brought over a tray of sandwiches, and Dino opened a bottle of wine.

"You know," Meg said, "this is a much nicer way to spend the day than playing golf with a lot of businesspeople."

"Hear! Hear!" Stone said.

4

*G*ino and Veronica Bellini sat in first class, enjoyed a drink and lunch, then, an hour out of LaGuardia, each disappeared into a restroom with a backpack, and when they emerged, Gino was wearing a business suit, tie, and toupee, and the pillow under his belt was in the toilet tank with his old clothes and his backpack. Veronica wore a stylish dress with her long hair down, and they emerged from the airplane without luggage. Immediately outside the door two obvious police detectives were waiting in the rampway and hardly gave them a glance.

When the last passengers had left the airplane the bemused detectives went aboard and searched it thoroughly and left just as bemused, while the Bellinis drove away in a chauffeured black Mercedes, rented. They were driven to a five-star Fifth Avenue hotel and checked into a large suite.

"What now?" Veronica asked.

"We'll get another shot at her," Gino replied.

"Is it worth it, Gino?" Veronica asked.

"It's worth it to me."

"Why don't we go to Europe for a while?"

"Maybe, we'll see. Now, we both have some shopping to do, and I have a few chores to take care of." He held up a computer thumb drive.

BACK IN KEY WEST, Stone and his guests had moved on to cocktails, and Viv and Meg were planning dinner.

Dino's cell rang. "Bacchetti. Yeah? What do you mean?" He listened for a minute, then hung up.

Before Dino could speak, Stone's cell rang. "Hello?"

"Stone, it's Harry Kaufelt."

"Yes, Harry?" He put the phone on speaker and set it on the table between him and Dino.

"I just got to New York, and a couple of New York cops met me. The Carews or Bellinis or whoever the fuck they are weren't on the airplane. And I know goddamned well they got on it and took off."

"Harry, Dino is right here. Tell us what you want to do."

"What can I do?"

"I can put out an APB on them," Dino said, "and we can check the hotels, but it's a big city with thousands of hotels."

"Thanks, Commissioner, but I don't think we have enough evidence to ask your people to make that kind of effort. We still haven't found the weapon. We'll have to go another way."

"Call me if I can help. I'll be here the rest of the week, then in my New York office after that."

"Yes, sir." Everybody hung up.

"Well," Dino said, "that's cute—they changed their appearance on the airplane and walked right past my guys."

"It wouldn't have taken much," Stone said. "Ditch their clothes down the toilet and put on something they brought in their backpacks. And I would imagine that anybody that clever and with that much money would have a new identity or two all set up, as well."

"Meg will be safe here this week," Dino said, "but somehow I get the feeling that she'll be flying to New York with us this weekend."

"I'll admit that crossed my mind," Stone said. "Let's see how it goes."

"That would put her in the same city as the Bellinis," Dino pointed out.

"That crossed my mind, too. She'd best stay with me, I guess."

"I guessed," Dino replied.

VIV AND MEG were making dinner while Stone and Dino talked.

"You know," Meg said, "I'm glad I met you all. This is a lot more fun than dining with the crusty board of the Steele Group."

"Thanks, we're enjoying you, too."

"Stone seems to be almost too good to be true," Meg said. "Is there anything I should know about him?"

"Stone used to be on the NYPD, and he and Dino were partners in the old days, so they've been best friends forever. Stone, believe me, is a perfectly straightforward man. He's what he seems to be."

"I'm delighted to hear it," Meg said. "I had a marriage that didn't survive the first year of my start-up, and I didn't have much of a social life while I was building my company. Since the buyout, everything has changed but isn't necessarily better. Anybody who reads the *Wall Street Journal* knows how rich I am, and I've had to be very careful about the men I meet."

"I can understand that," Viv replied. "I don't think Stone is as rich as you are, but he's very well off, indeed. He doesn't need your money."

THEY HAD PASTA at the outdoor dining table.

"I know you're in software," Stone said to Meg. "What are you working on these days?"

"A lot of things," she replied, "but the one that's taking up most of our resources is the self-driving car. We've stolen a march on most of our competitors, and our system is in the final stages of testing."

"Have you tried it out in New York yet?" Stone asked. "That should be a challenge for it."

"As we speak," she replied. "We have six vehicles—four cars and two delivery trucks—on your streets. And we're going to put on a demonstration for the Steele board this week in Key West."

THE BELLINIS were now using the name Beresford on passports and credit cards, which Gino thought sounded classy. They dined at the 21 Club early and then went to see *Hamilton*. "These seats were twenty-five hundred each from the hotel concierge," he said to Veronica. "But who gives a fuck? We may not be as rich as we ought to be, but we're rich enough for right now."

"I'm happy," Veronica said, "but you're not going to be until Meg is dead and buried."

"But then I'll be very, very happy," he said. "I'll keep suing them until they come up with a big settlement. With Meg gone, they'll fold."

"I hope you're right," Veronica said.

AFTER DINNER, during which a couple of bottles of wine were consumed, they all ended up in the spa, and Stone was impressed with how comfortable Meg was, being naked with new friends.

She had a shower in the master bathroom, then dressed.

"I was hoping you'd stay," Stone said.

"Not tonight, but I won't keep you waiting long."

"I'll drive you to the Casa Marina."

"That won't be necessary," she said. "I called for a car. Just lead me to your front door."

He did so, and a sleek car with a small antenna array on top was parked just outside. As they approached it, the rear door slid open, and Meg got in. "This is my pride and joy," she said, giving him a kiss.

The door slid shut, and the car moved silently away, turning at the corner.

Stone went back inside. "Is Meg gone?" Viv asked.

"Her car came for her," Stone said. "No driver, just the car."

TEN MINUTES LATER, the front doorbell rang, and Stone answered it.

Meg stood there, looking unhappy.

"I hope the car didn't have an accident," Stone said, bringing her in.

"It didn't," Meg replied. "It just stopped. One of my techs is with it now."

"You look as though you could use a drink," Stone said.

"I certainly could," she replied, and he poured her a gimlet.

"Did the tech figure it out?"

"He thinks it's a software problem," she replied.

"Software is what you do, isn't it?"

"It is, and we have rewritten it half a dozen times over the past two years. I would think it was impossible that we would still have a bug, but while the tech was there, he got a call. All six of our vehicles in New York stopped, too."

"So, they all have the same software bug?"

"So it seems," she said. "I've already called a team into the office to get to work on it." She yawned. "I'm tired," she said.

"Then why don't you stay the night?"

She looked up at him. "Are your intentions honorable?"

"Only as honorable as they need to be," Stone replied.

5

On Monday morning the directors of the Steele Group reassembled at the golf course.

"How's Al Harris?" Stone asked Arthur.

"On the mend. He insisted that we play today, and he swears he'll be at the board meeting on Friday."

"Did he have surgery?"

"Yes, and his arm will be in a sling for a bit."

"When you speak to him, tell him I wish him well and look forward to seeing him at the board meeting."

They had to wait five minutes for Meg to show up, and when she did it was in a taxi. Stone supposed she was saving her driverless car for its demonstration to the board, if it was working again.

"Sorry about that," she said to Arthur. "I don't need to warm up. I did my stretches in the backseat of the cab."

"You have the honor," Arthur said, ushering her onto the tee. She hit it straight for a good two hundred yards.

Stone still sliced his drive, but not into the rough. He had a shot at the green with a good lie.

Arthur's went straight and landed a yard behind Meg's.

Arthur Jr. hooked into the deep rough.

"I can't get him to take lessons," Arthur said to Stone as their cart trundled down the fairway. "He's convinced he can teach himself, like that left-handed pro who says he's never had a lesson. What's his name?"

"Bubba Watson," Stone replied.

"Tell me," Arthur said, "how do you like your rental house?"

"It's wonderful," Stone said. "I've had to resist finding out who the owner is and making an offer."

"That's right, you have the house-buying disease, don't you?"

"I'm afraid so. I did sell one, though."

"Which one?"

"Washington, Connecticut. I just wasn't using it."

"Do you think you'd use a house here?" Arthur asked.

"A warm place in winter is very inviting," Stone replied, "even if it's only for long weekends."

They all hit their second shots and drove on.

AT THE FINISH, Arthur reviewed their scorecards, and Meg had won it on handicap. Arthur was second, and Stone was third.

"I guess we had the lucky foursome," Arthur said.

Stone was putting his and Meg's clubs into the convertible when the now-familiar police detectives drove up.

"Back already?" Stone asked. "What's new?"

"We didn't get the Bellinis, but our guys found the weapon," Harry Kaufelt reported. "It's a goddamned Kalashnikov. I wonder what that means."

"Probably nothing," Stone said. "It was available, and the guy bought it, and it might have been a lucky thing for us. A lot of those weapons are old and war-worn, and its accuracy may have suffered."

"Did you hear more than one shot?" Harry asked.

"No, I think that's all there was. Have you located the vehicle?"

"Got that, too, stolen and abandoned near the airport, and it was cleaned of any evidence. We got Bellini's phone number in California and called it. A housekeeper said the Bellinis are on vacation in Europe, and she doesn't know when they'll be back."

"They've certainly had time to get to Europe," Stone said.

"I'm just glad nobody's dead," Harry said. "Visitors here get hurt a lot—motor scooter accidents, scuba diving, bikes hit by cars—and about once a year some drunken spring-breaker will take a dive off the end of the White Street Pier into three feet of water and break his neck, never mind all the shallow-water-no-diving signs. But this is the first time I can remember when a sniper took a shot at somebody, and it rankles. The only hired killers we've ever dealt with were brought in by drug dealers to kill other drug dealers, and their practice is to walk up behind a guy and shoot him twice in the head."

"Is that still happening?"

"No, the drug trade here is pretty much small-time, now. Oh, once in a while a few bales of marijuana wash up on a beach or a fisherman is found with a fish stuffed with a few kilos of cocaine, but that's about it."

"Anything Dino or I can do to help?"

"No, I just thought I'd tell you about the weapon and the car."

"Thanks, Harry, I'm glad to hear how it's going." Stone got into his car, where Meg was waiting, and told her what Harry had said.

"Maybe it wasn't Bellini," she said. "Maybe it wasn't me the shooter was aiming at."

"That's possible, but when I take you back to New York, we're going to pretend you're in terrible danger."

"Are you taking me back to New York?"

"You said you wanted to look at apartments, didn't you?"

"Yes, I did, so I should consider this an invitation?"

"Unless you want me to just throw a sack over your head, sling you over my shoulder, and carry you onto the airplane."

"As romantic as that sounds, I think I'll just accept your invitation."

"Good idea," Stone said.

6

Stone woke up beside Meg Harmon, and he thought for a moment how nice it was to share a bed.

Meg's eyelids fluttered. "Where am I?" she asked.

"In New York," Stone replied. "Don't you remember? I threw a bag over your head, slung you over my shoulder, and flew you out of Key West."

She sat up and looked around the room. Stone admired her breasts. "This isn't New York," she said.

"My mistake—we're still in Key West."

"I'm glad to hear it. I'm not tired of Key West yet."

"I hope that's not all you're not tired of," Stone replied. "What would you like for breakfast?"

"Whatever you're having."

Stone picked up the phone and buzzed Anna in the kitchen. "The usual," he said, "but for two."

"You are very hungry today," Anna replied.

"Two plates, please." He hung up and turned to Meg. "What would you like to do until breakfast arrives?"

"Watch TV," she replied. "Ask me again after breakfast." She fell back onto the bed.

Stone turned on *Morning Joe.*

AFTER THE BREAKFAST DISHES had been removed from the bed, Stone asked Meg again, and she made a different suggestion. After he had respected her wishes and cooled down, Stone excused himself and picked up the phone.

"The Barrington Practice," Joan said, "sometimes known as Woodman & Weld."

"It's me," he said.

"I know, I recognized your breathing."

"Who owns the rental house in Key West?"

"It's the rental agents' policy not to reveal the name of the owners. I think they're afraid that, next time, you'll call them direct."

"Please call them and ask if the house is for sale."

"I don't need to call them, they told me at the outset that it was for sale."

"Why didn't you tell me?"

"I didn't want to set you off on another house-buying jag."

"I buy houses one at a time, not in jags. How much are they asking?"

Joan told him.

"Offer them twenty-five percent less, and tell them I won't consider a counteroffer, just yes or no."

"Whatever you say, boss."

"Call me back when you have the owner's answer."

"Roger." They hung up.

"You're going to buy the house?" Meg asked.

"No, I've offered them too little, and when they turn me down I'll forget about it. It's how I keep from buying too many houses."

"Your mind works in weird ways."

"What's weird about that?"

"It's weird to make an offer for a house you don't want."

"I suppose it's a little unusual, but I wouldn't go as far as weird."

"Trust me, it's weird," she said. "Where do you presently have houses?"

"In Los Angeles, Paris, London, and the south of England."

"How about New York?"

"Yes, in New York. Oh, and Maine—I forgot Maine."

"Why so many houses?"

"I don't like hotels, so when I go somewhere I like, I'd rather stay at home. But I like my houses to be run like hotels."

Meg shook her head. "This just gets weirder and weirder."

"How long have you been a billionaire?" Stone asked.

"A few months."

"How many houses have you bought since then?"

"Only one."

"But now you're shopping for something in New York?"

"Yes, but that will only make two."

"And you think you'll be finished when you have two houses?"

"Well," she said, "I think I might like a place in Ireland."

"Where else?"

"Maybe the South of France."

"All right, you're up to four houses."

"But I haven't bought that many."

"Only because you haven't had time," Stone said. "Stick around."

The phone rang. "Hello?"

"It's Joan. They've accepted your offer."

"What?"

"You've just bought yourself another house."

"They accepted twenty-five percent off the ask?"

"Yes, and that includes the car and the golf cart, too."

"When do they want to close?"

"Today," she said.

"Nobody closes today."

"They said that Jack Spottswood has all the paperwork ready to go. You can go in anytime today and sign the documents. I'll wire the funds right away. Anything else?"

"I can't think of anything," Stone muttered.

"Good. I'll get the utilities transferred to your name as soon as you have title."

"Thank you," Stone said weakly, then hung up.

"I take it you've just bought another house," Meg said.

"I didn't mean to," Stone said. "It was an accident."

"Any psychiatrist will tell you there are no accidents. In this case, you made an offer, and they accepted. It's really hard to buy a house accidentally."

"I didn't even have it inspected. What if it has termites? I've heard they have termites in Key West."

"You can have it inspected, and if you have termites, you can have it tented."

"What's that?"

"They throw a big tent over the place, run you out, and pump a lot of termite-killing stuff into the tent. Takes about a day."

"Oh."

"Anyway, the place seems to be in fabulous shape. The owner has probably already had it tented."

"I'll ask," Stone said. He called Joan.

"Hi there, what a surprise to hear from you."

"Yeah, yeah, call the rental agent and find out if the house has been tented for termites."

"It was tented last week," Joan said.

"Okay. Tell the agent that the house won't be rented anymore."

"Okay."

"And call Arthur Steele's office and have the house put on my homeowner's insurance policy."

"Already done. Anything else?"

"Yes. I want to know who the seller is."

"Arthur Steele."

7

Stone drove to Fleming Street, to the offices of Spotts-wood, Spottswood & Spottswood and climbed the steep stairs.

Jack Spottswood greeted him in his office with a handshake and a smile.

Stone settled into a chair and took a few deep breaths.

"Would you like a glass of water?" Jack asked.

"Thanks, I'm fine."

"There's an elevator, you know."

"I must have missed that. I'll tell you a law firm joke," he said.

"Shoot," Jack replied.

"A man calls a law office, and a man answers, 'Spottswood, Spottswood & Spottswood.'

"The caller says, 'May I speak to Mr. Spottswood, please?'

"'I'm sorry, Mr. Spottswood died some years ago.'

"'Then may I speak to Mr. Spottswood?'

"'I'm afraid Mr. Spottswood is on vacation this week.'

"'All right,' the man says, exasperated, 'may I speak to Mr. Spottswood?'

"'Speaking,' the lawyer replies."

Jack laughed. "Never heard that one." He reached for a stack of documents and plopped them down in front of Stone. "There's a condition report and an appraisal there," he said. "You'll be delighted to know that it appraised for half a million dollars more than you're paying for it."

"I'm happy to know that," Stone replied, starting to sign documents.

"And the owner had any problems mentioned in the inspection repaired at his expense."

"Arthur must have wanted to sell very badly," Stone said.

"He said he wasn't using it enough—he's owned it for three years and has been down here twice in that time."

"Arthur's crazy."

"Not entirely, Stone," Jack said. "He made a million dollars on the sale."

"Why didn't you tell me that?"

"I didn't know you were interested until the paperwork arrived this morning."

"This morning?"

"About eight-thirty."

"I hadn't even made an offer at that time."

"I guess Arthur figured you'd bite, once you'd spent a couple of days in the house. I think it's the most beautiful house in Key West, except for mine."

Stone handed him back the signed documents.

Jack's secretary leaned through the doorway. "We've received Mr. Barrington's funds," she said. "Shall I disburse?"

"You may disburse," Jack said. "Congratulations, Stone, you've bought the second most beautiful house in Key West. I hope we'll see you down here often. Would you like to join the Key West Yacht Club?"

"Yes, thank you," Stone replied. He had dined there a couple of times.

"I can arrange that for you. Would you like a berth? There's one going."

"I don't have a boat here."

"My advice is take the berth. Then, should you get the boat bug, you'll have a place to dock it. There won't be another one available until somebody dies."

"I'll take the dock," Stone said, rising and shaking Jack's hand. "Thank you for handling this so smoothly, Jack. I'll try and send something your way from Woodman & Weld."

"Always happy to have new business," Jack replied.

Stone took the elevator down. Why risk breaking a hip?

WHEN HE ARRIVED back at the house, Meg and Viv were having coffee in the outdoor living room. "Did you tell Viv?" he asked Meg.

"Tell her what?"

"Where I've been."

"Oh, yes," Meg said, "he's been to his lawyer's office."

"My God," Viv said. "Don't tell me he's bought this house."

"He has."

"That's funny," Viv said, "just last night Dino said to me, 'I love this house, why don't we buy it?' I gave him my list of reasons, including that we couldn't spend enough time here and that we couldn't afford it, then I said, 'If you'll just be patient for a few days, Stone will buy it, and then we can stay here whenever we like.'"

Dino arrived in time to hear that. "Did he buy the house?"

"He did," his wife replied.

"Can we stay here whenever we like?"

"You can," Stone replied.

"Can we retire here?"

Viv and Meg laughed.

"Of course you can," Stone said, joining the laughter.

"How much did you pay for it?"

"A million dollars more than Arthur Steele paid for it, but half a million less than he was asking."

"This was Arthur's house?"

"I'm so glad you didn't know that," Stone said, "because if you had, I'd have shot you."

"You don't sound all that happy about having this wonderful place."

"I'm overjoyed," Stone said, deadpan. "This was a conspiracy among Arthur, Joan, and Jack Spottswood."

"They only did it because they love you," Viv said.

Stone's phone rang. "Hello?"

"Hi, it's Jack. You're now a slip-owning member of the Key West Yacht Club. They'll send you a bill for the initiation fee and the first year's dues and slip charges."

"That was very quick."

"I'm a past commodore and my nephew Billy is the current one. We know people."

"Thank you, Jack."

"And I booked you a table for four for dinner tonight. There's an annual minimum charge for food and drink, and I thought you might like to start whittling it down."

"You're a fine attorney, a great proposer, and a lovely concierge," Stone said. "I thank you for all of that." They said goodbye and hung up.

"That was Jack Spottswood," Stone said. "I'm now a member of the Key West Yacht Club, and we're having dinner there tonight."

"Great," Dino said.

"I also own a slip. If I hadn't taken it I'd have had to wait for somebody to die."

"But you don't own a boat," Dino pointed out.

"It's only Tuesday," Viv said. "He'll be here for a few more days."

"I'm not buying a boat," Stone said.

———

THAT EVENING, Stone, Meg, Dino, and Viv arrived at Stone's new yacht club. Jack Spottswood greeted them from the bar. "Come outside," he said to Stone, "and I'll show you your slip in the marina."

Stone followed him out the door and across the parking lot, where a row of berths lay, each containing a boat.

"There you go," Jack said, pointing, "that's your slip."

Stone looked at it and saw that a familiar-looking boat was parked in it. "Whose is the Hinckley 43 in my slip?"

"Oh, that belonged to the previous owner of the berth," Jack said. "He died a couple of months ago, and his widow has put the boat up for sale."

"It looks quite new," Stone said.

"He had owned it for only a short time when he died," Jack explained. "I think the engines have something like fifty hours on them."

"Good evening, gentlemen," a woman's voice said from behind them.

Stone turned to find a handsome woman in her sixties standing there.

"Stone," Jack said, "this is Betty Koelere, who now owns the Hinckley."

Stone shook her hand. "How do you do, Betty? I was sorry to hear of your husband's death."

"Well, he had twenty-two years on me, and I guess it was his time," she replied, then handed him a thick brown envelope. "I thought you might like to look this over—it's the order form for the boat, listing all the equipment installed."

Stone accepted the envelope. "I'll have a look at it," he replied.

"Have a good evening," Betty said, then turned and walked back into the clubhouse.

"Jack," Stone said, "is this a setup?"

"You mean, you, Betty, and the boat being in the same place at the same time?"

"Let's not leave you out of the equation."

Jack laughed and took Stone's arm. "Let's go back to the bar. You can look over the specs later."

"You know," Stone said, allowing himself to be led toward where the bourbon was, "I own a Hinckley 43 already, which is at my house in England."

"I know that," Jack replied. "I guess that means Betty won't have to sell you on it."

"I am not buying a boat," Stone said.

8

S tone finished his Knob Creek just as the bartender set
down another. He took the papers out of the envelope
and scanned them quickly. The boat was equipped almost identically to his own, in England, but with a few extra
options.

"How much is Betty asking?" Stone said to Jack Spottswood.

"I believe a new one is going for around two million," Jack
replied.

"They've gone up the past couple of years?"

"Hasn't everything?"

"You didn't answer my question. How much is she asking?"

"I'll tell you the truth, Stone, she's all alone now, and she's cash-poor. I think she'll accept any reasonable offer."

"I don't want to take advantage of a widow's situation," Stone said.

"Just offer her whatever you think is fair."

Stone took another gulp of the bourbon, then a deep breath. "Offer her a million eight," he said.

"I'll be right back," Jack replied. He walked to the other end of the bar and exchanged a few words with Betty Koelere, then returned. "Betty gratefully accepts your offer," Jack said. He took the sheaf of papers and removed the last page. "Here's the contract I drew up for her." He wrote in Stone's name and the price. "Initial in the two places and sign right here."

Stone took another swig of the bourbon, then quickly read the contract, signed, and handed it to Jack. He got out his iPhone and tapped out an e-mail to Joan, then sent it. "Joan will transfer the funds to your firm's account tomorrow," he said to Jack.

Jack walked back down the bar, delivered the contract to Betty, who smiled broadly and waved. Jack returned. "Congratulations, Stone, and thank you for making that gentlemanly offer. And by the way, everything on the yacht is in perfect working order, the bottom is clean, and the boat is still under warranty for another four and a half years."

Dino waved at him from a table. "Join us for dinner?" Stone asked Jack.

"Thanks, but I'm meeting some people. Your copy of the contract is in the envelope."

Stone walked over to the table and sat down.

"Don't tell us," Dino said. "You just bought a boat."

Stone finished his drink and waved for another. "God help me, I did."

"Let's go look at it," Viv said.

"Tomorrow. Right now I'm starving."

"I've never seen anything like it," Meg said. "You started the day homeless, clubless, and yachtless in Key West, and you've put all that together in a single day."

Stone managed a weak smile. "I guess I have," he said.

GINO AND VERONICA BELLINI checked into the Royal Suite at the Dorchester Hotel in London. He plugged in his laptop and checked his e-mail. "My goodness," Gino said, "Miss Meg's driverless cars, six in New York and one in Key West, seem to have gone awry. Harmony Software has already reached out for my help."

"Isn't that a pity," Veronica said, lifting the back of his toupee and kissing his bald head. "Now, tell me what you're getting out of this."

"Satisfaction, pure satisfaction," Gino replied, "and a big settlement when I tell them how to fix it." His cell phone rang, and he answered it.

"Mr. Bellini, this is Frank Simmons at Harmony Software."

"Hi there, Frank. What can I do for you?"

"Did you get my e-mail? We've got a major glitch in the driverless car software, and we need your help."

"*My* help? Why, I thought you folks were getting along just fine without my help."

"Be that as it may, we'd like to retain you as a consultant on the project."

"On what terms?"

"One year, two million dollars."

"Sorry, Frank, I'm a busy man."

"What will it take, Gino? Tell me."

"Three years at five million a year, and I don't work on-site, just wherever I happen to be when you need me."

"Please hold for a moment."

"He's checking with Meg," Gino said to Veronica.

Simmons came back. "Done. I'll e-mail you a contract. You can sign it, scan it, and return it. Meg will do the same. Now we need you to go into the Beta version and fix whatever is causing the cars to stop running."

"Just as soon as I receive the contract, signed by Meg."

"Tomorrow morning."

"All right, Frank, I'll fix Meg's toy. It will be done by noon, Florida time, tomorrow. Oh, and I'll need the latest sign-ins and passwords."

"Thank you. Your contract is on the way to Meg."

"Nice doing business with you, Frank," Gino said, then hung up.

"It worked?" Veronica asked.

"To the tune of fifteen million dollars over three years," Gino replied, grinning.

MEG HUNG up her cell phone.

"You look glum," Stone said. "Anything I can do to help?" They were in the middle of dinner.

"No, I've just fixed the problem, but it cost me fifteen million, out of my own pocket."

"What does that fix?"

"The cars. We should be able to go on with the demonstration to the board. I'll need to borrow your computer and printer when we get back to the house."

Stone poured them all more wine. "Meg," he said, "I get the feeling that extortion may be involved here."

"And very likely, more to come," she replied.

THE BELLINIS DINED at Le Gavroche, possibly London's finest restaurant and holder of three stars from the *Guide Michelin*.

"I think you should do some shopping tomorrow," he said to Veronica.

"You've read my mind," she replied. "How much can I spend?"

"I never thought I'd hear myself say these words, but whatever you like."

"I never thought *I'd* hear you say those words," she replied, "but they sound very sweet."

"I'm a very sweet guy," Gino said, as the sommelier tipped more Chateau Lafite 1978 into their glasses.

9

Stone navigated his new boat out of its berth, across Garrison Bight, through Key West Harbor, then turned west, into open water, and pushed the throttles of the Hinckley 43 to 3200 rpms. Soon they were cruising at a little better than 30 knots.

"How long to our destination?" Meg asked from the big, comfortable seat beside him.

"It's about seventy miles, so a bit more than two hours. The calm seas will keep us fast and comfortable."

"What's it like out there?"

"It's better if you see it for yourself." Stone tapped in half a dozen waypoints on the moving map before him and engaged the autopilot, which took charge and pointed them at the first waypoint.

Dino and Viv came in from the cockpit. "It's getting pretty windy back there," Dino said.

"Grab a beer and make yourselves comfortable in the cabin."

Stone arranged himself in the helmsman's chair so that he could see both the moving map and Meg by shifting his gaze. "I'm concerned about you," he said.

"Oh? Why?"

"Well, I've known you for only a few days, but who I'm seeing now is not the happy person I saw earlier this week."

She sighed. "I'm just afraid that, by paying this . . . 'extortion,' as you put it, I'm buying into more problems than I'm solving."

"That's often the way it is with extortion or blackmail. It's very likely that he'll ask you for considerably more. What hold does he have over you?"

"The keys to the kingdom, you might say. Gino Bellini has what you might call a checkered background," she said. "He was a troubled youth, spent some time in reform school for hacking and computer theft, and narrowly avoided prison. He was rescued from that life by a mentor, a professor of computer science at Stanford, who got him a scholarship there. He didn't graduate—he was sucked out of there by a Silicon Valley start-up—not mine, not yet—and he began making more money than he would have ever imagined possible, half a million dollars a year, and more. Still, as I was to learn, he retained that part of his psyche that controlled criminality."

"He's a born criminal, you mean?"

"Not exactly. That was learned behavior, I think, but it still seems to remain an important part of the way he thinks. When I let him go and paid him off for his share of the company, I thought that would be the end to it. I mean, even after taxes he was sitting on more than a hundred million dollars. You'd think that would be enough to satisfy him, but no. It chafed on him that I was making more than a billion dollars on the deal, never mind that the concept was mine and that I had secured the financing, supervised his coding, and ran the business, while his job was to sit at his computer and make my ideas work. He still managed to believe that, somehow, I had wronged him, cheated him out of his fair share."

"I hope you had a good attorney when you were setting up the business and writing employment contracts."

"Oh, yes, the best legal minds in Silicon Valley were paid exorbitant sums to make sure that a situation like this could never arise."

"Sometimes good lawyers are worth whatever you pay them," Stone said, with a little reproval in his voice.

"Oh, I know that, and I don't question either the quality of their work or what I paid them. I just don't think they ever realized who they were dealing with in Gino's case—nor did I, for that matter."

"A good contract covers legalities," Stone said. "It's difficult to predict illegalities, though every attorney tries to. Has Bellini committed any criminal act that you know of?"

"I suspect so," Meg replied. "I suspect that he's planted little bombs in our software that can be triggered whenever he likes."

"Have you caught him at it?"

"My people can't even *find* the bombs, let alone prove that he put them there. I think what he's doing is using a password that he set up some time ago to get into the programs and set off the bombs. And now, because of the deal I've made with him, he has the current passwords necessary to do that—the aforementioned keys to the kingdom. He knew the demonstration to the Steele board was coming up and how important that would be to the company's success, and he's managed to turn that into fifteen million dollars in his pocket."

"Will there be other opportunities for him to do that?"

"Oh, yes. We'll be turning over our prototypes and our software to the State of California and the U.S. government soon, and it's critical that we get certification from both, otherwise we won't be able to go into production and do large-scale fleet testing of the vehicles. I'll tell you this, Stone, in the strictest confidence—last night I was thinking of trying to find someone to kill the man."

"Whoa," Stone said. "Even if that were successful, like the bribe you paid, it would create more problems for you than it would solve."

"My brain tells me that, but my gut wants him dead," she said.

"Let me explain how this would go," Stone said. "First of all, you'd have to find a contract killer, a hit man. Do you know someone who might know someone who does that?"

She laughed. "The only person I know who might know someone like that is Gino Bellini."

Stone laughed. "What happens when someone like you tries to find someone like that is that you have to deal with criminals, people who can't be trusted, no matter how much money they are being offered. Often, these people are already snitches for one or more police officers or FBI agents. They're out on parole, maybe, and they want to endear themselves to the people who have the power to send them back to prison. You'd find yourself handing over money in an alley or a bar somewhere to an officer of the law, who will then arrest you and charge you with conspiracy to murder. It's a losing game."

She shrugged. "Maybe I should just lure Gino into a back alley and shoot him myself," she said. "Then I wouldn't have to trust anybody, and I'd save a lot of money."

"And you would almost certainly spend the rest of your life in prison."

"Why? I'm smart, why couldn't I get away with it?"

"You're talking to a former homicide detective, and I can tell you from experience that there are so many ways to make mistakes and so many techniques available to the police for finding those mistakes that you'd have very little chance of success. All it takes is one little mistake, and you're done. The best you could hope for is to hire the world's most expensive defense lawyer who might, somehow, win at trial and get you off. You'd spend more than you've already given Bellini on your defense, then his wife would bring a civil suit against you for wrongful death, which you could easily lose, and for the rest of your life, at least half the people who know and love you would believe that you're a murderer, and that would be hard to live with."

"I suppose you're right," Meg said disconsolately.

"Ask O. J. Simpson," Stone said.

The autopilot turned the yacht toward the last waypoint and, ahead, low islands came into sight.

10

Gino Bellini switched off his laptop. "There," he said, "Miss Meg is up and running again. For the moment, at least."

"Have you given up on just killing her outright?" Veronica asked.

"No, I haven't," Gino replied. "Dirty Joe is still on the hunt in Key West."

"That didn't go so well last time—we had to run for it."

"I've instructed him to wait until he has a shot in some out-of-the-way spot, where the police can't be all over him in a minute."

"You're going to let her do her demonstration to the Steele board?"

"Of course. I want her to have the illusion of progress, until I can hit her again. Or until Dirty Joe can."

"Who is Dirty Joe? You haven't told me anything about him."

"Joe Cross. We did some time together in a California reform school when we were just kids, and we kept in touch. We called him Dirty Joe even then, because there was *nothing* he wouldn't do for money. When I was at Stanford he dealt marijuana on campus. When I was in Silicon Valley, he upped his game to cocaine, which was the propellant of choice there in those days. On the side, he'd do hits, and he always got away with it. He sort of retired to the Keys, living up in Islamorada, but he's always receptive to the opportunity for fast cash."

"And you think he can handle this?"

"He hasn't done a day of time since reform school, and that record was expunged when he was twenty-one, so he's on nobody's list of suspects, which is usually the problem when you want somebody hit. The police look at the record first."

"But he hit the wrong person in Key West. Doesn't that bother you?"

"It was a windy day, and that was as close as he could get. If we're patient, Dirty Joe will come through, and Meg's inferiors will be a lot easier to deal with."

DIRTY JOE CROSS and his girlfriend, Jane Jillian, known to her friends as Jungle Jane, sat back a mile or so in their offshore boat, a thirty-six-footer with three large outboards clamped to the stern, and Joe watched through his binoculars as the blue Hinckley rounded Fort Jefferson and picked up a mooring in the little harbor. "They're down for the night," Joe said, "and the light's going. We're not going to get a shot at them before tomorrow morning. We got anything to eat aboard?"

"No problem," Jane replied. "If you want fresh fish, I'll catch you something for supper."

"Good idea," he said. "Snapper, maybe?"

"Whatever the sea yields," she replied. "If you want to get picky, find yourself a fish restaurant. The nearest one is about seventy miles away."

"I'll eat whatever you put in front of me," Joe said.

THE HARBOR was empty of other boats, and Stone was glad of it. "Dino, Viv, and I were out here last Christmas," he said to Meg.

"Tell me about the fort," Meg asked.

"It was built sometime before the Civil War, and during the war it was used as a prison for Union deserters. The only reason a lot of people ever heard of it was when there was a yellow fever epidemic on the island, and Dr. Samuel Mudd was imprisoned here for the crime of aiding and abetting John Wilkes Booth after he assassinated Abraham Lincoln. Booth had broken his leg when he jumped from Lincoln's box to the stage at Ford's Theatre, and he fled into Maryland, where he stopped at Dr. Mudd's house for help along the road south. Mudd knew Booth but treated him anyway and didn't report him until the following day. As a result, he was convicted along with the other conspirators and sentenced to life in prison.

"He was sent to Fort Jefferson, and while he was here yellow fever broke out, and Mudd heroically saved many lives, for which he was eventually pardoned by the President."

"I hope there's no yellow fever now," Meg said.

"Nope, it's now a national park."

They had a drink, and Dino and Viv grilled steaks for dinner.

THE FOLLOWING MORNING, after a good breakfast and a Bloody Mary, Stone broke out the rubber dinghy from its locker and inflated it, then launched it over the stern and fastened the outboard to it.

Viv pleaded freckles, and Dino stayed with her, while Stone and Meg took the dinghy to Loggerhead Key, a mile or so away.

"It looks deserted," Meg said. "Can I go without a suit here?"

"I'm counting on it," Stone said. "Tan lines aren't allowed on Loggerhead." He pulled the dinghy up onto the beach; they left their swimsuits aboard and swam for a while, then got out and let the wind dry them as they walked up the beach.

DIRTY JOE CROSS and Jungle Jane Jillian approached Fort Jefferson slowly, then saw a couple leave the moored yacht in a rubber dinghy. He took a look through his glasses. "Bingo," he said. "And they seem to be heading for Loggerhead."

With Jane at the helm they motored slowly along on a route parallel to the beach, and Joe went below and came back with an AR-15–style assault rifle and shoved a banana clip into it, watching as the couple swam, then walked up the beach.

"Man, she looks good naked," Joe said.

"Watch out or I'll kick your ass," Jane replied.

He knew she would, too. "Okay, okay, just drift for a while. I can't hit anything if we're under way."

Jane did as instructed. "How close in do you want to be?"

"A hundred yards or so, and go at idle speed."

She slowly closed the gap between them and the beach.

"They haven't even seen us," Joe said. "This is going to be a piece of cake."

"Who's the guy?" Jane asked.

"Who gives a shit?" Joe came back. "If he gets in the way, he's dead meat. This is a good distance. Take the engines out of gear, but be ready to leave fast, toward Key West."

Jane put the engines into neutral, and they idled, adrift.

Joe tried standing, but couldn't get steady enough. He knelt and braced the rifle against the gunwale of the boat; he checked the wind and distance, adjusted the scope, and checked the view. Looking good.

STONE AND MEG walked along on the wet sand at the water's edge, then she stopped and pulled him around toward her. He took her in his arms and pressed her against his body, then kissed her.

JOE SIGHTED through the scope and took a good look. A head shot wasn't going to do it; even a little movement of the boat made that an unlikely hit. The woman's back was to him, and he placed the crosshairs between her shoulder blades, took a deep breath, let it out, then began to squeeze the trigger. As he fired he felt a breeze on the back of his neck and swore.

Stone felt a breeze, too, at the moment he heard the *crack* of the rifle. He swept Meg's legs from under her, and they both hit the sand.

11

Stone looked around for shelter; no trees, not even shrubs for fifty yards, and he didn't want to get any farther from the dinghy. He looked out at the boat off the beach: it had begun to turn slowly away from them. A man stood up, holding a rifle, and Stone could hear him swearing.

"TURN THE GODDAMNED thing back on course!" the man yelled at a woman who was at the helm. She put the engines into gear and started to turn back toward them.

"QUICK!" Stone said to Meg. He helped her to her feet, grabbed her hand, and they ran away from the beach, toward some dunes, diving behind the nearest one as the rifle could be heard again and flying sand scattered around them. "Keep your belly on the ground," Stone said to Meg, "and crawl back toward the dinghy. The dune gets higher as we go." Then he heard automatic fire and hugged the sand beneath him. The guy with the rifle was swearing again, yelling instructions at the woman. Stone looked up, and the boat was again stern to their position. "Okay, let's go," he said to Meg, and they began crawling as fast as they could. Shots rang out again, but hit the top of the dune behind them. The shooter had lost their position. "Lie very still, now," he said.

"WHERE ARE THEY?" Jane asked.

"How the fuck do I know?" Dirty Joe yelled back. "They're behind that fucking dune. And I need another magazine." He went below to get one.

THEN STONE heard a clattering sound from some distance away. He risked sticking his head up long enough to find its source. Dino was weighing the anchor they had put out to reinforce their mooring. Stone thanked Hinckley that raising the anchor involved only the pressing of a switch, not physical labor. He ducked back down. "Dino's on the way," he said to Meg.

"Does he know how to operate that JetStick thing you've been using?" she asked.

"Sort of," Stone replied. "He'll get the hang of it." The automatic fire started again, and the shooter was panning toward them, rounds ripping off the peak of the dune as they hit. "Stay down," Stone said, as if that were necessary. He heard the engines on the Hinckley start up, but he was afraid to check on Dino's progress.

"THEIR BOAT is moving!" Jane shouted, and Dirty Joe stopped firing and looked at it as it accelerated. He turned his rifle back toward the beach and got off another burst, then dropped the magazine and shoved in another. "This is my last one," he said to Jane.

Then there was a single shot from the direction of the blue yacht, and an almost simultaneous whack as the bullet struck the radome on top of his cabin. "Oh, shit, those people are armed. Let's get the hell out of here! Head for Key West!"

Jane did as ordered and shoved the throttles forward. The boat leaped ahead. "Why Key West? We don't want to go there."

"When we're out of their sight we'll turn for Islamorada," Joe replied.

STONE RAISED his head now and saw the boat roar away, its three outboards howling. He looked back at the Hinckley and saw Dino's head protruding from an open hatch in the cabin roof; he was standing on the skipper's seat, firing a handgun at the retreating speedboat.

STONE STOOD up now. "The shooter is out of here," he said to Meg. "Let's get to our dinghy." They ran down the dune and back up the beach, to where they had dragged the dinghy ashore. They launched it, climbed in, and Stone started the outboard. A moment later Dino had stopped the Hinckley, and they were pulling up to the stern boarding platform of the yacht, where Viv stood waiting to take their painter.

"Are you two hurt?" Viv asked.

"No, we're fine," Stone said, "just a little sandy." He tied up the dinghy, then got out the stern shower and adjusted the water temperature. He hosed Meg down as she stood on the boarding platform, then did the same for himself.

"How nice to have hot water," Meg said. "I'll get us robes." She went forward toward their cabin.

Stone went to the pilot's seat and turned the yacht back toward their anchorage.

"I'm sorry we didn't get here sooner," Dino said, clearing his weapon and laying it on the dashboard. "If we hadn't had that anchor out, we might have had a real chance of arriving in time to hit them. As it was, I think I got their radome. I didn't see the boat's name, did you?"

"No, there were three outboard engines blocking the view of the stern," Stone said.

"We had no chance of catching up to them," Dino said. "That thing probably does fifty knots with all that power. They're headed toward Key West, though. You want to go back?"

"What's the point?" Stone asked. "By the time we get there, they'll be tucked into a berth somewhere, and there are thousands of them. Did you recognize what kind of boat it was?"

Dino shook his head. "Nothing I've seen before."

"I never even got to my weapon," Viv said. "It was all too fast." Viv, like Dino, went everywhere armed; it was the ex-cop in her.

Meg brought Stone a robe, and he got into it, then they motored slowly back and picked up their mooring again. This time, he didn't lower the anchor.

Dino got out his phone. "I'll call this in, and maybe we can have them met in Key West." He stared at his phone. "Zero reception out here." He grabbed the VHF microphone, pressed the on button, and dialed in Channel 15. "Coast Guard, Coast Guard," he said. "Stone, what's the name of our yacht?"

"It doesn't seem to have one," Stone replied. "I guess the previous owner didn't get around to it."

"Coast Guard, this is Hinckley yacht, calling from Fort Jefferson. Do you read?"

"This is the Coast Guard," a voice came back weakly. "What is your condition and your request?"

"We're safely afloat," Dino replied, "but two people on another boat fired an assault rifle at two of our party on Loggerhead Beach."

"Anyone injured?"

"No, and the shooters departed in the direction of Key West, going very fast."

"Describe their craft."

"Maybe thirty-five feet, powered by three large outboards, very fast. We returned fire with a handgun, and I think we hit their radome."

"I'll alert our Key West station and the police," the man said. "Give me your name, address, and phone number."

Dino gave him his office information and his cell number.

"Do you require any assistance?"

"Negative," Dino replied.

"Leave your radio on Channel 15, in case we need to contact you," the man said.

"Will do. Oh, and you might contact Detective Harry Kaufelt at the Key West PD. He would be interested to hear about this."

"Roger, and out."

Dino turned to Viv. "Who do I have to fuck around here to get a drink?"

"I am that person," Viv replied, handing him a scotch. "How long do I have to wait to get paid?"

"Not long," Dino said, kissing her.

They were given a couple of snappers from a passing sports fisherman, and Stone got the grill fired up again.

12

When they were back in their berth at the Key West Yacht Club, Stone phoned his friend and Viv's boss, Michael Freeman, at Strategic Services, the world's second-largest security company.

"How are things in Key West?" Mike asked.

"Not the most fun I ever had," Stone replied, then told him what had happened.

"How can I help?"

"Meg Harmon—you know about her?"

"I do."

"She has a demonstration of her new self-driving car at the Casa Marina Hotel here, for the benefit of the Steele Group board. She's going to need some personal protection, given what happened."

"Is Viv there?"

"Right here."

"Put her on, and we'll work it out."

Viv sat down with the phone and had a brief conversation with Mike, then ended the call and handed the phone back to Stone. "We'll have a team of six at the Casa Marina by nine to-morrow morning," she said, "loaded for bear."

"That's a relief to know."

"I didn't think we would need security at your house."

"Quite right. I don't think this Bellini guy knows about the house."

Jack Spottswood ambled over from his boat and was given a drink. Stone didn't tell him about the shooter.

"Your funds arrived and were distributed to Betty," Jack said. "She's a much-relieved woman, and she thanks you."

"My pleasure. It's a wonderful boat, but then I already knew that, because it's my second one. You should come visit when I'm in England, Jack—you'd like it."

"You're in London?"

"No, on the South Coast, near Beaulieu and the Solent."

"Pretty country."

They were hailed from ashore, and Harry Kaufelt and his partner, Moe, came aboard. Jack listened intently while Stone related the events at Fort Jefferson.

"You didn't mention that," Jack said.

"I didn't want you to be concerned."

"The Coast Guard were ready for the return of the shooter," Harry said, "but the boat never showed up."

"They probably went somewhere up the Keys," Jack said. "There's a hundred and fifty miles of shoreline up there to hide them."

"Exactly right," Harry said. "If we had a better description of the boat, we might have a better chance of finding it. The three outboards are the only distinguishing feature we have, and there are lots of those on the water."

"Don't forget the damaged radome," Dino said. "I put a bullet in that."

Harry got on his phone and issued instructions to spread the word to electronics dealers in the Keys. He hung up. "How much longer are you staying?" he asked Stone.

"Anxious to get rid of us, Harry?" Stone asked.

"Not in the least. I just want to know how much longer I need to worry about you."

"I expect we'll wing our way north the day after tomorrow," Stone replied. "Ms. Harmon has some business to conduct tomorrow afternoon, then we'll be free to go. And don't worry, I've arranged security at the Casa Marina for her meeting."

"Is this the thing with the driverless car?"

"That's right."

"We were warned that one would be in the neighborhood and not to arrest the driver, since there won't be one."

"That's good advice," Stone said.

The cops left, and Jack Spottswood finished his drink and left, too.

When they got home, Anna had left a big pot of beef stew on the stove, so they didn't have to make dinner.

THE BOARD of directors of the Steele Group stood at the front of the Casa Marina Hotel and waited for something to happen. Men in suits with bulges under their jackets stood quietly by, also waiting for something terrible to happen.

"All right, gentlemen," Meg said, taking out her iPhone. "We've just finished a good dinner, and now we need our car." She opened an app and tapped a few keys. From around a corner, a bright red car with no driver in sight appeared, turned into the hotel's block, then stopped and flawlessly backed into a parallel parking spot. Two more cars, green and yellow, followed, then the three vehicles drove up to the front door of the hotel, stopped, and all their doors opened. "Ms. Harmon," a voice said from inside the lead vehicle, "your cars are here for your party." The board members got into the vehicles, and Stone rode in the lead car with Meg, who sat in what would ordinarily be the driver's seat. "Where to, Ms. Harmon?" the car asked.

"Key West International Airport," she said. "The departure set-down."

"Yes, ma'am," the car said, and the little caravan set off,

negotiating turns, stopping at stop signs and traffic signals, avoiding careless tourists crossing the road in front of them, and giving bicycles and scooters a wide berth. At the airport, the cars pulled up to where departing passengers would be set down. "You are at your destination," the car said. "Would you like me to call someone to help with your luggage?"

"No thank you," Meg replied. "We've decided not to leave, but to go back to the Casa Marina instead."

"Would you like a sightseeing tour on your way?"

"Why not?" she replied.

The cars set off again, while the car radio broadcast a continuous guided tour of the town, giving the riders a history, pointing out landmarks, and making a few jokes. Presently, they were driven back to the hotel, where the passengers got out, and the cars drove away. Meg got a big round of applause from the board.

"That's very impressive, Meg," Arthur Steele said for the group. "Do the vehicles always operate so flawlessly?"

"They certainly do," Meg said. "We're now ready to proceed from beta testing to fleet trials for the Department of Transportation and the State of California. We've also assigned vehicles to about two dozen officials for their daily commutes and normal uses."

"A smart move," Arthur said.

"Well," Meg replied, "it will be much better than waiting for them to read the written reports from their testing staff. There's nothing like a hands-off experience to sell a new idea."

That got a big laugh from the board, and everybody went inside for a cocktail party, joining selected investors of both the Steele Group and Harmony Software.

"That was spectacular," Stone said to Meg, as they followed the group.

"It kind of was, wasn't it?" Meg replied with a big smile.

"Tell me," Stone said, "what would have happened if one or more of the cars was involved in an accident?"

"First of all, no accident would have occurred that could be blamed on the cars, only other, driver-operated vehicles, and our cars are very good at anticipating errors by drivers of other cars. But if an accident had somehow happened, the cars would have collaborated with each other on an assessment of the injuries and damage, taking only a few seconds, then the police and ambulances, if necessary, would have been automatically notified. By the time they arrived, the cars would have printed out a completed standard-form accident report for the police and the insurance company, and the passengers would have been on their way again in record time."

"You've thought of everything, haven't you?"

"We better have," Meg replied.

13

The following morning Stone called Joan and let her know they were returning to New York a little early.

"Everything all right?" she asked.

"Yes."

"Do you want Fred to meet you?"

"Good idea. I'll be bringing a guest, and we'd be crowded in Dino's car."

"I'll let Helene know, too. Dining in tonight?"

"I expect so, just the two of us, in my study."

"You should know that when you arrive you'll find an unexpected guest waiting for you."

"Who's that?"

"You'll see," Joan replied, then hung up.

Stone wondered if that person could be of the female persuasion. He would not be comfortable with such a presence on this occasion. He nearly called Joan back and told her to clear the decks, but decided, instead, to rely on her discretion.

THEY ARRIVED at the Key West airport and left the car in the lot for George to pick up, then walked out to the airplane. Stone unlocked the baggage compartments and began loading luggage.

"You didn't tell me you had your own airplane," Meg said. "I was expecting an airliner."

"What's money for?" Stone asked.

"I don't see any pilots."

"There's just one, and you're looking at him."

She appeared a little uncomfortable.

"Are you concerned about my piloting skills?" Stone asked her.

"Not at all, except maybe when I'm aboard that," she said, pointing at the Citation.

"If you're uncomfortable, I'll be happy to put you on an airline, but it will be close to bedtime before you arrive, since you'd probably have to make a couple of stops to change airplanes."

Viv stepped in. "Meg, we've flown with Stone many times, and believe me, you will be in good hands. You and I can talk on the way about your security arrangements in New York."

Reluctantly, Meg climbed aboard the airplane and took a seat with Viv in the passenger compartment, while Stone conducted a preflight inspection. Dino took the copilot's seat; he didn't fly himself, but he liked to complain about Stone's flying.

They were first in line for takeoff, and a minute later they were climbing in a northerly direction, before joining Stone's filed flight plan. Within half an hour they were at flight level 400, or forty thousand feet. Stone adjusted the heating for comfort and let the autopilot do the rest, then turned on some classical music in the hope of soothing Meg. The air was smooth up high, and there wasn't a cloud in sight.

"A good day to have Meg as a passenger," Dino said, looking around. "God help us if she sees a thunderstorm or we fly through a cloud."

"You think I should have warned her that I would be flying? It never crossed my mind."

"I think that if you had, she'd be aboard an airliner now."

Stone opened the *New York Times*. "You're in charge," he said to Dino. "Let me know if anything awful happens."

They had a strong tailwind and flew at around 500 knots, over the ground for most of the trip. As they flew the arrival procedure for Teterboro, they descended through some clouds until they were at three thousand feet. Shortly, they picked up the Instrument Landing System for runway 6, and Stone put down the crossword puzzle.

CARS WERE not normally allowed on the ramp at Jet Aviation, but Dino's was, and Fred had managed to follow his car through the gates and out to the airplane. Dino went back and helped the women down the stairs, while linemen took their luggage to the appropriate vehicles. Shortly, they were on their way into the city, well ahead of rush-hour traffic, Dino and Viv in his car and Stone and Meg in the rear seat of the Bentley.

"You're very quiet," Stone said.

"I'm still calming down," she replied. "I mean, I relaxed a lot when we were high up, but when we began to come down and flew through those clouds, I got nervous again."

"Clouds are just collections of water vapor. Do you get nervous during airline flights?"

"No, not anymore."

"I hope you'll get used to flying with me. Did you ever consider a corporate aircraft?"

"I didn't really fly all that much on business for a long time, so it seemed unnecessary."

"You should think about it now. I'm sure the board would approve the expenditure, since all of them fly corporate."

"Do you fly yourself going overseas?"

"Yes, I have a house in England and one in Paris. I fly up to Newfoundland, refuel, then go nonstop from there. Coming back against the wind, I stop in Iceland or the Azores, as well, to refuel."

"You make it sound like a very ordinary way to travel," she said.

"It is for me. I don't enjoy the airport experience, and as you saw, we managed to avoid all that."

"It's certainly a convenient way to travel. And I will be crossing the country a lot."

"If you want to look into it, I can find a consultant to help you find an aircraft that meets your needs."

"I'll think about it."

THEY ARRIVED at Stone's house and left Fred to deal with the luggage, then went to Stone's office. Bob, his Labrador retriever, ran to him with tail wagging, and to Stone's surprise, a nearly identical Lab followed him, wagging all over.

"Who's this?" he asked Joan, after he had introduced Meg.

"That's your surprise visitor," she said. "Her name is Sugar, and she belongs to a lady across the street. We met when walking them, and she asked me to keep Sugar for a couple of days while she was away. Bob is agreeable to the arrangement, as you can see."

"I hope we're not going to have a lot of Lab puppies running around here anytime soon," Stone said.

"I don't suppose you've noticed, but Bob has been deprived of that function, and so, I'm told, has Sugar."

Stone took Meg up in the elevator and into the master suite, where her clothes had been unpacked and put into the second dressing room.

Meg inspected the premises. "I like the way you live," she said.

"Thank you, so do I."

"And now that I'm on the ground safely, I feel better about your flying arrangements. I don't think I'll have a problem with it next time."

"I'm glad of that. I'd rather fly with you than without you."

GINO AND VERONICA BELLINI got through baggage and customs and found a driver waiting for them. Once in the car, Gino said, "I'm going to buy a fucking airplane."

"That's fine by me," Veronica said, "as long as you're not flying it. I mean, when you had the little airplane, I kind of enjoyed flying with you, but anything bigger, I'd like a pro—no, two pros—up front."

"I'll start looking into it tomorrow," he said.

"How much does that sort of airplane cost?"

"New, somewhere between five and fifty million dollars, depending on your tastes."

"That's quite a price range."

"I expect we could get something suitable for ten or fifteen million."

"Why don't we wait until you screw a lot more money out of Meg Harmon," Veronica said.

"There won't be long to wait," Gino replied.

14

They dined before a cheerful fire in Stone's study. Bob and Sugar slept by the hearth, curled up together. "I like your house," Meg said. "How old is it?"

"Seventy years or so. I inherited it from my great-aunt, my grandmother's sister. I did most of the restoration work myself, just about everything that didn't require a license, like plumbing and electrics."

"How could you afford to live here on a police detective's salary?"

"I couldn't," Stone replied. "I was up to my ears in debt when an old friend from law school invited me to join his firm. I had never gotten a law license, so I took a cram course and passed the bar. He had it in mind that I specialize in handling the cases the firm didn't want to be seen handling—in short, the personal, often messy side of clients' lives. My experience as a cop helped."

"That doesn't sound as though it could make you rich enough to live like this."

"Oh, I did better and better, as time passed, and my clients got better, too. Then I married the widow of an actor—you remember Vance Calder?"

"Who doesn't?"

"Arrington and I had had a relationship for a while when she met Vance, and they were soon married. He had become extremely wealthy during his long career. Arrington didn't know it, but she was pregnant when they married. Our son, Peter, who took my name after Vance's death, is a film director in Los Angeles, and his partner is Dino's son, Ben."

"So you married a rich widow?"

"I did, and I helped her become richer before she was murdered by an ex-lover."

"And you inherited everything?"

"Oh, no, only about a third. The bulk of it went into a trust for Peter, which I manage. He's old enough now to take charge of it himself, but he's asked me to continue in that role."

"So, like me, you became suddenly rich?"

"Not quite. I was doing very well in my practice and I was made a partner in Woodman & Weld. While she was alive we lived mostly on my income, while continuing to build her fortune. I preferred it that way."

"But you experienced the shock of suddenly being able to have anything you want, just as I did."

"Not exactly—that took a while to dawn on me. That's when I started buying houses—my great weakness, as you have come to know."

"I could use some advice on how to conduct myself," Meg said.

Stone took a sip of his wine. "Go shopping," he said.

"I have already done so," she replied, laughing.

"Not just clothes and jewelry—art, if you like it, the airplane we talked about, a place in New York, and maybe a vacation house somewhere you love. The aircraft can take you there. Just keep remembering—you earned it, and you deserve it. That's more than I could say for myself."

"That's good advice. I didn't ask you about your family."

"Ah, they're an interesting story. My parents grew up together in a town in western Massachusetts called Great Barrington. They were, I think, third cousins, and their fathers were both in the textile business—woolens, mainly. When it became obvious that the young people were attracted to each other, their parents deeply disapproved."

"Why? Genetics?"

"No, politics. My father and, to a lesser extent, my mother held leftist views. My father was for a while a card-carrying Communist. He had no interest in his family's wealth or their business. I think he felt guilty that he had had such a privileged upbringing. He was at Yale when he discovered a love for woodworking, and he wanted to make that his trade. His father, of course, wanted him in the business, but he disdained that.

"After a couple of years at Yale, which he had spent seeing my mother as much as possible—she was at Mount Holyoke— they eloped, he dropped out of college, and they moved to New York to live a bohemian existence. My mother was a talented painter. Both their parents disowned them, my father for being a Communist, my mother for marrying my father."

"And your father became a woodworker?"

"Not at first—that required space for a shop and a lot of expensive tools. He began by going door-to-door in Greenwich Village with his toolbox, offering to do odd jobs. Gradually, he got small commissions—a bookcase, a dining table. My mother's paintings were selling, and together they saved enough to make a down payment on a house with room for a shop in the cellar. After a few years he had earned an excellent reputation as a designer and craftsman. In fact, he made just about every wooden thing in this house. I helped him when I was a teenager, and I learned the skills from him that helped me renovate this house. They're both gone now."

"What a lovely story."

"What about your family?"

"My father was an aeronautical engineer, and after Stanford he was hired by Douglas Aircraft and made a career there. He was on the design team for many of their models. My mother taught high school in Santa Monica, and they lived near her work and his. I was born late in their marriage—quite a surprise, I think.

"We were solidly middle class—I didn't have to work my way through college. I had a golden California girlhood, spent a lot of time at the beach with boys who were clearly not going to amount to anything, although a few of them did. One made a fortune building surfboards.

"I was interested in engineering, but more interested in electronics. I followed my father to Stanford, where I studied computer science, instead of airplanes. I worked at Apple for a while, then, when they showed too little interest in what I wanted to do, I started consulting, wrote a couple of pieces of successful commercial software, which made me some cash, founded Harmony, and the rest, as they say, is history."

FRED CLEARED their dishes, and Stone poured them both a cognac, then he leaned back in his chair and regarded her. "Why do I get the feeling that I haven't heard the whole story about you and Gino Bellini?"

"Well," she said, "I guess that's because I haven't told you the whole story."

"If I'm going to stop him from ruining your business and killing you, I think I should know everything."

Meg sighed. "I suppose it would be ungrateful of me not to tell you about it."

"Worse, it could be dangerous."

"All right," she said. "I guess it's time, and I've had just enough to drink."

15

Meg took another swig of her brandy, and, her tongue thus loosened, she began.

"Gino and I met at Stanford and had what, for that time, would pass as a torrid affair. He was more attractive then—less bullish-looking, slender, and at times, quite funny.

"He got me through my coding courses, being something of a prodigy, where I was klutzy. I had good ideas for what the software should do, but I was not good at telling it how. Gino sort of came behind me with a broom and a dustpan and made my ideas work. We were a good team, two sides of the same coin.

"I also took a lot of business courses, and I was way ahead of him in that regard. I planned for several years to do a start-up, and when I was getting ready I finally told him about it. He went nuts, accusing me of shutting him out of the profits that should come from his work. I took a hard line. I told him I would give him five percent of the company and he could buy another five percent, and that if he objected to that he could pay for the whole ten percent. He borrowed money to scrape up the investment. What I didn't know was that he borrowed it from a guy who was a loan shark.

"By the time we got the company operating smoothly, I had to loan Gino the money to pay off his lender, and his investment ended up costing him twice what it should have. I saw that his debt to me was paid from the proceeds of the sale, and I made sure that in the transaction, he didn't get to keep any of his stock, whereas I hung onto forty-five percent of mine.

"By the time of the sale I had managed to shunt him aside from the self-driving car to another product with much less promise. After the sale, my new partners insisted I drop development on that product, and Gino was just sitting at a desk, doing not much of anything. I hadn't cheated him, but I hadn't been very kind to him, either. Our affair had ended a couple of years before, and he had married Veronica, a very sharp cookie who brought out the worst in him. She's certainly a partner, or even a moving force, in any criminality he's involved in.

"Finally, I made it impossible for him not to resign, and he did. What I didn't know was that he took copies of all the software on the car project, and although I had changed all the passwords, he managed to hack into our system and steal them."

Stone interrupted: "That's when you should have called the police."

"I couldn't do it," Meg replied. "Not because I didn't want to or didn't have the guts, but because I was in hot negotiations to sell the company. The kind of news we would have made in Silicon Valley would have blown that for me, and I didn't have the development money to continue the project without a sale. So I didn't call in the authorities, and my lawyers tell me it's too late now, that Gino could make a case for at least partial ownership of the software, thus having the right to access it. Now I'm stuck with Gino lying in wait around every corner, metaphorically speaking."

"Not entirely metaphorically," Stone said. "He's already made two attempts on your life, and the last one came very close to success. If Dino hadn't had the presence of mind to interfere, and the weapon, you and I would both be food for the gulls on Loggerhead Key."

"That was very timely of Dino," Meg agreed.

"And not for the first time," Stone said. "He and I have a history of his pulling my fat from the fire, not to mention my ass."

"That's a good friend to have," Meg said. "I wish I had one like him."

"Stick around," Stone replied.

GINO SAT at his computer in his and Veronica's hotel suite. "Meg is in New York," he said, pointing at his screen.

"Where?" Veronica asked, looking over his shoulder. "A hotel?"

"Let me try Google World," Gino said, then watched as the satellite shot zoomed in on the signal from Meg's cell phone. "I can't figure out what this is," he said. "It's not marked as a hotel—it must be a house, a town house."

"Well, after we've looked at apartments today, let's see if we can find it. The desk just called—the car is waiting for us downstairs."

Gino grabbed his jacket. "Then let's go find a place to live."

IT WAS a condo on Park Avenue, in a new building. Gino had steered the agent away from a co-op, since the board would do a background check and demand tax returns, an area where his background was spotty.

This condo was promising: around four thousand square feet on two floors, high up, if not quite the penthouse. The views were up and down Park Avenue, west to the park and east to the river. It was the show apartment for the building and was, thus, nicely furnished.

"What do you think?" he asked Veronica.

"I think it meets our current standards," she replied. "We can always move up later." Gino haggled for the furnishings, then signed a sales contract. "When can we move in?" he asked the salesman.

"The minute your check clears," the man said.

Gino wrote a nine-million-dollar check, signed it, and handed it over. "Walk this to your bank and get it cleared," he said. "We'll wait here."

"I should mention that there are no linens included—sheets and towels—if you're planning to sleep here tonight."

Veronica spoke up. "While you're clearing the check, I'll run over to Bloomingdale's and stock up. Do we need pots and pans, too?"

"Yes, and small appliances—toaster, coffeemaker."

"Bloomie's has it all." She rode down in the elevator with the salesman.

"Is his check really going to clear?" he asked her.

"You bet your ass it is," she replied. "He's an impatient man, so be quick about it."

He introduced her to the man on the desk and the doorman, then shook her hand and hailed a cab. Veronica got into their rented Mercedes and headed for Fifty-ninth and Lex.

GINO STROLLED around the apartment, taking another look at it. There was a nice study with bookcases filled with some books-by-the-yard; they each had a dressing room and bath; he liked the mattress. Home, sweet home.

Half an hour later, the agent walked in, handed him the ownership documents, the rules of the building, and a fistful of keys. "Nice doing business with you, Mr. Bellini," he said, and got out of there.

———

VERONICA GOT hold of a personal shopper at Bloomingdale's and roamed the store while the shopper made lists of her purchases. When she couldn't think of anything else to buy, she wrote a check for her goods, extracted a promise of immediate delivery, and left for their hotel, where she quickly packed their bags and checked out.

Back at her new building, she asked the concierge to find her a housekeeper, then went upstairs, where she found Gino, opening boxes from Bloomie's.

"Everything go okay?" she asked him.

He tossed her a set of keys. "We're in business, babe, and Miss Meg will soon be out of business."

16

Stone had awakened that morning and discovered two dogs in bed with them. He moved them gently off, so as not to wake Meg, then ordered breakfast from Helene. Shortly the dumbwaiter chimed, and he woke Meg with a kiss on the ear.

"What's that I smell?" she asked.

"Homemade sausages," he replied, "and scrambled eggs, orange juice, muffins, and coffee." He switched on the morning news shows.

"You're an information freak, aren't you?" she asked.

"You betcha. I have to know what's going on. Shall I tell you how your day is going to work?"

"Please do."

"Fred is yours for the day. Let me explain about him. He's

British, but he came to me from a French friend who gave me a year of him. Within the first week I had hired him permanently."

"What's his background?"

"Military. He was a regimental sergeant-major in the Royal Marines, and after retirement did some security work. He's a lot tougher than his size and appearance would indicate, and absolutely fearless."

"Can I borrow a gun from you? I'd feel better carrying it."

"Do you have a New York City license to carry a concealed weapon?"

"Of course not."

"Then you may not have a gun. Unlicensed possession in this city carries a prison sentence. Fred, however, is licensed, and a crack shot into the bargain, and the Bentley is very nicely armored."

"Why do you have an armored car?" she asked.

"I bought my first one from a Mercedes dealer who had ordered it built for a client who needed it sooner than he had planned. It was arranged for me to buy it from his widow. I was in an awful accident with it, and the armor saved my life. Strategic Services sold me the Bentley—they have a division that armors vehicles."

"They're the ones who provided security for us in Key West?"

"Correct, and they will discreetly follow your car and accompany you in and out of shops, or wherever else you want to go. They are also armed, and they have photographs of Gino

Bellini." He handed her a business card. "If you want to look at apartments or houses, call Margo Goodale, who will set that up for you."

"Sounds like I'll have a full day," Meg said.

"Feel free to make calls from any phone in the house. If you need secretarial services, see Joan—she's the very best at what she does."

"If I find an apartment I like, what's the procedure?"

"You sign an offer and give Margo some earnest money. Condos are the easiest to buy quickly. Co-ops require a lengthy application process, sight of your tax returns, and a personal interview with the board. It can take two or three months, but I may be able to help hurry the process along, depending on the building, and of course, you already have living quarters here, if you're comfortable with that."

"Of course I am."

"Feel free to give this address as your own."

"Thank you. May I hire you as my attorney?"

"Of course. I'm happy to have you for a client, and when you mention my name, always say that I'm with Woodman & Weld. That carries some weight around town."

"I'll remember."

"We'll likely dine with Dino and Viv this evening. I'll let you know about that."

"I'll look forward to seeing them."

"If you want an office to work from, Arthur Steele will arrange one in his building. You're entitled to that as a board member, when you're in town. If you buy a residence here, you'll have to make your own office arrangements, or better yet, have a home office."

"You're full of advice," Meg said.

"If my friends would just follow my advice," Stone said, "their lives would be so much richer, fuller, and happier."

"Do your friends resist your advice?"

"Almost always."

"Why?"

"Because they think it can't be all that great if they're not paying for it."

"I'll keep that in mind," Meg said. "So far, your advice has been impeccable."

"I like that word," Stone replied.

"MEG IS on the move," Gino Bellini said to Veronica, holding up his iPhone. They were in the rental Mercedes, driving down Park Avenue.

"And just when we were about to pin her down," Veronica said.

"Wait a minute." They were stopped at a traffic light at Fifty-seventh and Park. Gino pointed across the intersection. "She's right there," he said. "She must be in the green Bentley." The light changed and their driver moved on.

"Make a U-turn as soon as possible," Gino said to their driver.

The driver did so.

"Now step on it. Look for a green Bentley."

The driver moved into the right lane, which was clear for the moment, in order to catch up. A few blocks up Park, he did catch up, but the Bentley was in the left-hand lane, turning left.

"Shit!" Gino yelled.

"I'm sorry, sir, they switched lanes on me just as I was catching up to them."

"Can you figure where they're going?"

"They're driving west on Sixty-sixth Street, so they could either turn downtown on Fifth Avenue or cross Central Park on that street."

Gino watched his iPhone. "They've turned down Fifth Avenue," he said. "How long to catch up with them?"

"No way of telling, sir, in this traffic."

"Oh, the hell with it," he said. Gino's cell phone rang.

"Yeah?"

"It's Joe Cross," a man's voice said.

"Dirty Joe, how are you?"

"Not so good. I missed another chance."

"I'm not surprised to hear it. She's in New York. What happened?"

"I caught her and this guy on a little island west of Key West, but the wind and water didn't cooperate, and they had a friend on another boat who was armed. We had to get out of there fast, and as it was, the guy put a bullet in my radar, an expensive repair."

"Add it to your bill," Gino said, "and get your ass to New York." He gave the man his new address. "Find a hotel nearby and be at my place at ten AM tomorrow."

"Done. Can I overnight a package to myself at your address?"

"Containing what?"

"Firearms. I can't buy them there, and I don't know yet where my hotel will be."

"Sure, you do that." Gino hung up.

"You're going to use him again?" Veronica asked.

"How many hit men do I know?" he whispered to her, conscious of the driver's big ears.

17

Meg returned to Stone's house a little after five, and Fred hauled several shopping bags and boxes up to the master suite. Stone was at his desk, and he made them a drink from his office bar.

"A good day, I hope?"

"A very good one. Tonight I'll be a new woman—you won't recognize me. In fact, I may be a new woman every night for a week."

"You bought that many clothes?"

"I did."

"Look at any apartments?"

"Didn't have time for that—another day. Where are we dining?"

"At Patroon, a favorite restaurant of ours. You'll like it."

"Can I dress to kill?"

"Sort of. It's not all that formal, though, so don't overdo it."

"You give such good advice," she said.

"Told you so."

DIRTY JOE and Jungle Jane were packing for their trip. "Did you get the weapons off?" she asked.

"On their way. They'll be at Gino's house."

"Where are we staying?"

Joe sat down on the bed and did some Googling. "Best deal that's close to Gino's is the Lombardy, on East Fifty-sixth Street, off Park Avenue. There's a suite available."

"Sounds good," she replied. "Gino is paying anyway."

"I booked for a week. If we get it done, we can take a few days off, see a musical or something."

"How will I be armed?"

"The little .380. I'll have a .45, both with silencers and three magazines."

"Sounds good."

"If Gino can nail her down, we'll both take her. She won't survive the crossfire."

"Good deal."

THEY WERE SETTLED into a booth at Patroon, with drinks and menus before them.

"How was your day?" Viv asked Meg.

"Just lovely."

"How did your security detail work out?"

"They were perfect. I felt safe at all times. You do good work."

"Thank you, ma'am," Viv said.

"Did I tell you," Stone said to Meg, "that Strategic Services is the second-largest security company in the world?"

"Nope. Who's the largest, Viv?"

"I keep trying to forget their name," Viv said.

"What's your job there?"

"Executive VP for security. I used to be chief operating officer, but I didn't like the business side, so I asked for the change."

"She's a happier woman since then," Dino said.

"I worry less," said Viv. "I didn't like thinking about the bottom line all the time. I just assemble the right teams for the work in hand."

"Viv was quite a cop," Stone said. "She saved Dino's life, took out an assassin, and on another occasion, she fired a single shot from a handgun at a terrorist driving a car packed with explosives, from nearly a block away, and put the round through the back window and into the back of the driver's head. The bomb, if it had gone off, would have taken out a big chunk of Second Avenue. She got a medal and a big reward for that one."

"I didn't know policemen could accept rewards," Meg said.

"As it happened, she had resigned from the NYPD that morning to marry Dino later that same day."

"Good timing, Viv!" Meg said. "Can an ex-cop carry a weapon in this city?"

"There are two sitting at this table," Stone said, "not to mention one serving officer."

"Once again, I'm well protected!"

"You also have an excellent steak knife handy, if things get out of hand," Stone said.

GINO AND VERONICA BELLINI glided to a halt in front of the restaurant. "Here we are," he said, and he waited for their driver to open the door for them.

"And how do you know this place?"

"I don't. I read about it in a novel."

The door opened, and they went inside the restaurant and Gino gave his name. They were escorted to a table against a wall and sat side by side with a good view of the whole place. Drinks and menus were delivered.

"Holy shit," Gino said.

"You put that so gracefully, Gino," Veronica said drily. "What does it mean?"

"Look across the room, center booth, under some photographs on the wall."

"I see two couples having dinner."

"Exactly. The blonde is Meg Harmon."

Veronica stared across the room. "Holy shit," she said softly. "What do we do?"

"First of all, stop staring at them. Look anywhere else in the room but there."

"Okay, now what?"

"Tell me what you'd like for dinner."

"A steak and a Caesar salad," she replied.

The headwaiter materialized at their table and inquired if they'd like to order.

"Two Caesar salads, two strip steaks, medium rare," Gino responded.

"Would you like any vegetables?"

"Onion rings and green beans," Gino said.

The man handed him a wine list. "I'll be back in a moment to take your wine order." He vanished.

"Are you looking at them?" Gino asked.

"I'm trying not to," Veronica replied.

"Look for other interesting faces in the room—imagine who they might be."

The headwaiter returned. "Have you chosen a wine, sir?"

Gino glanced at the wine list at the high end of the price range. "A bottle of the Opus One," he replied.

"An excellent choice. May I decant it for you?"

Gino looked at him blankly.

"The wine is twenty years old; it's likely to have some sediment at the bottom."

"Yes, do that, thanks."

"I see an actor I recognize," Veronica said, "but I can't think of his name."

"Good, keep checking him out until the name comes to you."

The headwaiter returned with a bottle of wine in a basket, a candle, and a corkscrew. He uncorked the wine, sniffed the cork and handed it to Gino, who aped him.

The headwaiter held the bottle with the candle under it and carefully poured the wine into a decanter. "There," he said, and poured some for Gino to taste.

Gino tasted it. "Yeah, okay."

The man poured two glasses. "I'll be back shortly to make your salads," he said, then went away.

Gino got out his cell phone, Googled the Lombardy Hotel, and rang the number. "Joseph Cross," he said to the operator.

"Hello?"

"You're in—good."

"About ten minutes ago," he said. "We're about to go out for dinner."

"Write this down—Patroon, 160 East Forty-sixth Street. Call them and make a reservation, then get here as soon as possible. I'll call you after you're seated."

"Right," Joe said, then hung up. "We've got a restaurant recommendation from Gino," he said to Jane.

18

*T*he headwaiter returned with a small cart, with a bowl and several ingredients on top. Gino and Veronica watched as he expertly mixed egg yolks, crushed garlic, oil, a little vinegar, anchovies, Parmesan cheese, and a teaspoon of mustard. When the mixture was smooth he poured the dressing over torn leaves of romaine lettuce, sprinkled croutons on top, and served them.

"Great," Gino said, tasting a bite. Veronica approved as well. "Here we go," Gino whispered, looking up at the entrance.

Dirty Joe and Jungle Jane appeared at the dining room door, nicely dressed, and they were seated at a table to Gino's right and ordered drinks.

Gino tapped in Joe's number, and Joe picked it up.

"Yes?"

"You're sitting on the south wall," Gino said. "We're on the west wall. On the east wall there is a table with four people, sitting under some photographs. Got it?"

"I think so."

"The blonde is who you came to town to see."

"Got her," Jo replied.

"Now stop looking at her. They're already on their main course, so you don't order a starter. Eat something before they finish dinner, then go outside and wait until they come out. Follow them and find out where she's staying."

"Gotcha. We don't have our tools yet."

"Don't do anything, just follow her. When she's safely inside you can go anywhere you like. Be at my place at ten tomorrow morning."

"Gotcha." Joe hung up.

"So that's Dirty Joe?" Veronica asked.

"And his girl, Jungle Jane, the cleaned-up versions. We're not going to have to hunt down Meg—Joe will take care of that. Tomorrow, after he's armed, he can take care of her."

"Gino, you are so smart."

"Sometimes it's better just to be lucky. Tonight we got lucky."

STONE AND HIS PARTY finished their dessert, paid the bill, and left the restaurant.

———

JOE AND JANE sat in a taxi, the motor running, and watched as the two couples got into a large black SUV. "Driver," Joe said, "follow that car."

"Jesus," the driver said.

"What's wrong?"

"That's a cop car," he said, "and it's got the police commissioner's license plates. You want me to follow *him*?"

"Exactly. You can hang well back, I just want to see where the car goes."

They followed the SUV down to First Avenue, took a left on East Forty-ninth Street. The big vehicle continued across Second Avenue and stopped on the right, in the middle of the block.

The cabbie stopped, too, well back. "Well?" he asked.

"We'll get out here," Joe said, handing the man a twenty. "Keep the change." They got out of the car and walked slowly up the opposite side of the street as the occupants of the vehicle dismounted and went inside a town house. As Joe and Jane passed, he made a mental note of the house number. "Got 'em," he said. "This is going to be easier than I had thought."

STONE TOOK his guests into his study, and Fred brought them espressos, while they sipped cognac or Grand Marnier.

Dino's phone buzzed and he glanced at the caller's number before answering. "What?" he said, then listened for a moment. "Are they still in sight? Okay, don't worry about it." He hung up.

"What was that?" Stone asked.

"A cab followed us from the restaurant, and two people, a man and a woman, got out of it down the street and walked past your house. The guy appeared to write down your house number, then they walked up to Second Avenue and got another cab."

"Let me get this straight," Stone said. "They got out of a cab down my block, then walked another block and got into another cab?"

"Right, and the guy wrote down your house number. My driver is an on-the-ball cop. I do not like this. Do you like it?"

"I do not like it," Stone said.

"Wait a minute," Meg said, "is this about me?"

"Could be," Dino said. "I don't think this one is about Stone."

"There's something I didn't want to tell you while we were in the restaurant," Meg said.

"All right," Stone replied, "shoot."

"While we were having dinner, Gino and Veronica Bellini came into the place and were seated across the room from us, on the opposite wall."

"Why didn't you speak up?" Stone asked. "I'd have liked a look at the guy."

"Because I didn't want Gino to know I'd spotted him. Gino made a phone call, and a few minutes later a couple came into the restaurant and were seated to my left, a few tables away. Gino made another call, and the man of the couple answered, then both he and the woman took a good look at me, but only once. They ate something, but left before we did."

"Describe the couple," Stone said.

"The man was tall—maybe six-three or six-four—and thin, with thick, curly, salt-and-pepper hair, not recently cut. The woman was, maybe, five-eight and curvaceous, and here's the thing—they were both deeply tanned."

Dino spoke up. "You're describing the people in the boat who shot at you."

"I am?" Meg replied.

"I hope you're both wrong," Stone said.

"I saw them in the boat, too, and neither of us is wrong," Dino replied.

"And they were waiting outside in a cab when we left the restaurant, and followed us."

"Right," Dino said, "and as soon as they had your address, they got into another cab and drove away."

"This is disturbing," Viv said. She had not spoken until now. "I think we're going to need someone in the house, to answer the door if anyone calls."

"Good idea," Dino said.

"I think so, too," Meg replied.

Stone spoke up. "I have a better idea."

"Let's hear it," Dino said.

"I think we should get out of here early tomorrow morning and leave Dino's people to pick up this couple, if they drop by again."

"And where would we go?" Meg asked.

"Maine is nice this time of year," Stone replied. "And I'm running out of houses."

19

Stone and Meg had breakfast in bed, with Bob and Sugar playing on the rug nearby.

"Why Maine?" Meg asked. They had been too busy exhausting each other the night before for her to ask.

"Because I have a house there, it's convenient and secluded, on an island. Our only other option is L.A., and that's too far away."

"How small an island?"

"The largest in Penobscot Bay," Stone said. "The village is Dark Harbor, and it's big enough for shops and restaurants and to fill out your wardrobe, if necessary. Otherwise, there's L.L. Bean."

"I'd better pack," Meg said. "What will I need?"

"Casual stuff—a sweater or a light coat for the evenings,

which will be cool. I'm sorry you won't get to wear any of your new things. Save them for our return."

"And when will that be?"

"When it's safe. Dino is going to put people in the block, and if the couple shows up again, they'll be arrested."

"On what charge? They haven't done anything."

"They've done something in Florida—they tried to kill us, and Dino can identify them. So can you, for that matter, but I was too busy ducking at the time."

"Then why don't we just stay in the house until Dino's people arrest them?"

"Because we don't know when they'll show up—today, tomorrow, or next week? They may even know that you made them, and if that's the case, they're going to be very cautious."

"Then I'll pack," Meg said. "Is there a washer and dryer at your place?"

"There is, and a housekeeper to operate them." He picked up the phone. "I'll call them now and let them know to expect us. Seth can arrange for our second flight."

"We have to change planes?"

"There's an airstrip on the island, but it's too short for my airplane. A smaller plane will take us from the Rockland airport. It's a ten- or fifteen-minute flight."

"I like small planes even less than bigger ones," she said.

"I'll blindfold you." He called Seth Hotchkiss at the Maine house and let Joan know they'd be leaving.

"You want to take one dog or two?" she asked.

"Doesn't Sugar have a mother?"

"You mean besides me? Yes, she does, but I had a call yesterday, and she won't be back for another few days. She begged me to keep Sugar, and it didn't take much begging."

"Then this will be a two-dog trip." He hung up and picked up the *Times*.

"Aren't you going to pack?" Meg asked.

"I have a wardrobe in situ."

FRED LOADED them into the Bentley while it was still in the garage, then drove quickly out, closing the garage door behind them, while Stone looked up and down the street.

"I don't see anybody," he said.

AN HOUR LATER they were rolling down runway 1 and lifting off. After a departure procedure they were pointed at Maine, and the flight to Rockland took little more than half an hour. Bob and Sugar sat on a rear seat each, looking out the window.

When they turned off the runway at Rockland and taxied to the FBO, a Cessna 182 was waiting for them. They transferred Meg's luggage, emptied the dogs and boarded, and they were soon flying at a thousand feet over the largest and most beautiful bay in Maine, if not the world.

Meg seemed entranced rather than frightened. "Maybe small planes are not so bad," she said.

"That's Islesboro, dead ahead," Stone said, pointing. "See the airstrip?"

"Oh, it's paved," she said. "I was expecting something more primitive, like dirt."

"It's a very civilized runway, it's just short, only two thousand four hundred and fifty feet. I once offered to pay for lengthening it another thousand feet, and the locals were horrified. They don't want jets flying in, and, anyway, this is a small inconvenience."

They set down on the Islesboro strip and taxied to where Seth awaited, standing next to the house car, a 1938 Ford station wagon, beautifully restored. Stone introduced Meg, and Seth put her luggage into the car, then drove them to the house.

"Oh," Meg said, as they drove up. "It's bigger than I had expected."

"You expected a dirt runway and a tarpaper shack?" Stone asked.

"Well, just something more rustic." She liked the interior, too, and the bedroom. Seth's wife, Mary, was introduced and asked their preferences for dinner.

"It has to be lobster," Meg said. "I can never get enough lobster."

Stone's cell phone rang, and he answered it.

"Hi, it's Dino."

"What's happening?"

"They haven't turned up, but I've identified them."

"How the hell did you do that?"

"I had a sketch done, scanned, and sent to the Monroe County sheriff's office in the Keys. Somebody in the Islamorada office recognized them immediately. One Joseph Cross and his girlfriend, Jane, no last name yet, known to the locals as Dirty Joe and Jungle Jane."

"They're nothing if not colorful," Stone said.

"He's let it be known that he's a retired businessman from San Francisco," Dino said. "Nobody knows what business, but I can guess."

"I expect it involves weapons," Stone replied.

"That's my expectation, too, but the guy has no criminal record in California, Florida, or anywhere else, and we can't run a check on the girl without a last name."

"Did you cross-check him with Gino Bellini?"

"Yeah, and no match."

"Meg told me that Gino did some juvie time, but that could have been expunged if he kept his nose clean. Still, Gino and Dirty Joe could have met there and kept in touch."

"Let's not take our guessing too far," Dino said.

"Have you put out an APB on them yet?"

"That's too much of a stretch at this point, but we've checked the hotels and come up with nothing. Of course, they could have registered under an assumed name, if they have IDs and credit cards for that."

"I wouldn't be surprised," Stone said. "If the guy's a pro he'll have all the tools."

"Are you in Maine yet?"

"We're at the house."

"I hope Meg likes it."

"She was expecting a hovel, so anything would have impressed her. She's upstairs getting unpacked now."

"Okay, I'll keep you posted. Go eat a lobster."

"Will do." Stone hung up.

20

Dirty Joe and Jungle Jane arrived at Gino Bellini's apartment building and were sent up to the twenty-ninth floor in the elevator. A uniformed maid met them at the door and ushered them into the living room.

"Wow," Joe said, "what a view!"

"Nice, isn't it?" Gino replied. "Coffee?" There was a silver service on the table before the sofa.

"Thank you, both black," Joe replied. They took a seat.

"I assume you've tracked Miss Meg to the house."

"We have."

"Whose house is it?"

"There's a brass plaque on the street-level door that says 'The Barrington Practice,' followed by 'Woodman & Weld.'"

"Is the house owner's name Barrington?"

"That's our assumption."

"Have you been to the house this morning?"

"We were there at eight o'clock," Joe replied, "for an hour and a half. Nobody left."

"Then they must have left very early," Gino said, "because they're not there anymore."

"Then where are they?"

Gino set an iPad on the coffee table. "They're in Maine," he said.

"Maine?"

Gino pointed at the blue circle on the Maine map. "On an island called Islesboro, in a town called Dark Harbor."

"How'd they get there so fast?"

"We had them at Teterboro Airport for most of an hour, so either her host has an airplane or they've chartered something. You're a pilot, Joe."

"That's right—Jane and I both fly a Beech Baron."

"Did you fly your airplane to New York?"

"No, we flew commercial—that's why I sent the tools to you."

"So, rent an airplane and fly up there."

"How do we find them?" Joe asked.

"It's a very small town, a village, really. Ask around."

Joe shook his head. "Can't do that. When we get the job done, people will remember we were asking."

Gino zoomed in on the map. "The house is next door to the yacht club," he said, pointing. "You got an iPhone?"

"Yes."

"Then use that to find the house—should be easy."

"We'll need to book a room somewhere."

"Now, that's a problem. There used to be an inn on the island, but it's closed. I checked."

"Then we'll have to be in and out on the same day."

"There's an airfield there."

Joe got out his phone and Googled the island. "Short strip—twenty-four hundred feet. That's good for light aircraft."

"Where can you rent an airplane?"

Joe did some more Googling. "There's a Bonanza available at Teterboro," he said, "but how are we going to get from the airfield to the house?"

"Rent a car."

Joe shook his head. "If there's no inn on the island, I doubt if there'll be a car rental agency, either." He did some more Googling. "No, there isn't."

"I recall that you've had some experience with stealing cars," Gino said.

"You have a good memory. Let's hope we can find something near the airport, then."

Jane spoke up. "This is all too insecure," she said. "We don't know who, if anyone, will be at the airfield. We don't know where the nearest car is to steal. In a small village we stand too good a chance of being spotted and remembered. What we need to do is to spend a day or two on the island, get the lay of the land, find out where the fuck we're going and how we're going to get back to the airfield after the job's done. We need to know if there are cops in the village, and if so how many and how many cars."

Gino stood up, walked to the window, and gazed at the view for a moment. "You could rent a house or a cottage," he said. "How about that?"

"Not a good idea. We'd have to land on the mainland, rent a car, take a ferry, and meet a rental agent. We'd be seen by too many people, coming and going."

"How about this?" Jane said. "We do all that, then we leave the island without doing the job."

"That kind of misses the point, doesn't it?" Gino asked.

"Then we rent a boat and go back to the island. You said the house is next to the yacht club, so it's on the water, right?"

"Smart girl," Joe said, "but why rent a house when we can just rent a boat, one we can sleep on, if necessary."

"Where are you going to rent a boat?" Gino asked.

"It's Penobscot Bay, for Christ's sake," Joe said. "The whole area is lousy with boats—we'll research it."

"We should buy a rifle with a scope," Jane said. "It's Maine, people hunt, so it shouldn't be a problem. We don't want to just walk up to the front door and shoot whoever opens it."

"She's right," Joe said. "The boat idea will work, but this is going to be a three- or four-day project, and it's going to be expensive."

"I can afford it," Gino said. He placed a stack of hundreds on the table. "Get it done."

———

STONE PICKED UP the phone and dialed a local number.

A gruff voice said, "Who the fuck is this?"

"Hello, Ed," Stone said. "It's Stone Barrington. You free for dinner tonight?"

"Where?"

"My house."

"Are you having lobster?"

"Yes."

"I'm sick of fucking lobster. I'll bring my own steak."

"Not necessary, we possess a steak."

"Just you and me? Is that the best you can do?"

"Just you and me, and a pretty girl."

"That's more like it."

"Seven o'clock, if you want a drink first."

"Better your liquor than mine," Rawls said, then hung up.

"Who's coming to dinner?" Meg asked.

"Friend of mine named Ed Rawls, lives on the island."

"What does he do here?"

"Whatever he likes. He retired from the CIA some years back, then moved here. There used to be a little group of ex-Agency guys here, called themselves the Old Farts, but one by one they died off. Ed is the only one left."

"What's he like?" she asked.

"Indescribable," Stone replied.

21

A t precisely seven o'clock the doorbell rang, and Stone answered it. "Good evening, Ed," he said, shaking the man's hand.

"It better be," Rawls replied gruffly, "to get me out of my comfortable chair."

"There's a comfortable chair right over there," Stone replied, nodding. "Right next to the pretty girl. Meg, this is Ed Rawls. Ed, Meg Harmon."

Rawls shook her hand. "Of Harmony Software?"

Meg looked surprised. "That's right."

"We get the *Wall Street Journal* up here, you know—the *New York Times,* too."

"And I thought this was the far north," Meg said, laughing. "I suppose you're on the Internet, too."

"Couldn't live without it," Rawls said, accepting a glass of Knob Creek from Stone. "I do most of my shopping online, and all of my correspondence."

"Ed is surprisingly computer literate," Stone said, "for somebody as ancient as he is."

"You'll be ancient one day, too, Stone," Rawls said, raising his glass and taking a deep swig of the bourbon. "But not you, Meg."

"You'd better not leave me alone with this guy, Stone," Meg said, laughing.

"Damn right," Rawls replied. "I'd have your knickers off before you knew it."

Stone laughed. "Ed, I think you've been spending too much time alone."

"Oh, I've got a widow stashed in Camden, gets over to the island most weekends. I keep my hand in—so to speak."

"Stone tells me you were CIA," Meg said.

"Oh, I had a careerful of that work, until I got sent to prison."

"Stone, you didn't tell me Ed was an ex-con," Meg said.

"Damn right I am. I got life and did a few years of it, until the truth came out and I got a presidential pardon. Now I'm back in everybody's good graces—everybody who counts, anyway." Rawls looked at Stone. "So, pal, what're you doing up here? Somebody after you?" He turned back to Meg. "Stone only comes up here when somebody is after him."

"Not this time," Meg said. "They're not after Stone, they're after me."

"Who are 'they'?"

"A guy who was once my business partner, who thinks he should be as rich as I am."

"Is this a shootin' war?" Rawls asked.

"I'm afraid it is," Stone said. "The ex-partner has hired somebody. If you see a couple around here—he's six-three or -four, skinny, curly hair, going gray. She's five-eight, with the usual equipment—sing out, will you?"

"These people have names?"

"Dirty Joe Cross and Jungle Jane, no last name. He's a pro, but fortunately not the ultimate pro. He's tried twice and failed."

"That's encouraging," Ed said. "An inept assassin's not much good to anybody."

"That's so," Stone agreed.

"But if he keeps at it," Rawls said, "sooner or later he'll get lucky, and lucky is just as good as good."

"You're a pessimist, Ed," Meg said.

"I'm so sorry," Rawls replied, "am I casting a shadow of gloom over the party? I hope the fuck so."

"No, Ed, you're right," Stone said. "We're taking precautions."

"Well, this house is a good start, as precautions go," Rawls replied. "Has he told you about this house, Meg?"

"No," she said, "but maybe it's time he did."

"The house was built by my first cousin," Stone said. "He was a higher-up in the CIA, so the Agency took an interest in how it was built and contributed to its design and construction."

"That means the framing is steel clad," Rawls interjected, "and the windows are bulletproof."

"He left the house to a foundation that contributes to the welfare of the families of agents who died in the line of duty," Stone explained, "but he also left me lifetime occupancy. Eventually, when I could afford it, I bought the place from the foundation."

"And added it to the Barrington collection?" Meg asked.

"No, this was before the collection. It was my first second home."

"We don't see near enough of him up here," Rawls said. "Like I said, he only shows up when somebody's after him—or in this case, after you."

The tinkle of a silver bell interrupted them.

"That's dinner," Stone said. "Ed, I hope you're still taking your steak rare."

"I like it too weak to move around," Rawls replied.

They went in to dinner.

JANE LET herself into their hotel suite and found Joe at the computer.

"You find some clothes for Maine?" he asked her.

"Enough. What did you find?"

"I nailed down the Bonanza at Teterboro," he replied, "and I found us just the right boat for charter in Rockland."

"What kind of boat?"

"A Hinckley picnic boat, a thirty-four-footer with a little galley and a double berth."

"Fast?"

"It's got twin 320s, and it'll crank out thirty-five knots, in a panic, a little less at cruise rpms. The renters were impressed with my Coast Guard captain's license."

"Is there a gun shop in Rockland?"

"Is there a town anywhere in this country where there isn't a gun shop?"

"Right," she said. "What's our schedule?"

"We pick up the airplane at nine AM. I've booked a car and driver to get us to Teterboro. I'll have to do a little pattern work to show them I can fly the thing, but we'll be headed north before lunch."

"How long a flight?"

"An hour or so, I guess. I've booked a rental car at the Rockland airport, then we'll take possession of the boat, and you can go gun shopping. We'll sleep aboard, then case Islesboro from the water the following morning."

"And then?"

"And then we'll make a plan. Oh, one other thing—there's an operating quarry near Rockland. We might be able to put our hands on some explosives tonight. That will give us more options."

"Options are a good thing," Jane said, "but I'd settle for one clear shot at Miss Meg."

"So would I," Joe replied.

22

S tone, Meg, and Ed Rawls sat before a roaring fire and swirled the brandy in their glasses. The dogs lay in a pile in front of the fireplace.

Ed was the first to speak. "What precautions have you taken, Stone?"

Stone took a sip of his brandy. "Precautions? We left New York City and came to Maine."

"Is that enough, do you think?"

"Yes," Meg chimed in. "Is that enough?"

"Well, let's see," Stone muttered. "We drove out of my garage at, what, seven-thirty this morning? We drove to Teterboro, and we weren't followed. We flew something over three hundred nautical miles to Rockland, changed planes, then flew to an island in Penobscot, Maine, and we're sitting in a well-armored house, drinking Rémy Martin. Is that enough precautions?"

Ed shrugged. "Maybe. How well do your pursuers know you?"

"Not at all, I hope."

"How did they find you to make the two earlier attempts on Meg's life?"

"Well, the first time, they knew Meg was attending a Steele Group board meeting, and they probably checked the activities board at the Casa Marina Hotel and found out she was on the list to play in a golf tournament, and there's only one golf course in Key West."

"And the second time?"

"They followed my boat from the Key West Yacht Club to some islands west of there."

"I didn't know you had a boat in Key West."

"I didn't, until the day before we left."

"So how'd they ascertain that you were leaving on a boat for some island?"

"The yacht club is in plain sight of a main road—it would have been easy to spot us. Also, we stopped for fuel in Key West Bight, and we could have been seen there, then followed."

"Where'd you go?"

"Out to Fort Jefferson, about seventy miles west of Key West."

"How'd they know where you were going? A boat isn't like an airplane—you don't file a flight plan."

"I suppose they followed us from a discreet distance. I wasn't looking for a tail."

"Were you looking for a tail this morning?"

"I checked out the block as we drove away, and I didn't see anybody."

"But somebody could have seen you leave, then followed you to Teterboro?"

"I suppose that's possible."

"Then anybody with a smartphone could look up your tail number and check your flight direction and destination."

"Once again, yes, I suppose so."

"It would be harder to figure out where you were going after Rockland, unless, of course, these people know you better than you think and know about this house."

"Oh, all right, Ed, I concede your point. Now, do you have another point?"

"It occurs to me that a moving target is harder to hit than a stationary one."

"Another very good point. Are you suggesting we move around?"

"I recollect that you are a partner in a very nice floating object."

"That's right, I am," Stone said. "I had not forgotten. I thought we might even take a little cruise."

"What a good idea," Ed said drily.

"Is this floating object as nice as the one in Key West?" Meg asked.

"Much nicer," Stone said.

"I'm up for a Penobscot Bay cruise," she said.

"I'll see what I can do," Stone said. "I'll call our captain tomorrow morning. How would you like to come along, Ed?"

"You got an easy chair aboard?"

"Several of them."

"Then I'm available."

THE FOLLOWING MORNING after breakfast Stone phoned Bret Todd, his captain. After an exchange of pleasantries, he inquired about the availability of *Breeze*, the 125-foot motor yacht he and two business partners had bought from the estate of the former owner.

"We put her in the water the day before yesterday," Bret said. "We've pulled her apart for a major cleaning, now under way, but we could have her ready by noon tomorrow. Where did you want to go?"

"Oh, just a bay cruise for a few days."

"Then I'll get the crew cleaned up, too, and we'll pick you up at your dock at noon?"

"Noon would be very good," Stone said.

"How many guests?"

"Two—one of them will be bunking with me."

"Then we'll see you at noon tomorrow."

JOE CROSS presented himself at the charter FBO at Teterboro and showed them his pilot's license, medical certificate, and logbook. He did a walk-around of the Bonanza, a six-seat, single-engine aircraft, then he flew the charterer around the traffic pattern, landed, and taxied to the ramp. Half an hour later they took off for Rockland and landed an hour and a half after that.

They drove their rental car into the town, and on the way, passed a gun shop. Joe waited while Jane went inside. Half an hour later she came out with a long gun pouch and a brown bag, and she got into the car.

"Find what you were looking for?"

"A very nice Remington 700 and a box of 30-06 ammo," she replied. "I fired a few rounds on their range, and it sighted in well."

"Then let's go take a look at the granite quarry," he said, checking his phone map. A few minutes later they parked at the roadside near the fence and looked at the pit. "There," he said, pointing at a little shed. "That's where it will be."

They stopped at a hardware store on the way back into town and bought a pair of bolt cutters and a crowbar, then continued to the marina.

"That's lovely," Joe said, pointing at the picnic boat, "and it blends in perfectly around here. There must be dozens in Penobscot Bay." They checked in with the office, Joe presented his captain's license, and a young man gave them a tour of the boat, showing them the engines, charts, and other equipment aboard. They settled in, then went to dinner at a local restaurant. It was dark when they left.

Cutting through the quarry fence, then using the crowbar on the shed's hasp was simple enough, and Joe took half a dozen sticks of dynamite, some fuses and detonators, and they were back aboard the boat before midnight.

Joe sat down and spread out the chart of Penobscot Bay. He tapped the chart. "That's our target area," he said.

23

The following day at noon, the yacht's tender pulled up to Stone's dock, and the three of them handed their things aboard, and the dogs scampered willingly into the launch.

Ed Rawls's gear included a long gun pouch. "I thought we might shoot some skeet," he said to the crewman.

"Of course, sir. We have all the equipment aboard, including the shotguns."

"Thanks, I prefer my own gun," Ed said.

They motored quickly out to where *Breeze* lay at anchor, her boarding steps lowered, and soon they were seated in the sunshine on the fantail, enjoying Bloody Marys.

The anchor rattled up and was secured, as were the steps, and the yacht glided away from the harbor.

DIRTY JOE CROSS stood in the cockpit of his chartered picnic boat and watched her depart through his binoculars. "Well, shit," he said.

"Surely we can keep up with something that size," Jungle Jane said.

"I guess that's our only choice," Joe said. "We have no idea how long they'll be aboard."

"I hope they're not doing a transatlantic," Jane said.

ONCE THEY were under way, the captain, Bret Todd, came aft. "Did you have a destination in mind for today?" he asked Stone.

"It's a calm day, why don't we go out and have a look at Monhegan Island? Maybe we could anchor off for the night, if conditions allow."

"Certainly we can, if the seas remain calm. As I expect you know, there's no sheltered mooring at Monhegan."

Stone nodded, and Bret went back to the bridge.

"Where's Monhegan Island?" Meg asked.

"Pretty far out. We may not be able to go ashore, but we can get a look at it. It's where Andrew Wyeth did many of his paintings."

Ed Rawls seemed more interested in other boats than Monhegan. He used binoculars to scan each one as he sighted them.

"What are you looking for, Ed?" Meg asked.

"Pirates," Rawls replied.

DIRTY JOE FELL in half a mile behind the yacht and set the autopilot to their heading.

Jane handed him a sandwich and a beer. "How fast are we going?"

"Twelve knots or so. I guess that's cruising speed for them."

"Well, we've got a nice day for a hunt."

"Couldn't be better. If the wind doesn't come up, we might get a shot at them when they anchor for the night. You'd better make up our bunk, I guess."

"SO THIS FELLOW, Gino Bellini, doesn't like doing his own shooting, huh?" Rawls asked Meg over cocktails, late in the day.

"He doesn't have that kind of guts," Meg replied. "He prefers to do his damage at his computer keyboard." She told him about the testing of the driverless cars that was about to start.

"If you're a passenger in one of those things, how do you tell it where you want to go?"

"You press a button and speak to it," Meg said, "or if you prefer, you can type your request on a rear-seat keyboard."

"What's the range, before you have to plug in again?'"

"We've got it up to around three hundred miles, now, about what it would be for an engine-powered car. If you're in town you'll use less power, of course. The idea is more for commuting than long trips."

"How does it avoid collisions with other vehicles?'"

"With very precise radar. The car can change directions or stop faster than a human driver. Its reactions are just about instantaneous. You'll never hit a pedestrian or a deer while being driven, and, of course, it has all the seat belt and airbag protection that any modern car does."

"What's the top speed?'"

"Well, if you're on the German autobahn, about a hundred and twenty mph. In the States, a hundred, and the car will automatically slow to the speed limit if it detects police radar within half a mile."

They were approaching Monhegan now, and Stone noticed that there was a small swell running in from the Atlantic.

"We'll anchor in the lee of the island," Stone said, "and with the stabilizers running, we should be comfortable for the night."

JOE SLOWED DOWN. "They're headed for Monhegan Island," he said to Jane, pointing ahead. "I expect they'll anchor for the night."

"What will we do?'"

"We don't want to anchor in this swell, we might get dumped out of bed in the night, and we can't get too close to them. We'll run down to the next island and find some shelter there."

STONE TOOK MEG up forward for a look at the bridge. "It's getting hazy," he said, and noted that Bret had the radar on.

"We might be in for some fog as the day cools," Bret said.

"Do we have any problem with anchoring if we're fogged in?" Stone asked.

"Not really. We can set a radar alarm to go off if another boat gets too near us. That turns on the foghorn and warns them off." He slowed the yacht and made ready for anchoring. The sea was a little flatter in the lee of the island. "There's been a boat showing in our wake on radar," Bret said, pointing at the screen. As he did so, the other boat made a turn to the left. "He's a lot smaller than we are. He might be looking for shelter on another island."

"How long was he following us?" Stone asked.

"I first noticed him a few minutes out of Dark Harbor. He could just be letting us do his navigating for him."

Stone stepped off the bridge and onto the port deck and scanned the horizon. The haze was getting worse, and he could see nothing.

Stone and Meg went to dress for dinner, and when they came up there was no more than a hundred yards of visibility. They lit a fire in the saloon and closed the doors to keep out the fog.

"I didn't get much of a view of Monhegan Island," Meg said.

"Maybe it will be better in the morning," Stone said, but he hoped not. He didn't like the news of a following boat, and the lack of visibility was to their advantage.

They had a drink, then were called to dinner.

24

Stone was nearly lifted out of his berth by *Breeze's* foghorn.

Meg sat up in bed. "What the hell was that?" she asked.

"Our foghorn going off," he replied.

"I thought a boat only used a foghorn if under way," she said.

"Normally, but our radar has an alarm that blows the foghorn if another vessel gets too close to us in the fog."

"How close is too close?" she asked.

"I don't know." Stone was pulling his pants on and looking for his deck shoes. Pulling on a polo shirt, he trotted up the companionway, then walked forward to the bridge. The fog was thick and heavy, with almost no visibility, and the sea was calm. Captain Bret was already there.

"Good morning," Stone said. "How close is he?"

"A quarter of a mile and closing," Bret replied, gazing at the blip on his screen, the only one moving. "He has radar, too," he said. "He's avoided a couple of anchored boats to the west. I've turned off the stabilizers. The swell died during the night."

Stone looked at the blip; it was still closing from astern. He left the bridge and walked to the fantail, where he found Ed Rawls on his knees on the built-in seat, looking astern. He was clutching an extraordinary rifle with a fat silencer screwed into the barrel, a big scope on top, and a banana clip that Stone reckoned held thirty rounds. "See anything, Ed?"

"My hand before my face," Rawls replied, "but only barely."

Stone could hear engines now. "Radar shows he's closing."

"I don't need radar to get that," Rawls replied. "I've got ears."

"It doesn't sound very big," Stone said.

"No, and it's too quiet for a lobster boat."

Suddenly, the engine noise stopped.

Stone peered into the fog. "I still can't see him."

"Well, that means he can't see us, either. Thank God for small favors."

Stone heard a metallic click from the fog. "What was that?"

Ed took hold of the banana clip on his weapon, released and extracted it, then slammed it home again. "That answer your question?"

"I guess it does," Stone replied.

"You should either take a seat or get down on the deck," Rawls said.

Meg walked up behind Stone, startling him. "What's going on?"

Stone got down on one knee and pulled her down beside him. "There's another boat out there, nearby."

"I can't see a thing," Meg said.

"Be quiet and listen," Stone whispered.

There was nothing for a full minute, then the engine noise came up again and, gradually, seemed to fade a little. "Is he leaving?" Stone asked Rawls.

"He is. I think he must have heard our response," Rawls said.

The departing engines made more power, and the boat seemed to be moving away.

"I expect he's got radar that allows him to move around in this fog," Rawls said. "That, or he's just nuts. I expect there are other boats anchored out there."

"Not in that direction," Stone said, "from what I saw on our radar."

Bret joined them at the fantail, and Stone and Meg got to their feet.

"He's left us," Bret said.

"How close did he get on the radar?" Stone asked.

"Thirty meters."

Rawls unscrewed the silencer and returned the rifle to its scabbard. "That's close enough," he said. "The fog was on our side."

"Are you expecting an assault?" Bret asked.

"It's a possibility," Stone replied. "We came up here to get rid of somebody who took a shot at us a few days ago, in Florida."

"All we've got aboard is two shotguns for skeet, but I do have some buckshot, if it's needed," Bret said. "And I've got a nine-millimeter handgun in my cabin, but I think Mr. Rawls is better armed for the occasion."

"It would seem so," Stone said. "Anybody hungry?"

"Everybody, I expect," Rawls said.

"The cook's at work on breakfast," Bret replied. "I think we'd better serve it at anchor, and wait for the sun to get a bit higher and burn off some of this fog before we weigh anchor."

"Agreed," Stone said.

A MILE or so away, Joe cut the engines to idle and set the Jetstick to "Hover." "There, that will keep us pretty much in the same spot," he said.

"What about current?"

"The GPS will communicate that to the boat's computer and it will be taken into account."

"How close did we get to them?"

"Fifty, sixty yards, maybe. If the fog had been a little less thick, we might have gotten a shot off."

"She's probably still in her bunk," Jane said.

"I heard a couple of male voices, once, but I couldn't make out what they were saying. I heard somebody ram a magazine home, though, so I can't say they weren't expecting us."

"That's bad news," Jane said. "What do you want to do?"

"They're just on the edge of my radar screen," Joe said. "We'll wait here for them to make a move, then we'll follow very, very discreetly."

"If we can see them on radar, then they can see us," Jane pointed out.

"Yeah, but when the fog lifts they'll be easy to find, given their size, which is something over a hundred feet. We'll be harder to pick out among the pleasure boats and lobstermen. How many days' food do we have aboard?"

"Three, unless you want to go on a diet."

"If they go a lot farther afield, we'd be better off to reprovision somewhere, then just pick up a mooring at Dark Harbor and wait for them to come back."

"Agreed," she said.

AFTER BREAKFAST STONE sat down to read the *Times* online and wait for the fog to clear. Meg came and sat down beside him.

"What's our plan?" she asked.

"Wait for the fog to lift, then continue our cruise," Stone replied.

"Won't they follow us?"

"Maybe, but they know we're armed now, so they'll be cautious. They might even drop the chase."

"I hope so," Meg said.

"We can hope."

25

B y lunchtime the fog had been reduced to a haze, and they had, maybe, a mile of visibility. Rawls resumed his position on the fantail and unsheathed his weapon again, this time affixing a small tripod under its barrel.

A steward brought him a Bloody Mary, but he declined it. "I love 'em, but they don't improve my accuracy," he said.

"Do you shoot a lot?" Stone asked.

"I've built an indoor range in what used to be a swimming pool on my property, which is good for handguns, and I bulldozed myself a big berm in the woods that gives me up to two hundred yards of clear shooting with the rifle. With the silencer, I don't disturb the neighbors. I've shot a few moving targets, deer that have wandered onto my range, and I've distributed the meat to my neighbors, and that helps keep them calm. As I recall, you have a handgun range in your basement in New York."

"True, but I haven't fired a rifle for a long time, and I'm not sure what I could hit with it."

"Firing a rifle accurately is pretty much having the time and patience to sight properly—and especially with a telescopic sight, it's easier than a handgun."

"What is this firearm you've got here?" Stone asked.

"A few dozen were made for the Agency a while back, and I managed to 'lose' this one on an operation. It's sort of a combination sniper/assault weapon. A guy named Teddy Fay, who worked in Tech Support, designed it and built the prototype. As I recall, you knew him."

"A little," Stone said.

"The combination of extreme accuracy and the ability to go full automatic make it possible for a man to hold off an assault by, say, a platoon, if he has enough ammo. It has a nice feature I hadn't seen before—you can set it to fire two rounds with one trigger pull. I think it increases the chances of getting a hit on a target, especially one that's moving."

"I'll go check the radar," Stone said. He went forward to the bridge and found Captain Bret making 12 knots again. Stone checked the radar. "Any sign of our pursuer?"

"He seems to be in and out of the picture, or it could just be more than one boat back there. It's hard to know if we're being followed. Stone, I hope it doesn't get to be necessary to kill somebody. The state cops would be all over us for a week, and your cruise would be over."

"I hope it doesn't come to that, Bret, but we're not going to set ourselves up as targets. And having spent a lot of years as a cop, I know how to deal with them."

"I'll leave it to your judgment, then," Bret said.

They dropped the hook off a small island for lunch, then Captain Bret came to ask where they wanted to go next.

"I think we'll go home," Stone said. "There's no point in continuing if we've got somebody in our wake, ready to take a shot at us. The situation doesn't lend any pleasure to cruising."

"Right," Bret said, "and I take your point. We'll have you back on your dock by, say, six o'clock this evening."

"That sounds good," Stone said.

JOE TOOK another look through his binoculars at *Breeze*. "They've weighed anchor and are headed back in the general direction of Islesboro," he said to Jane.

"Then why don't we use our speed advantage to get back there and be waiting for them?" Jane asked.

"I think that's the thing to do. They obviously know we're trailing them, and they know we're armed. As you say, just one clear shot is all we need." He turned the boat and shoved the throttles forward. Soon they were making 32 knots.

———

STONE AND MEG went below for a nap after lunch but didn't get much sleeping done.

"I don't remember the last time I made love in the afternoon," Meg said.

"Well, if we can keep you from working too hard, we can do more of this."

She pulled him on top of her. "Let's start now," she said.

BY HALF PAST FIVE they were approaching Dark Harbor, and they dropped anchor on one side of the approach to get the tender in the water. Stone gave their bags to a crewman and went up on deck. To his surprise, Ed Rawls was still on the fantail, his weapon at the ready.

"We're about home now," Stone said.

"Right now is our most vulnerable time," Ed replied. "We're dead in the water, and there's no fog to protect us. I can see four Hinckleys from here, any one of which could be the one shadowing us. They could just be lying in wait, ready for a clear shot. I think it would be a good idea if you got Meg into a jacket with the hood up. Her blond hair would be too easy to spot."

"Good idea," Stone said. She came on deck and he sat her down and asked her to wear a jacket.

"Are we still in danger?"

"Until we're inside the house again," Stone said.

Captain Bret approached. "The tender is ready, and your bags are aboard. We can take you ashore anytime you like."

ED RAWLS put his rifle in the single-shot mode and slowly swept the line of boats moored outside the yacht club.

"OKAY," DIRTY JOE said to Jungle Jane, "you want to take your shot?"

"I've got her in my sights," Jane replied. "I'm just waiting for the captain to move away from her."

THREE THINGS HAPPENED in quick succession: Captain Bret dropped a pen and bent to pick it up, Meg stood and began to move toward the boarding steps, and a *crack* was heard, simultaneous with the sound of breaking glass. Stone yanked Meg to the deck.

ON THE FANTAIL, Ed Rawls sighted, took a deep breath, let half of it out, and squeezed the trigger. A woman was the shooter, and there was a man behind her at the helm. His rifle made a tenth of the noise the rifle had. He stood up. "Somebody's down over there," he said, pointing toward a picnic boat a couple of hundred yards away.

STONE LOOKED back toward the yacht's saloon: a corner window had a fist-size hole in it and around the corner there was an exit hole, bigger. He followed Rawls's finger to the picnic boat, which seemed adrift now. "Bret," he said, "I think you'd better call the state police and ask them to come by the boat and bring a stretcher."

THE MAINE STATE POLICE didn't arrive by boat; they were there in twenty minutes in a helicopter, which they set down on the water on its pontoons. Half a dozen people climbed out, and Captain Bret sent *Breeze*'s tender for them. Instead of coming directly to the yacht, they motored over to the picnic boat in question, weapons at the ready.

Stone could see them climbing aboard, and he picked up the binoculars. Everybody in the picnic boat's cockpit was looking down. Then two of them got back into the tender and it motored back to the yacht.

Stone knew one of the men from a couple of years before; they shook hands. "That boat has been stalking us since yesterday," Stone said, "and after we anchored we were fired on"—

Stone pointed at the holes in the saloon windows—"and we felt it necessary for our safety to return fire." Ed Rawls came over with his weapon, popped the magazine, cleared the breach, and handed it to the cop.

"What have you got over there?" Stone asked the cop, nodding in the direction of the picnic boat.

"We've got two corpses," the man replied, "both dead of gunshot wounds."

"I think you'll find they were both struck with the same round," Ed said.

"How's that?" the cop asked.

"At the moment I fired, immediately after they did, they were lined up, just for a millisecond, and I fired only one round. The shooter was the woman."

"What round does this thing take?" the cop asked, checking out the weapon.

"A .223."

"Well, that would have enough muzzle velocity to take down both of them. What sort of weapon is this?"

"It's custom-made," Rawls said. "Until now, it's only been fired at targets and deer that got in the way."

"We'll need it for a while for ballistics. Your round ended up in the man's chest, after traveling through the woman's head, so the ME can recover it."

"Keep it as long as you need it," Rawls said, "but I would like to have it back when you're done."

Stone addressed the cop. "Is it all right if we go ashore, to my house? You can catch up with us there if you have more questions."

"Sure, go ahead, and I expect we will have."

Stone, Meg, and Rawls boarded the tender and were taken back to his dock. Once inside the house, he lit a fire and gave everybody a drink.

"That's three rounds to us," Stone said to Meg. "Any idea what Mr. Bellini might try next?"

"Not a clue," Meg replied.

26

Stone took the two policemen through Meg's history with the assassins. "We didn't know they had traced us here, until our captain noticed, on radar, a boat following us half a mile back. Then we got fogged in. This morning they were only thirty meters away, but still hidden by the fog. We heard a magazine being shoved home—you know how sound carries across water—and then we headed for home. They followed, then disappeared. Apparently they used their speed to get ahead of us and wait for us to anchor."

Both cops were taking notes and nodding. "And you think they were hired by this Gino Bellini fellow?"

"We do, but we can't prove it, now that Joe Cross and his lady friend are dead."

"My report will go in tomorrow morning," the lead cop said, "and it will say justified homicide, self-defense. I've no doubt that the lethal round came from Mr. Rawls's very impressive weapon, but that will be affirmed by our lab."

"In that case," Stone said, "would you like to switch from coffee to something more soothing?"

"I'd like to," he replied, "but our chopper's waiting, along with the rest of our crew and the two corpses. We'll take them back to our headquarters for processing." They stood up, shook hands, and Stone escorted them to the door.

He came back to find Ed Rawls at the bar, pouring. "I don't think that could have gone more smoothly," he said, handing glasses to Stone and Meg and resuming his comfortable chair before the fire. "Except that they got off a round before I fired my shot."

"Her round made it self-defense," Stone said, "and your round executed their sentence. I'm glad we don't have to put Meg through a trial."

"You know, I've only killed one person before today, and that was in a firefight in Finland. I'm glad I've kept up my shooting skills, though."

"So am I," Meg said.

"And what are you going to do about Mr. Bellini?" Rawls asked Stone.

"Well," Stone said, "I doubt if we'll get a chance for you to shoot him."

"No," Meg echoed, "Gino isn't the type to do his own dirty work—he needed Dirty Joe and Jungle Jane for that, and I doubt if he knows any other assassins."

"That reminds me," Stone said, picking up his phone and pressing a number from his favorites.

"BACCHETTI," Dino said.

"Hi, there."

"Hi, yourself. How's Maine?"

"Dangerous, until about an hour ago."

"How so?"

"Bellini's people from Islamorada managed to follow us here and took a shot at us about an hour and a half ago."

"Did they hit anything?"

"Just a cabin window aboard *Breeze*. You remember Ed Rawls?"

"Sure, give him my best."

"He took them both out with a single round."

"You're kidding."

"I kid you not. The state police are flying their bodies to their morgue as we speak."

"So it's over?"

"As far as Dirty Joe and Jungle Jane are concerned, yes, and you can notify the authorities in the Keys that they are no longer being sought."

"Will do. But you've still got to deal with Bellini?"

"Right. I think we're safe in our beds for the time being, though. You and Viv want to come up here for a few days?"

"I'm afraid the boss won't give me any more time off for a

while, and Viv is somewhere in darkest California, doing good work for Strategic Services."

"See you when we get back, then."

"Looking forward." They both hung up.

"You're staying for dinner, Ed." It wasn't a question.

"You talked me into it, but I'll have to go home and get a steak."

"Mary will find something that meets your requirements."

Mary came into the living room, wiping her hands on her apron. "I heard that," she said. "What's your pleasure, Mr. Rawls?"

"I'm easily pleased," Rawls replied.

"How about a nice crown roast of lamb?"

"Sold, thank you very much."

"Dinner's in an hour," she said, then went back to her kitchen.

Stone poured them another drink, while they waited.

THAT NIGHT, in bed, Meg said, "I'd like to go back to New York tomorrow, if that's convenient for you. I still have to look at apartments, and I'm not through shopping."

"You've had enough of Maine?"

"Well, let's see, pursuit, gunfight, and fatalities, not to mention the fog."

Stone laughed. "Your reasons are good enough. We'll have a good breakfast, and I'll call for the light plane to come get us. We'll be at my house by noon."

"I like the sound of that," she said.

"In the meantime, let's see what we can do to take your mind off Maine." He dove under the covers and did what he could to amuse her.

THE FOLLOWING MORNING they loaded their luggage and the dogs into the Cessna and took off for Rockland. The fog was gone, and they had a glittering Maine day for their flight.

Fred awaited at the airport, and Stone took the shotgun seat, leaving the broad rear seat for Meg and the puppies.

Joan greeted everybody as they got out of the car, while Fred took their bags upstairs. "And how are my dogs?" Joan cried, kneeling to greet them. She received many kisses.

"Anything to attend to in the office?" Stone asked.

"Always," Joan replied.

"I'll go call your friend Margo and talk apartments with her," Meg said.

Stone went into his office and sat down at his desk. "What's up?"

"Are you and Meg still being hunted?" Joan asked.

"The hunters became prey and are out of the picture, their remains in the custody of the Maine State Police."

"I'm glad to hear it," Joan said, plopping a stack of mail and messages onto his desk. "Now, you play with that for a while, then we'll talk responses."

27

Gino Bellini sat in his New York living room and tried Dirty Joe's cell number again. This time, a man answered.

"Hello?"

"Joe, this is Gino Bellini."

"Hey."

"You sound funny."

"Well, Mr. Bellini, that's because I'm not Joe Cross."

"Who is this?"

The man repeated a phone number. "Is that the number you're calling from?"

"Yes."

"My name is Green. I'm a lieutenant with the Maine State Police. How are you acquainted with Mr. Cross?"

Gino's mind was racing. Joe had gotten himself arrested.

"Oh, we're just acquaintances," he replied. He checked his recent calls. "Actually, he called me, and I was returning his call."

"It's important that you and I sit down together for a few minutes," the lieutenant said.

"I'm in New York," Gino said.

"Then I'll come to you. Would this afternoon be convenient?"

"Lieutenant, I'd hate for you to make a trip to New York for nothing. Why don't we just talk now? Is Mr. Cross in some kind of trouble?"

"Well, I guess you could say that. He's dead. So is his wife or girlfriend. Can you straighten me out on their relationship?"

"I'm afraid not," Gino said. "Were they sick or something?"

"No, sir, they were shot."

Gino felt relieved. "I'm sorry to hear that. Have you made an arrest?"

"Oh, there won't be an arrest. They were shot while trying to shoot someone else. Are you acquainted with someone called Meg Harmon?"

Gino wasn't going to start lying now. "Yes, but I haven't seen her for months."

"What is your relationship to Ms. Harmon?"

"We used to work together. She made me a rich man, and I'm very grateful to her."

"Do you know where she is at the moment?"

"No, but she lives in San Francisco, or did the last I heard."

"Are you acquainted with a gentleman named Stone Barrington?"

"No, I've never heard that name."

"May I have your address, Mr. Bellini?"

Gino gave him the New York address.

"If I should happen to be in New York soon, may I stop by to see you?"

"Normally, yes, but I expect to be traveling a lot for a while. I'm really just stopping here for a few days to get over jet lag. I've just come from London."

"Do you have another address, Mr. Bellini?"

Gino gave him his San Francisco address.

"And your e-mail address?"

Gino gave him that.

"Do you have Mr. Cross's address?"

"I believe he lives somewhere in the Florida Keys. I haven't seen him for many years."

"And how did you first make his acquaintance?"

"In high school."

"Can you think of any reason why Mr. Cross would have your business card in his wallet?"

"What business card?"

"At Harmony Software?"

"I used to work there, but the company was sold last year. Oh, I remember now—I ran into Joe Cross at the airport, and I gave him my card. That must have been two, three years ago."

"Have you seen him or spoken with him since?"

"No."

"Well, it's kind of odd. I'm speaking to you on his cell phone, and he called your number half a dozen times over the past few weeks."

"As I said, I've been out of the country, and I didn't take the phone with me, and there weren't any voice mails from him when I got back."

"When did you get back?"

"Yesterday," Gino lied.

"He called this number three days ago."

"I wasn't here then. Lieutenant, I'm afraid you're going to have to excuse me. I have an appointment I have to keep."

"All right, Mr. Bellini. I'll be in touch."

"Anything I can do," Gino said. "Goodbye." He hung up, and he was sweating.

"That didn't sound good," Veronica said.

"It was somebody from the Maine State Police. Joe and Jane are dead, shot by somebody while they were trying to shoot Miss Meg."

"Oh, shit. How'd they trace him to you?"

"They have his cell phone, and there were calls to me on it. You heard my answer to that."

"You think we're in the clear?" she asked.

"If we weren't, they wouldn't be calling—they'd be pounding on the door."

"Still, that's too close for comfort. Maybe you should lose that cell phone, Gino, and get another one with a new number. The Apple Store is just a few blocks away."

"Then let's get over there," Gino said, rising.

———

STONE'S PHONE BUZZED. "A Lieutenant Green on the phone, from Maine."

Stone picked it up. "Hello, Lieutenant."

"Mr. Barrington, I thought you'd like to know that we've got Joe Cross's cell phone, and he made some calls to a man named Gino Bellini."

"That's the gentleman who would be the suspect for hiring Cross," Stone said. "He's pursuing Meg Harmon."

"Have you got any evidence to connect him with Cross?"

"Let me put it this way—Gino Bellini has a hot grudge against Meg. He believes she cheated him in a business deal, which is nonsense."

"So we'd have her testimony of hard feelings between them?"

"Right."

"But nothing to connect Bellini with hiring Joe Cross to kill her?"

"Nothing that I'm aware of."

"Well, I'm going to stay on this at my end. I'd appreciate it if you'd let me know if anything arises on your end that could help us make a case against Bellini."

"I'll certainly do that," Stone replied. The two men said goodbye and hung up.

28

Stone had cleared his mail and messages and was about to join Meg for a drink, when there was a soft knock on his door. He looked up to find Lance Cabot standing there.

"Joan is away from her desk," Lance said. "I hope I'm not intruding."

Stone had a history with Lance Cabot, who had been a CIA operative in London when they first met. He had risen at the Agency over the years and was now director of Central Intelligence. And, Stone knew, Lance didn't give a shit if he was disturbing him.

"You may as well come the rest of the way in, Lance," he said, and as he did, he heard the outside door open and close.

Lance walked to a chair, and Joan stuck her head inside.

"Sorry, boss, I was returning Sugar to her rightful owner, and Mr. Cabot got past me. Shall I shoot him?"

"Perhaps later," Stone replied, and Lance managed a chuckle.

Stone glanced at his watch. "Join me in a drink?"

"If you have some very, very good single malt, I'd be delighted," Lance said.

Stone went to his office bar and pressed the button that exposed the bottles behind the paneling. "I have a Talisker and a Laphroaig," he said.

"Oh, the Laphroaig," Lance replied. "Like it says on the bottle, with just a little cool water."

Stone poured the whiskey, added a squirt of water, poured himself a Knob Creek on the rocks, and handed Lance his drink. He sat down. "Lance, what brings you to see me that we couldn't have talked about on the phone?" He had the odd feeling that the man had choppered in from Langley just to speak to him face-to-face.

"Oh, I was just in town and thought I'd drop by." He took a sip of his scotch and smiled a little. "Always goes down well."

"Doesn't it?" Stone didn't speak further; he just waited for Lance to get around to it.

Finally, the silence got the best of him. "There is just this one thing," Lance said. He waited another moment for Stone to respond, decided he wasn't going to, and continued. "An acquaintance of ours has turned up dead on your doorstep, in Maine. His girlfriend, too."

"Not quite on my doorstep," Stone replied.

"Ah, yes, I believe he was aboard a small boat."

"Correct, and his girlfriend was firing a Bushmaster at my yacht. She broke a window—two windows, in fact."

"And was that grounds for terminal action on your part?"

Stone shook his head. "No, that would have required scratching the varnish."

"Quite," he replied. This was a British locution favored by Lance, who had received his early education at Eton and had never quite gotten over it. In this case it meant either "I believe you," or perhaps, "I don't believe you."

Stone didn't much care which.

"My recollection of your shooting skills does not include an ability to kill two birds with one .223 round," Lance said.

"If you had such a recollection, it would be accurate," Stone replied, "but a guest who practices that sort of thing happened to be aboard."

"And armed."

"Quite," Stone replied.

Lance smiled his small smile again. "May one ask, with what?"

"With a higher and better iteration of the weapon to which it responded," Stone said. "I didn't see the maker's name on it."

"If it was in the possession of our old friend Mr. Rawls, I don't expect you would have. I really must remember to have someone collect that bird and return it to its natural habitat."

"That might turn out to be a dangerous endeavor," Stone said. "Ed seems to have proprietary feelings toward it."

"During the years of his service quite a number of items belonging to his employer seem to have leaped into Mr. Rawls's hands, as if by magnetism."

"I don't doubt it," Stone replied. "Dare I ask how you came to be acquainted with such vile assassins as Dirty Joe and Jungle Jane?"

"That is an unkind characterization," Lance said, with mild reproval. "Mr. Cross served his country well for many years before he took his pension."

"And then decided to augment it with the sort of work that earned him his sobriquet," Stone pointed out.

"Our alumni sometimes turn a hand to one thing or another in retirement, after acquiring skills in our service."

"Tell me," Stone said, "where would the Agency find such a recruit as Joe Cross?"

"From a source more common than you might think," Lance replied. "A reform school warden with an eye for talent."

He held out a hand and examined his manicure. "Which brings me to our other subject."

"What subject is that?" Stone asked, in spite of himself.

"One Gino Bellini."

"Oh, my God," Stone said, "don't tell me he's one of yours, too."

"He was. Gino had a yen for luxuries he couldn't afford on what we could offer him, so he didn't serve out his term with us. His gifts found a higher market value elsewhere."

"I know a state police officer in Maine who would be very grateful for that knowledge," Stone said.

Lance looked at him sharply. "Stone, this conversation, like all of our conversations, is to be held in the strictest confidence. Surely I needn't explain that to you each time we meet."

"So you expect me to sit back and allow Mr. Bellini to assassinate my friend and colleague?"

Lance's handsome countenance betrayed a tiny trace of concern. "And who might your friend and colleague be?"

"You disappoint me, Lance. A crack has appeared in your image of universal knowledge."

"I'm afraid I must require an answer to my question," Lance said.

"I refer to Meg Harmon."

"Ah, the estimable Ms. Harmon! Inventor and entrepreneur!"

"All of that and more," Stone replied. "What, isn't she an old girl of your school?"

"I fear not. We can't take on everybody."

"And you're telling me that you weren't aware that Gino Bellini wanted her dead and recruited Dirty Joe to do the dirty work?"

"If he did so, he was way, way out of bounds," Lance said. "I shall have to speak to him about that."

"And give him ten of the best with your trusty cane, Headmaster?"

"Perhaps I had better expand your knowledge of things just a bit," Lance replied.

29

S tone took a sip of his bourbon. "I am always ready to have my knowledge expanded," he said.

"Perhaps you—and Ms. Harmon—are unaware that Gino Bellini's skills were sought by . . . well, let us say, a competitor?"

"Ms. Harmon's competitors possess deep skills already. Why would they seek Mr. Bellini's?"

"Perhaps they were late to the gala," Lance replied.

"How late?"

"Quite late—so much so that they need a great leap forward and are willing to purchase it at a premium."

"From what little I know of Mr. Bellini, he would be unlikely to decline such an offer," Stone said.

"He did not, strictly speaking, decline. Let us say that we declined on his behalf."

"I didn't know that you allowed your organization to meddle in the affairs of American businesses," Stone said.

"We do not," Lance replied. "We have not."

"Ah," Stone said, "my knowledge expands. So this business is offshore."

"Not a business," Lance replied. "Shall we call it a nation-state?"

"Why are we being so delicate, Lance? Why not call it what it is?"

Lance sighed. "Very well, if you insist—China."

"So China doesn't have a self-driving-car project?"

"Not one that is sufficiently advanced to compete with Ms. Harmon's. And an offer that would seem rich to Mr. Bellini would jingle in the pocket of such a buyer."

"So they find it cheaper to buy the technology than to originate it?"

"They would, if we allowed it."

"And how do you prevent such a transaction between a foreign government and a private individual?"

"Now you're sounding like a lawyer, Stone."

"I do not represent either the seller or the buyer."

"I hope you can understand that it is not in the interests of the United States government to allow a technology of such inestimable value to fall into the hands of what might charitably be described as a 'competitor.'"

"I believe I grasp that. Did our government outbid the competition?"

"Certainly not. My betters would not stoop to dealing with a thief in such an important matter, and a thief is what Mr. Bellini is. I am reliably informed that when he left the employ of Harmony Software, his pockets were filled with proprietary information—designs and specifications—of the product which Ms. Harmon has so recently submitted to the Department of Transportation for certification."

"I knew that he was capable of subverting her software, but I was unaware that Mr. Bellini had walked out the door with the crown jewels."

"How well you put it, Stone! The crown jewels, indeed!"

"I am appalled," Stone said.

"As well you should be, as an upright and patriotic American!"

"Then why do I feel that I am about to be taken advantage of?" Stone asked.

"Stone, your country needs only your assistance. It does not seek advantage of you."

Here it comes, Stone thought, reflexively crossing his legs. "What sort of assistance are we talking about, Lance?"

"Your relationship with Mr. Bellini gives you certain advantages in dealing with him," Lance replied.

"Lance, I have no relationship with Gino Bellini. I have never clapped eyes on the man."

"Of course you have, you dined at the same restaurant only a few nights ago."

"He was not pointed out to me, so I didn't know he was there until later."

"Still, he recognizes you as someone who might deal for Ms. Harmon."

"Deal? With someone whose company's most valued possession he has stolen?"

"Stone, you are surely aware that when a thief has stolen something of great value—and, incidentally, has been prevented from selling it abroad—his most likely market is the victim of the theft. Or, perhaps, its insurer."

Now Stone was beginning to see. "And I just happen to serve on the board of Meg Harmon's insurer."

"My, you *are* quick, Stone."

"And you are just a bit slow, Lance."

"Oh? And how is that?"

"Harmony Software has not filed a claim with the Steele Group, so why would Arthur Steele wish to involve himself in buying back something he has not been asked to pay for?"

"Do you think he would prefer to pay a claim in full, or to forestall the claim by buying back the stolen goods at a substantial discount?"

Stone had recently been involved in such a transaction with Arthur Steele involving a stolen work of art. "Perhaps the latter," he said.

"With that in mind, don't you think that Arthur Steele might be willing to get into bed with a whore? I mean, he would just be haggling over the price, would he not?"

"Lance, I don't think that is a metaphor Arthur would appreciate."

"Then don't put it to him that way, Stone. Speak to the man as a lawyer and a member of his board."

"And who is going to speak to Gino Bellini?"

"Why, you are, of course. Who better to operate in medias res?"

Stone did not immediately reply.

"Oh," Lance said apologetically, "would you like to look that up?"

"I know what it means, Lance," Stone replied with some heat.

"So you'll get in touch with both parties?"

"I don't exactly have Mr. Bellini's phone number, Lance."

Lance placed a card on the desk. "As a matter of fact, earlier today Mr. Bellini got himself down to the Apple Store and bought a new phone with a new number, and he is likely to be *very* impressed to learn that you already have it. That might put him off balance just a bit, don't you think? Give you a leg up in the negotiations?" Stone looked at the card as if it were a coiled viper. Lance pushed it closer to him. "Can't hurt to give it a try, can it?"

"Lance, how the hell do you get information like this so quickly?"

"I have twenty-one thousand six hundred and sixty employees to do the research," Lance replied.

"How much did the Chinese offer Bellini for the crown jewels?" Stone asked.

"That information is a bit more difficult to come by, but I should think somewhere in the region of twenty-five to fifty million dollars," Lance said. He shrugged. "Just a guess, of course."

"I think that Arthur Steele is going to find that a difficult starting point for a negotiation," Stone replied.

30

Stone and Meg had dinner in his study. Bob, now bereft of Sugar's companionship, dozed fitfully beside the fire.

"You know," Meg said, "I think I prefer dining in this room to any restaurant I have ever gone to."

"Thank you," Stone said.

"I should thank Bob, as well. He makes it feel like home. Why have you deprived the poor dear of Sugar?"

"Sugar, alas, is a member of a family across the street, and I don't think they would accede to Bob's wishes in the matter."

"I'm sure Sugar misses Bob, too."

"Then she will have to find a way of expressing her desire to her family before we are likely to enjoy her company again."

"Maybe dogs should be acquired in braces," she said.

"As fond as I am of Bob, I'm not sure I could handle two of him."

"Oh, well."

"There's something I have to tell you about," Stone said.

"Uh-oh."

"Not something bad, necessarily, just something I think you would prefer to know about now rather than later, when you might blame me for keeping it from you."

She looked at him suspiciously. "Does this knowledge involve another woman?"

"No, no," Stone replied quickly. "It's entirely a business matter."

"Oh."

"I had a visit from a fr . . . an acquaintance late this afternoon who has managed to learn that Gino Bellini left Harmony Software with more than his talents and skills in his pocket."

"What, did he steal the silver?"

"Worse—the crown jewels."

"And what would those consist of?" she asked.

"All the designs and specifications of your driverless car," Stone said.

She stared at him, speechless. "And how did your acquaintance come by that knowledge?" she asked finally.

"He has a rather large staff devoted to the unearthing of such information."

"Do you regard his information as reliable?"

"About as reliable as one can get in an unreliable world."

"But what could Gino do with it? It would take him months, maybe years to build a duplicate car. By that time, we'd be in full production."

"His intent, apparently, is to sell the files," Stone said.

"But . . ."

"Abroad."

"I'm trying to think who would be a buyer capable of using the design."

"Keep thinking."

Her eyebrows went up. "Russia?"

"I don't think they would have the technical capacity. There is a story that, during World War Two, an American bomber crew were forced to land their disabled B-17 Flying Fortress in Siberia. Stalin ordered the airplane confiscated and reproduced, down to the last rivet."

"And?"

"And when the Russians were finished, their airplane weighed so much it could not fly."

"I think the Russians have become more technically adept since that time."

"And so has the technology become more daunting."

"The Koreans might manage it, I suppose."

"Think bigger."

"The Chinese?"

Stone nodded.

"The Chinese have the designs for my car?"

"No, my acquaintance managed to block such a sale. Don't ask how—I didn't."

"So Gino is looking for another buyer?"

"It would seem so. My acquaintance has suggested another means of blocking a sale."

"How?"

"Let me ask you—Harmony is insured by the Steele Group, is it not?"

"We are."

"And in the event of a theft of technology, Steele would have to pay?"

"They would."

"What are the limits of your policy, in such a case?"

Meg wrinkled her brow. "I believe it's a hundred million dollars. They'd have to lay off half of it to Lloyd's of London."

"My acquaintance has suggested that I approach Arthur Steele with the notion of buying your designs and specifications back from Gino. With Steele's money."

She thought about it for a minute. "What a good idea!" she said, brightening.

STONE MET Arthur Steele for lunch at a club on the Upper East Side of which they were both members, one so low-key that it didn't have a name. It was called "The Club" by its members.

Arthur shook out his napkin and spread it over his lap. A

waiter took their order and Arthur took another sip of the martini he had started at the bar. "Now, Stone, what's on your mind, and how much is it going to cost me?"

"Let me put it this way, Arthur—it's going to save you seventy-five million dollars."

Arthur looked at him suspiciously. "You sound like my late wife telling me how much she saved me, shopping the sales."

"She saved you seventy-five million dollars."

"I'm not sure I can afford to save that much money."

"Well, it beats the alternative," Stone said.

"And what is the alternative?"

Stone explained, as gently as he could, what had occurred, not mentioning any names. "I'd like to offer Bellini twenty-five million. Your company's liability, as you know, is seventy-five million."

"Is Lance Cabot involved in this?" Arthur demanded.

"Lance is the source of my information, but he is going to great lengths not to be involved in it. He has already managed to prevent a sale to China, but now he is walking backwards as fast as he can."

Their food was served, and Arthur tried his Dover sole. "Meg has not filed a claim, has she?"

"No, but it would take her less than a business day to do so."

"I can't go to the board and tell them that one of its members has filed a huge claim. It would be huge, I expect."

"She places a value of half a billion dollars on the stolen

property, which means given your liability limit, you'd save four hundred million. Can you afford to save that much?"

Arthur suffered a brief fit of coughing. "God, it's difficult to be in the insurance business these days," he said. "What should we offer this Bellini, Stone?"

"Offer twenty million and settle for twenty-five million."

"I was afraid you were going to say that."

"You might remember, Arthur, that your group owns a very large chunk of Harmony Software. If the designs were sold, you would suffer a great deal more than what it costs to buy off Bellini. Harmony's stock would plummet, and you know what you paid for your share."

Arthur gulped down the rest of his martini and chased it with another gulp of his wine, then he set down his glass and applied his napkin to his forehead. "Oh, Christ, go ahead," he whimpered.

31

Stone drove back to the offices of the Steele Group with Arthur, then they went up to his office.

"All right," Arthur said, "how do you want to do this?"

"I want you to cut me checks for ten, fifteen, twenty, and twenty-five million dollars, made out to 'bearer.'"

"And if you should get mugged on the way to see Bellini, or should you yield to temptation and take a South American vacation, it will cost me, let's see, seventy million dollars?"

"Should either of those things occur, Arthur, you can always stop payment," Stone replied. "Do you have a check format that is very official-looking?"

"The checks on our claim account satisfy that requirement."

"Good. Let's not keep Mr. Bellini waiting."

Arthur picked up a phone and pressed a button. "Mr. Harvey, this is Arthur Steele. Please cut four checks on our claims account in the amounts of ten, fifteen, twenty, and twenty-five million dollars, and hand-carry them to me for my signature." He listened for a moment. "Yes, those are the correct amounts, and please hurry." He hung up and looked at Stone. "I expect that Mr. Harvey has suffered a coronary and that someone is calling nine-one-one, as we speak. If he does show up, be prepared to wait while he argues with me."

"I'll summon all my patience," Stone said. He picked up a *Wall Street Journal* from Arthur's desk and began perusing it. Arthur sat, drumming his fingers on his desk.

After ten minutes of this, a man walked in carrying a file folder. He was wearing an ordinary business suit, but Stone imagined him in a green eye shade and sleeve garters, with ink-stained hands.

"Good afternoon, Mr. Steele," the man said.

"Good afternoon, Mr. Harvey." He nodded toward Stone. "This is Mr. Barrington."

Harvey turned and stared at him.

"I'm the delivery boy," Stone said.

Harvey handed the file folder to Steele, but didn't immediately release it from his grip. "I'll need a signed claim payment memo for each of these checks," he said.

"Mr. Harvey," Arthur replied, "let go of the fucking file." He gave it a yank, and it slipped from Harvey's grip.

"Mr. Steele—"

"That will be all, Harvey. Don't let the doorknob hit you in the ass on your way out."

Harvey backed his way to the door, let himself out, and closed it softly behind him.

"You'll have to forgive Mr. Harvey," Arthur said, opening the file. "He lets go of money reluctantly."

"I noticed," Stone replied.

Arthur spread out the checks, took an expensive pen from his pocket, uncapped it, and let it hover over the desk as he carefully read the amounts on each.

"Arthur . . ."

"All right, all right," Arthur spat, then signed each check. He took an envelope from his desk, tucked the checks into it, and handed it to Stone. "They are arranged in ascending amounts," he said to Stone. "Don't, for God's sake, hand him the wrong one, or even worse, all of them."

Stone tucked the envelope into an inside pocket, stood up, and shook Steele's hand. "At the next board meeting, Arthur, I'll tell them how reluctant you were to let go of these checks."

"I want three of them back by the close of business today," Arthur said.

Stone went downstairs and got into the rear seat of the Bentley, then he got out his cell phone, found the card Lance had given him, and gave the address to Fred. Ten minutes later Fred pulled up to a tall, skinny building; Stone got out, went inside, then dialed Bellini's number.

"Hello?" a male voice said hesitantly.

"Mr. Bellini, this is Stone Barrington. I think you are acquainted with the name."

"How did you get this number?" Bellini asked incredulously.

"It was posted on the public bulletin board at the Apple Store," Stone replied, "with a thumbtack."

Bellini made a gargling sound.

"I'm downstairs in your building, and I have a great deal of money for you. Please buzz your front desk and instruct them to admit me."

"I don't understand."

"If the desk clerk doesn't pick up his phone in ten seconds, I'm leaving and taking the money with me." He hung up.

Five seconds later, a phone on the front desk rang, and the attendant picked it up. "Yes, Mr. Bellini? Of course, sir." He hung up. "Are you Mr. Barrington?" he asked Stone.

"I am."

"Will you please take the elevator to the twenty-ninth floor?"

"Thank you." Stone walked to the elevator and pressed the button. The car rose, creating a g-force that pressed Stone into his shoes, then glided to a stop. The door opened directly into a vestibule, and a thickly built man about six feet tall, dressed in black trousers and a white shirt, no tie, and clutching a semiautomatic handgun, addressed him. "What do you want?"

Stone brushed past him, ignoring the gun, walked into a large living room with spectacular views, selected a chair next to another, and seated himself. "I'm Stone Barrington. Shall we get down to business?" he asked, indicating the other chair.

Bellini walked over and sat down, placing the pistol on the coffee table, within easy reach.

"Let me begin," Stone said, "by stating some irrefutable facts. You have taken, without authorization, the designs and specifications of a self-driving automobile from Harmony Software, and attempted to sell it to the Chinese."

"No, I—"

"Shut up," Stone said. "I'll tell you when it's time to talk."

Bellini shut up.

Stone took the envelope from his pocket, extracted the first check, and handed it to Bellini. "Read this," he said.

Bellini read it.

"That is an official check on the account of the Steele Group of insurers in the amount of ten million dollars. It is in payment for the return of all the files you stole from Harmony. You may hand them over to me now and keep the check. I assure you, it will not bounce."

"I'm afraid—" Bellini began.

"That is the carrot," Stone said. "Now the stick. If you are unwise enough to reject this offer and produce the files forthwith, you will be arrested and charged with hiring one Joe Cross and a companion to murder your former employer, Ms. Harmon."

"But—"

"I should tell you that, before Mr. Cross expired, he told two police officers and an emergency medical technician that you had hired him to commit murder. Those two police officers are waiting downstairs in a car to arrest you."

"But I don't—"

"However," Stone said, "if you accept this arrangement and produce the files, I am authorized to tell you that the testimony of the witnesses will be withheld, and you will not be prosecuted for murder by hire. Time to decide, Mr. Bellini. Do you accept?"

"But," Bellini said—and this time he was not interrupted— "I've already sold everything."

32

Stone's first impulse was to grab the weapon on the coffee table and strike Bellini on the head with it, but he restrained himself. "All right, Mr. Bellini," he said, "let's see if we can extricate you from your fatal error. Did I mention that Maine still has the death penalty?" Stone had no idea whether this was true, but he was becoming desperate.

"No," Bellini replied, "you did not."

"Once you are in custody, which action will take about three minutes, all will be lost. Do you understand?"

"But what can I do?" Bellini whined. "The designs are gone."

"To whom did you sell them?" Stone asked.

"To a man named Owaki."

Stone tried not to let his jaw drop. "Selwyn Owaki?" Stone

had read about this man; he was reputed to be the largest seller of illegal arms in the world.

"That is correct."

"How long ago?"

Bellini looked at his wristwatch. "About twenty minutes before you arrived."

"For how much?"

"Twenty million dollars."

"And how did you receive these funds?"

"They were wired to an offshore bank account."

"Did you deal with Owaki personally?"

"No."

"With whom did you deal?"

"A man named Beria, a Russian."

"Mr. Bellini, Lavrentiy Beria is dead. He was shot by the NKVD many years ago."

"Not Stalin's Beria, this one is Stanislav, a distant cousin, I believe."

"In what form did you give him the files?"

"I transferred them to a laptop computer he brought with him."

"But the original files are still on your computer?"

"No, he insisted I erase them while he watched."

"Mr. Bellini, you must be very careful to tell me the truth now. Your freedom and, eventually, your life are at stake. Do you understand that?"

"Yes, I understand."

"You still have all the files in your possession, do you not?"

"Well . . ."

"What medium are they on? Disks? Thumb drives?"

"A one-hundred-gigabyte thumb drive."

"Where is it?"

Bellini reached into a trouser pocket, produced a fat black thumb drive, and set it on the coffee table.

"Where is your computer?" Stone asked, pocketing it.

"In my study," Bellini replied, getting up. "This way."

Stone followed him into an adjoining room, where a laptop computer sat on a desk. Stone sat down and inserted the thumb drive into a slot and displayed its contents. He opened several files at random and found drawings and schematics of electronics. He removed the drive, put it back into his pocket, then did a search of the computer for the files, without success.

"I told you," Bellini said, "he made me erase all the files from my computer."

"Here is what you are going to do," Stone said. "You are going to call Stanislav Beria and get him back here with his computer. Give him a plausible technical reason. Last chance to save yourself, Mr. Bellini."

Bellini produced an iPhone and did a search for a number.

"Wait," Stone said. "Send me the contact before you call him." He produced his own phone and gave Bellini the number.

Bellini texted him the contact.

"Now, call him, and get him back here."

Bellini called a number. "Stanislav? This is Gino Bellini. Have you opened the files yet? Thank God. Do not open them on any account or they will be automatically destroyed, and you have the only copy. Bring your computer back here and I will remove the danger and make the files accessible without destroying them. I know, and I'm sorry about that. It was a simple oversight that I can fix in ten minutes. Thank you." He hung up. "Beria is on his way back here. We will be lucky if he doesn't kill us both."

Stone went back into the living room, took the pistol from the coffee table, checked the magazine and the breach, and tucked it into his waistband, then he had a good look around the room and decided that behind the curtains was the best spot to hide.

"He said he was five minutes away," Bellini said.

"Can you cause the files to be destroyed if he opens them?"

"Yes," Bellini said. "I can even make it possible for him to open them once, but not a second time without destroying them."

"Then that is what you will do. Ask him to open the files to be sure they are safe."

"All right."

Stone picked up the check on the coffee table and tucked it back into the envelope in his pocket.

"Am I not to be paid?" Bellini asked.

"You have already been paid by Beria," Stone said.

"He will kill me," Bellini replied.

"I'll be behind the curtain with your gun. I'll see that it doesn't happen."

The phone rang, and Bellini picked it up. "Please send him up," he said, then hung up. "He's on the way up," he said to Stone.

"Is he alone?"

"I don't know, I didn't ask."

"Is there a service elevator in this apartment?"

"Yes, in the kitchen. It opens onto a small lobby downstairs that opens onto the side street."

Stone nodded. "Play this straight," he said, "or you are finished."

"I will follow your instructions to the letter," Bellini said. The doorbell rang, and Stone went and stood behind the curtain.

He heard the door open, and more footsteps on the marble floor than he had expected. What sounded like Bellini and another man came into the living room.

"You were very foolish to do this, Gino," a man said.

"It was entirely unintentional, Stan, believe me. Give me your computer and I'll fix everything."

"In your study," Beria said. "I want to see your computer first."

Stone hadn't counted on this. He realized that he could see the study door from his position, and that meant that they would be able to see him from the study.

Bellini, Beria, and another, much larger man walked across the living room and entered the study. Beria sat down at

Bellini's computer and began typing. "The files are not here," he said.

"I told you that," Bellini replied.

"Now, you fix my computer so that I can open the files safely," Beria said.

Stone could see Bellini as he sat down, opened Beria's laptop, and began typing. After a couple of minutes of this, Bellini said, "There, it's fixed. You can open the files now. Try it, if you like."

Beria sat down and opened some files. "It works," he said. Now you sit down at your computer."

Bellini did so.

"Now we will transfer the twenty million I sent you back into my account. Don't worry, when I have had this checked out, I will rewire it."

At this moment, Stone heard the front door open and the click of high heels on marble. "Gino?" a woman's voice called.

"I'm in the study," Gino called back. "I'll be there in a minute."

The woman walked across the living room and into the study. Stone realized that, when they finished doing what they were doing, everyone would come back into the living room, and they would see him. Everyone in the study was standing behind Gino, watching what he did on his computer. "Now is the time," Stone said to himself. He slipped out of his shoes, held them in one hand, and the pistol in the other, then started walking quickly and soundlessly across the living room.

"There, it's done," he heard Gino say.

"Done is correct," Beria replied, then a single gunshot rang out, and the woman screamed.

Stone ran flat-out for the kitchen, and as he did, there was a second gunshot. He found the service elevator and pressed the button. The lights on the panel told him the car was on the ground floor. It began to rise, too slowly to suit Stone. He pressed the button again, hoping to hurry it, then he heard the footsteps of two men walking from the study back into the living room. He saw them go to the coffee table, and that meant that if they turned, they could see him, and there was nowhere to hide.

The elevator still had fifteen floors to go.

33

Stone stared at the floor numbers of the elevator as they slowly changed.

"LET'S GET OUT of here," Beria said to his companion.

"Better see if there's a back way," the man replied.

THE ELEVATOR DOOR opened; Stone stepped into the car and began looking for the correct number. Finally, he found G and pressed it, then slipped on his shoes and tucked the gun into his waistband. The door slid silently shut, but the car did not move.

Stone was about to reach for the button again, but the door

slid open and two men stood there. Beria was maybe six feet and 190 pounds; the other man was taller and a gorilla by any measure, maybe three hundred pounds. They stared at Stone.

"Good morning," Stone said, backing up until he was leaning against the rear wall. "Going down?"

"Thank you, yes," Beria said, stepping onto the elevator, followed by the gorilla. The door slid shut again, and after another pause the car started down.

Beria, who was leaning against the wall on Stone's left, said, "You live upstairs?"

"No, just visiting," Stone replied. The elevator seemed to inch down.

"Quite a building, eh?" Beria asked.

"Spectacular views," Stone replied.

"Who lives upstairs?" Beria asked.

"A woman of my acquaintance," Stone replied.

"And her husband?" Beria asked slyly.

"I'm afraid so. Fortunately, he's out of town."

Beria gave a short laugh, and the elevator stopped. The door slid open, and the two men got off. "Be careful," Beria said.

"Don't worry," Stone said, following them out of the elevator, but more slowly, hoping to put more distance between them.

The two went through the outside door and turned right, toward Park Avenue. Stone turned left, got out his phone and called Fred, who was waiting on Park.

"Yessir?" Fred said.

"Meet me on the corner of Fifty-ninth and Lex."

"Yessir."

Stone put away the phone and continued walking. As he did, a black S-Class Mercedes drove past him, and Beria waved from the rear seat. As Stone approached Lexington Avenue, the light changed and the Mercedes stopped. The rear window slid down, and Beria said, "Can I give you a lift somewhere?"

"Thank you, but my car is just around the corner," Stone replied with a little smile. He turned left, just as Fred drew up. The light changed, the Mercedes turned right and drove down Lex. Stone got into the Bentley. "Fred," Stone said, "follow the Mercedes, but keep well back."

"Which Mercedes, sir?"

"The black S-Class."

"Which black S-Class?" Fred asked.

Stone looked ahead of them and saw two Black Mercedeses driving a block down Lex ahead of them.

"Shit," Stone muttered.

"Let me know when you decide," Fred said

"Do you know which one entered Lex from the direction I came?"

"I'm not sure," Fred replied.

"Be sure to keep up with the changing lights," Stone said. "We don't want to get stuck. If we get a red light, run it."

"As you wish, sir."

As Stone watched, the Mercedes in the left lane turned left on East Forty-ninth Street, and the other continued straight ahead. "Follow the one that turned," Stone said, taking a flier.

"Yessir."

The Mercedes continued east, stopping for a couple of lights, then, as it approached First Avenue, it pulled over and stopped.

"Stop," Stone said.

Fred pulled over. "The car has diplomatic plates," he said.

From half a block back, Stone watched as Beria and the gorilla got out of the Mercedes and went up the front stairs into a building. The Mercedes drove away.

"Continue," Stone said, "but I want to see what that building is, so go very slowly."

As they passed the building Stone saw two brass plaques, one on each side of the large doors. The one on the left was unintelligible to him, since it was in the Cyrillic alphabet; the other, in English, read: PERMANENT MISSION OF THE RUSSIAN FEDERATION TO THE UNITED NATIONS.

"Okay," Stone said, "home." He waited until he was at his desk before he called Dino.

"Bacchetti."

"It's Stone."

"I figured."

"How did you figure?"

"I don't know. I get a creepy feeling sometimes when the phone rings, which means it's you."

"I want to report a double murder."

"Then call the police," Dino said.

"Has the mayor fired you?"

"Not yet."

"Then *you* are the police."

"Yeah, but all I'm going to do is call Homicide and tell them to get on it, so why don't you just call nine-one-one?"

"Because I don't want to have to explain why I was where the murders took place."

"You're going to have to explain that to *me*," Dino pointed out.

"I have no problem with that. You're taking the call, then?"

"Yeah, okay, let me get a pencil."

Stone heard drawers opening and closing, then Dino came back on the line.

"Okay, go."

Stone gave him the address and floor number of the building.

"Okay, who got offed?"

"A man named Gino Bellini and his wife, Veronica."

"The guy who hired Dirty Joe?"

"That's the one," Stone replied. "Did I tell you that Dirty Joe and his girl are dead? They were shot while tracking us in Maine."

"Yeah, you told me. That's Maine's problem," Dino replied. "Who killed the Bellinis?"

"A man named Stanislav Beria and an unsub."

"I know the name," Dino said. "Beria is with the Russian UN mission."

"Well, yes, I saw him go inside the mission, but he also works for Selwyn Owaki."

"He can't work for Owaki. Beria is a legitimate Russian

diplomat," Dino said. "I met him at a cocktail party at the Russian Embassy."

"I don't question that, but Gino Bellini told me he works for Owaki."

"Was this before or after Bellini was murdered? We could use a witness."

"Before, obviously, and I'm a witness to both murders."

"You actually saw them happen?"

"Yes. Well, more correctly, I heard them happen, one shot, followed a moment later by another."

"So you're not a witness?"

"Beria and his gorilla were the only other people in the apartment, besides Bellini and his wife."

"And you. You were in the apartment."

"Yes, Dino, I was."

"Were you in the room?"

"I was in the living room. Everybody else was in an adjoining study."

"So you're not a witness."

"I heard the shots."

"From the next room."

"Dino, Beria, his gorilla, and I were the only people in the apartment still standing, and I didn't kill them, so who's left?"

"Why didn't they kill you?"

"I was hiding behind a curtain, and while they were still in the study I made a run for the service elevator, in the kitchen."

"Why didn't you take the regular elevator?"

"Because I didn't want to be seen by the front desk staff leaving the building."

"Why? You say you didn't kill them."

"That doesn't mean they wouldn't think I did."

"Go on."

"Then I rode down on the elevator with Beria and the gorilla."

"Let me get this straight. You heard two people shot in the next room, then you rode down on the elevator with the shooters?"

"I was in the kitchen, waiting for the service elevator to arrive on my floor. I got in, the door closed, then it opened again and Beria and the gorilla got in."

"And they didn't notice you?"

"They did. I pretended to be visiting a woman upstairs."

"What woman?"

"There was no woman, Dino. Beria asked if I lived upstairs, and I said no, I was visiting a woman whose husband was out of town."

"Was this something derived from your own experience, Stone? Visiting a woman whose husband is out of town?"

"No, Dino, I made it up so Beria wouldn't shoot me."

"So where are the dead bodies?"

"Where they fell, in the study, I imagine. I suggest you get a team over there right now, then arrest Beria."

"Beria is a Russian diplomat, and as such, he carries a diplomatic passport and is immune from arrest, even for a double murder."

"Then arrest the gorilla."

"You want my people to appear at the Russian mission and ask for a gorilla?"

"I suggest you put a couple of men outside the mission. Since he and Beria appeared to be joined at the hip, when Beria leaves, arrest the gorilla."

"I'm going to have a hard time getting an arrest warrant for a gorilla," Dino said. "I don't think I'd even like to mention a gorilla to a grand jury, under oath."

"I have done my duty as a citizen," Stone said. "You want dinner tonight? P. J. Clarke's at seven?"

"Is Meg still there?"

"Yes."

"I'd love to have dinner with Meg. See you then." Dino hung up, and so did Stone.

34

Stone sent Fred over to Arthur Steele's office with the checks Arthur had signed. As Fred left for Steele's office, Joan buzzed Stone. "Arthur Steele on one."

Stone pressed the button. "Hello, Arthur, your checks are on their way back to you by hand."

"Which checks?"

"The ones you signed and gave to me."

"Which one did you give Bellini?"

"The one for ten million, but he gave it back, sort of."

"You're sending me all four checks, then?"

"That is correct."

"Did you get the computer files you wanted?"

"Yes."

"Without paying for them?"

"Yes."

"Stone, forgive my asking, but how did you do that?"

"It's complicated, Arthur. I'll explain when I see you again."

"Stone, did you do something to Bellini? I don't want to be a party to anything like that."

"No, Arthur, and Bellini is dead, so I couldn't do anything to him."

"Did you kill him?"

"Of course not—someone else did."

"I'm confused."

"I told you it was complicated, Arthur. All you need to know for now is that your checks are being hand-delivered to you now, and I got back the computer files, so there won't be an insurance claim."

"This sounds too easy, Stone. What are you keeping from me?"

"Arthur, please do this—pretend that we didn't have lunch today and that you didn't give me any checks. You'll feel better."

"But what about Bellini? Am I going to be questioned by the police?"

"No, Arthur, you are not, trust me. Have a drink and relax. Goodbye." Stone hung up.

STONE AND MEG had a drink in his study before leaving to meet Dino. "I have good news for you," Stone said, digging in his pocket and coming up with the thumb drive.

"What is that?" Meg asked.

"It contains the designs and specifications that Dino Bellini stole from you."

She went to the computer on his desk, plugged in the thumb drive, and examined some of the files. "How did you get them?" she asked, returning to her chair.

"Bellini gave me the drive."

"Why?"

"Because I gave him a check for ten million dollars."

"Your own ten million dollars?"

"No, it was from Arthur Steele, but I've since returned the check to him."

"Gino gave you back the check?"

"I persuaded him to."

"How did you do that?"

"I told him that Dirty Joe had confessed to two Maine State Police officers and an EMT that he had been hired by Bellini to kill you, and that the two Maine cops were downstairs in his building waiting to arrest him."

"But that wasn't true. Was it?"

"No, I lied."

"And that worked?"

"Yes."

"So what happens now? Is Gino still coming after me?"

"No, Gino is dead. Veronica, too."

"Good God, Stone! Did you kill them?"

"No, I did not kill them. You are the third person to whom I've had to deny that, and I'm getting tired of it."

"Stone, if you had killed Gino and Veronica, would you deny it to me?"

"No. Yes. I mean, I didn't kill them, so there's no need to deny it."

"But you just did."

"Because I didn't."

"Are you telling me the truth?"

"Yes, and that's the last question I'm going to answer on the subject."

"If you didn't kill them, who did?"

"I just said I wouldn't answer any more questions about it."

"Stone . . ."

"Listen very carefully. Gino and Veronica were killed by someone he had sold the stolen designs to—a man named Beria, who works for an arms dealer."

"None of those names mean anything to me."

"It's not important that they do."

"Wait a minute, you said that Gino sold this man the designs?"

"Yes, but he got them back."

"How? Why are you keeping this from me?"

"Tell you what—tomorrow morning, when I'm sober and less tired, I will explain everything to you in detail. In the meantime, all you need to know is that you have your designs back, Arthur has his check back, Gino and Veronica are dead, and I didn't kill them. May we leave it that way until tomorrow morning?"

"I guess so."

"Thank you very much." Stone looked at his watch: "It's time we left for dinner."

"With Dino and Viv?"

"Yes. Or at least, with Dino. Viv travels a lot on business, and she could be out of town. I didn't ask."

"Do I have to keep this business about the designs from Dino?"

"No, I've already explained it to him."

"Why Dino? Why not me, first? I mean, they're my designs."

"I had to report the murders to the police, so I called Dino as soon as possible."

"Gino and Veronica were murdered?"

"Yes, I told you that."

"You said they were dead."

"Well, they didn't simultaneously drop dead of heart attacks."

"But you didn't kill them?"

"If you ask me that again, I'll have to kill myself," Stone replied.

"You're going to have to explain all this to me later, Stone."

"I have already promised to do so. Shall we go?"

"Oh, all right."

35

They found Dino at the bar at P. J. Clarke's, half a drink ahead of them.

"Where's Viv?" Meg asked.

"Somewhere in darkest California, on business. Happens all the time. Our table is ready. You want to order your drinks in the dining room?"

"Sure," Stone said, and steered Meg that way.

When they were seated and the drinks had been served, including another for Dino, he said, "I assume Meg knows about this?"

"About what?" Meg asked.

"Yes, she knows." He turned to Meg. "About what I told you a few minutes ago."

"Oh, that."

"My people are taking Bellini's apartment apart as we speak," Dino said. "They were both in the study, as you said. One each in the head."

"Oh, God," Meg said. "I'm going to be sick."

"Why?" Dino asked. "You didn't get shot."

"No more details, please."

"I forgot to tell you," Stone said, "I took Bellini's gun from the apartment. I'll send it to you tomorrow."

"Why did you do that?"

"It was lying on the coffee table when the doorman rang to say Beria was on his way up, and Bellini was already in the study, so I stuck it in my belt. A little later, when I had to sneak out of there, with my shoes in my hand, I thought I might need it for self-defense if Beria saw me. Then, in the elevator, I was glad I had it."

"Give it to my homicide detectives," Dino said.

"Which detectives?"

"The ones who will be calling on you first thing in the morning to question you about the murders."

"I had hoped to avoid that by going straight to the top," Stone said.

"You hoped in vain. We have procedures, remember?"

"Yes, yes."

"Stone," Meg said, "if you didn't kill them, why are the police questioning you?"

"Because Dino somehow neglected to tell them that I didn't kill them."

"I couldn't do that," Dino said. "They have to draw their own conclusions from evidence and the witnesses." He turned to Meg. "Stone is the only witness, so it's standard practice that he is the immediate suspect, until the evidence clears him."

"What kind of evidence will clear him?" she asked.

"Beats me," Dino said. "I haven't visited the crime scene."

"Lack of motive," Stone said to her.

"I wouldn't lean too heavily on that," Dino said. "After all, you went to Bellini's apartment to get something he stole from your client. An objective person might conclude that he was reluctant to give it to you, and in the ensuing argument, you shot Bellini, then his wife, because she was a witness."

"An objective observer would not think that if he knew that I went to see Bellini with seventy million dollars in checks of different amounts, in order to buy the stolen designs back from him, and he accepted one for ten million."

"They didn't find any checks," Dino said.

"That's because I returned the checks to Arthur Steele, who gave them to me for the purpose of buying back the stolen designs."

"In that case, an objective observer might conclude that you murdered them to get back the ten million," Dino said, "and a jury might very well accept that conclusion."

"Stone is going to trial?" Meg asked.

"I am not," Stone said. "When Dino's detectives have heard all the facts, they will move on to the next suspect, who is the person who killed them, one Stanislav Beria. I am your witness to that."

"You didn't actually see Beria shoot them, and my people didn't find him in the apartment," Dino said.

"Of course not. I trailed Beria and his gorilla to the Russian mission. They'll find him there."

"No, the Russians won't let them in, and even if they should find Beria off the reservation, he will decline to answer any questions because he's a certified diplomat and has a diplomatic passport to prove it."

"Back to you, Stone," Meg said.

"I also have an excellent character witness," Stone said, "who will tell the detectives that I would never murder anyone."

"They would discount my testimony," Dino replied, "because they know that we are very good friends, and that I would probably lie for you."

"Probably?"

"Probably."

"The ballistic evidence will show that the bullet did not come from any weapon I own."

"Of course not," Dino said. "You would have been unlikely to use a weapon that could be traced to you. In cases like this, the murderer often obtains an untraceable weapon, and anyway, he would ditch it at the first opportunity."

"The doorman at Bellini's building will testify that Beria and the gorilla went up to Bellini's apartment," Stone said.

"He will also testify that *you* went up to Bellini's apartment," Dino said blithely.

"Your detectives will find no gunshot residue on my person or clothing," Stone said gamely.

"You've had plenty of time to scrub your hands and send your clothes to be cleaned."

The waiter brought menus.

"I recommend the steaks," Stone said to Meg.

"I think I've lost my appetite," she replied. "You should have the steak, though. I understand the food is terrible in prison."

Stone took a deep breath and let it out.

"Don't lose your temper, Stone," Dino said. "There are half a dozen people here who know you and could testify that you have trouble controlling yourself."

The waiter came to take their order.

"Terry," Stone said to the man, "have you ever known me to lose my temper?"

"Well," Terry said thoughtfully, "there was that time when your steak arrived too rare, and you threatened to murder the chef."

"Heh, heh," Stone said. "You know that was entirely in jest."

"You didn't seem to be jesting," Terry replied. "And you were sort of fondling your steak knife."

"I rest my case," Dino said.

Stone ordered, through clenched teeth.

Dino and Meg ordered, too.

"And a bottle of that cheap Cabernet that Stone always orders when he's buying," Dino said to the waiter.

"Gotcha," Terry said, then left.

"Well, Dino," Meg said, "I don't think Stone was very convincing about his anger problem."

"Neither do I," Dino replied.

Stone polished off his drink and began to fondle his steak knife.

36

Stone was stonily silent in the car on the way home, and Meg didn't disturb him. Back at the house they undressed and Stone came to bed wearing a nightshirt, while Meg was naked, as usual.

"That's amusing," she said, nodding at the nightshirt.

"You are easily amused," Stone replied. "You've been amused all evening by Dino, who was, as usual, very amusing."

"You thought I was serious about suspecting you of murder?"

"Were you not?"

"I was not, but perhaps I should revise my opinion."

"Which is?"

"There you go—I was trying to amuse you, and you took it the wrong way, of course."

"What do you mean, 'of course'?"

"You've been intent all night on taking everything I said the wrong way."

"I suppose I had trouble discerning between your speaking the wrong way and your speaking the right way," Stone said.

"Hasn't it occurred to you that I would never suspect you of murder?"

"No, it has not, given the circumstances, and Dino had trouble coming down on the right side of that question, as well."

"Are you mad at me or mad at Dino?"

"Can't I be annoyed with you both, simultaneously?"

"It's very unattractive when you are."

"I plead guilty to being unattractive, but not to murder."

Meg got out of bed, went to her dressing room, and came back wearing a nightgown. "Good night," she said, climbing into bed, pulling the covers up to her chin, and turning on her side, away from Stone.

"Sleep well," Stone grumbled. It seemed to him that Meg fell asleep immediately, which made him even angrier. He got very little sleep that night.

STONE WOKE from a fitful sleep with sunlight streaming through a window where he had forgotten to close the curtains. He reached for Meg but found Bob instead, his tail thumping against the bed. Stone could hear Meg's shower running. He rang Helene and ordered breakfast, then found the *Times* where it had been slid under the door and got back into bed, switching on *Morning Joe*, and pressed the remote control that sat him up and pointed him at the TV.

Meg came out of the bathroom in a terry robe, toweling her hair.

"Good morning," he said.

"Good morning."

"I ordered breakfast for us."

"I'm not very hungry."

"That's what you said last night and you ate a steak, then some of mine."

"Do you think I'm getting fat?"

"I don't know, I haven't seen your body for about thirty-six hours."

She whipped off the robe and posed for him. "There, dear, is that better?"

Stone looked up from his paper. "You're not getting fat," he said.

"I'm so relieved."

Breakfast came and they both ate everything on the tray.

"Now I'm getting fat," she said.

"Don't worry about it."

"Are we still angry with each other?" she asked.

"I'm not angry," Stone replied. "I'm disappointed."

"Disappointed in me?"

"I don't know what you want," he said. "I've kept you from

being shot twice, I've recovered half a billion dollars of computer files, and kept those files from being sold to a notorious arms dealer who could have sold them to anybody. Oh, and I murdered the man who ordered you killed. Is that not enough?"

"You murdered Bellini?" she asked, horrified.

"Of course not, that was a joke."

"It wasn't very funny."

"Funny, I thought it was."

"I didn't think it was funny, and I have a great sense of humor."

"That's what people with no sense of humor always say."

She sighed. "I'm tired of this," she said.

"We have that in common, if little else."

"Stone, I am no longer comfortable with this contentiousness."

"Then may I suggest, in the kindest possible way, that you not put up with it anymore and conduct your search for an apartment from a hotel? I'll have Fred drive you to any one you like."

She threw off the covers and marched into the bathroom. The hair dryer could be heard for a while, and it was followed by the sounds of suitcases being opened, packed, and closed again.

Stone buzzed Fred and asked him to get the car ready and to come and get her luggage. "Then take Ms. Harmon wherever she likes," he said, and hung up.

Fred knocked on the door just as she was leaving the dressing room, fully dressed.

"Come in," he shouted.

Fred came in. "Yessir?"

"Her luggage is in the dressing room."

Fred collected the bags and took them downstairs.

"Well," she said.

"I hope you find what you're looking for," Stone said.

"So do I," she said, walking out of the room and slamming the door.

"I meant an apartment!" he shouted after her. He muted Joe Scarborough's daily rant about small government, then went back to his *Times*.

AN HOUR LATER, as Stone was getting dressed after his shower, the phone buzzed. "Yes?"

"There are two homicide detectives down here," Joan said, "and they want to see you."

"Tell them to go—"

"No, no, no!" Joan said. "I'm not telling them that; they might arrest *me*."

"Have they shown you an arrest warrant?" he asked.

"Not yet."

"Tell them I'll be right down." He knotted his tie and slipped on his jacket.

———————

"GOOD MORNING, gentlemen," he said, walking into his office to find the two men on his office sofa, drinking his coffee. "How can I help you?"

"Good morning, Mr. Barrington," one of them said. "We'd like to ask you some questions about a couple of corpses on Park Avenue."

Stone refreshed their coffee cups. "Get out your notebooks, gentlemen," he said, "and your recording devices."

They did so, and Stone launched into an account of his every moment since meeting Meg Harmon in Key West, covering every detail of his visit to Gino Bellini's apartment and the events taking place there. An hour later he went to his desk, took out Bellini's pistol, and handed it to one of them. "Do you have any questions?"

The two men looked at each other. "I don't believe so," one of them said, tucking away his recording device. "We'll call you if anything comes up." They shook hands with him and left.

Five minutes later, Joan buzzed him. "Dino, on one."

Stone pressed the button. "What?"

"Were you nice to my detectives?" Dino asked.

"I gave them coffee and bored them rigid for an hour," Stone replied.

"Are you still pissed off about last night?"

"Certainly."

"Did you take it out on Meg?"

"Probably."

"Can I speak to her to ascertain whether she's still alive?"

"If you can find out what hotel she's staying in."

"And how would I do that?"

"Start with The Pierre and work your way down."

"Dinner tonight?"

"Will Viv be there?"

"No, she's still in California."

"Call me when she gets back. I'll need someone to talk with over dinner."

"Have a nice day," Dino said, then hung up.

37

Tommy Chang stirred from his sleep, wondering what had awakened him. The doorbell rang a second time. Tommy struggled out of bed and padded to the front door of his small house in his boxer shorts and bare feet.

A uniformed messenger of some sort stood there, holding a box. Tommy opened the door. "You need a signature?"

"Yes, please," the man replied, holding out an electronic device with a pen attached.

Tommy signed, took the package, and went back inside. He considered diving back into bed for another couple of hours, but a glance at the clock on the wall told him that he had already used up that time. He went into the kitchen, began the coffee by switching on the drip pot, then put an English muffin into the toaster oven and pressed the start button.

He looked at the box and could not find a return address. He figured it must be from Dirty Joe, because who else would be sending him things by overnight delivery? He hefted the package, and it felt as if there might be a book inside. He wondered for a moment if he had made anybody mad enough at him to send him a bomb, decided he had not, then found a box cutter and opened the box. Inside was a shipping envelope, sealed and pre-addressed, plus a business envelope. He opened the business envelope and read the letter inside, which appeared to have been printed from a computer file. It did not begin with a salutation or end with a signature.

I don't know if you read newspapers or watch television news, so I may be the first to tell you that Joe and Jane were killed by the Maine State Police in a gunfight yesterday.

Tommy was shaken by that news. They were his friends, and he and Joe were business partners. Yesterday, as mentioned in the letter, would have been the day before yesterday. He took a deep breath and began to read again.

Joe told me a while back that his will is in the safe at your office, and that you and Jane are his heirs. If she is deceased, then everything goes to you.

Tommy thought about that. He and Joe were partners in a flying school and air charter service at the Marathon Airport, and they also owned a small marina and boatyard nearby. His next thought was that they were cash poor, and that Joe had told him he was going to New York to remedy that, which meant to Tommy that Joe had taken a contract on somebody, and that he had probably been killed in an attempt to execute it. He read on.

There is $100,000 in hundred-dollar bills in the envelope contained in this package. There is also some information regarding the individual who was the subject of Joe's attention at the time of his demise. If you wish to replace Joe in the effort in which he was involved, you may secure the money and get on with it. If you do not wish to accept, you need only return the cash in the envelope provided, and you will hear no more from me. Should you accept the offer, you must complete it within ten days of receiving this package, or return the money.

Details of the subject and of Joe's death are in the package. The subject is in New York City as I write this, and the last known address is a private town house on East 49th Street, owned by a person known as Stone Barrington, a lawyer, whose office is on the ground floor. There is a thumb drive in with the cash. Download it to your computer, and it will automatically populate your iPhone. The app keeps constant surveillance at all times and will display the location on a map.

I do not wish to hear from you again and you will not hear from me. I wish you good luck on your assignment and a prosperous year.

The letter was not signed, but Tommy knew the sender to be Gino Bellini, with whom he and Joe had shared a cell for a few months in their extreme youth.

Tommy had no intention of returning the money.

He opened the shipping envelope, which was addressed to a building on Park Avenue, apartment 30, and found, as promised, ten packets of one hundred hundred-dollar bills, and two news stories, one from a newspaper, the other from a business magazine. The first, from a Maine newspaper, apparently downloaded from the Internet, described the circumstances of Joe's and Jane's deaths on a boat at an island in Penobscot Bay called Islesboro. The second was an article from a business publication, with two photographs, about a businesswoman named Meg Harmon, who had recently sold a large share of her company and netted something more than a billion dollars. He knew that Bellini had made a large sum, himself, on the transaction.

Tommy called his office, and his chief pilot, Rena Cobb, answered. "Bad news," he said, "Joe and Jane are dead."

There was a brief silence at the other end, then she said, "Holy shit."

"Yeah, I know. Day before yesterday, in Maine. I just heard a few minutes ago."

"Are we going to be okay?" Rena asked. She was aware of their cash-flow problem.

"Yeah, we are. I'm going to want you to make a deposit today—tomorrow at the latest. I'll be there in a few minutes. I

have to fly to New York for a few days, so have the Baron refueled, and you take the Cessna 210."

"Okay, see you soon."

Tommy hung up, then downloaded the app to his computer
and checked his iPhone to be sure it was working properly. A
blue dot appeared at New York City. He showered and shaved,
packed a bag, dressed, locked up, and headed for the airport.

HE PARKED in his usual spot and went into the office. Sheila, his
secretary, was at her desk. "Tomorrow you can start paying
bills," he said. "Rena will confirm when the money's in the bank."
He went into Rena's office, opened the shipping envelope and
took $10,000 for expenses, then gave the rest to Rena.

"I can fly this afternoon and be at the bank by noon tomorrow," she said. The procedure was to fly to Nassau, then depart
there on a flight plan to Jamaica, then, an hour out, change the
destination to Georgetown, in the Cayman Islands.

"Okay, I'll be back in a week or so." He took his bag into the
hangar and stowed it in the baggage compartment of the Beech
Baron, then he went to a steel locker in the hangar and removed
an aluminum case on wheels containing two handguns, a fold-
ing sniper rifle, and ammunition for all. He stowed that in the
Baron, then hooked up the tow to the airplane and pulled it out
onto the ramp. He used his cell phone to check the weather,
which was good, and file a flight plan for Brandywine Airport
in West Chester, Pennsylvania. At the appropriate moment, he

would cancel his flight plan and land, instead, at Essex County Airport, in Caldwell, New Jersey, and from there, take a car service into New York.

Tommy did a thorough preflight inspection of the airplane, then started the engines. He entered his flight plan into the Garmin 1000 flight computer, got his IFR clearance from the tower, then taxied to the runway, where he was immediately cleared for takeoff. He lifted off, retracted the landing gear and flaps, switched on the autopilot, and let the Garmin 1000 begin flying the programmed route. Soon he was at cruising altitude, and he set the fuel mixture for best economy. He had a four-hour flight ahead of him. Plenty of time to make a plan.

38

tone had lunch at his desk and pretended to work, but he was depressed about how things had gone with both Dino and Meg. His iPhone chimed, and he looked to see who the e-mail was from. There was only one, and he opened it.

Dear Stone,

I'm so sorry for how things went last night and, especially, this morning. Dino was giving you a hard ride, and I made the mistake of climbing on board. Big mistake.

I want you to know how truly grateful I am for the way you have protected me over the past days. I would be dead if you hadn't been there, and I would not have liked that. I enjoy your company so much—not to mention the sex—and I *want to go on seeing you. Maybe you'll be able to forgive me after a while, and we can meet for dinner. I'm at The Pierre, in a suite with a nice view of Central Park from a low floor. I'm going to start seeing apartments this morning with your friend Margo Goodale, who sounds very nice and very knowledgeable on the phone.*

Again, I offer my sincere apologies for my behavior, and I hope you will accept them.

Stone read it a second time and melted a little. He wrote back that he would call her soon.

A TEXT CAME from Dino. "Sorry about last night, pal," he said. "Viv's coming in late this afternoon, so you'll have somebody to talk to over dinner. Can we meet at Rotisserie Georgette at 7:30? I'll book. I'm buying, to make up for the hard time I gave you yesterday."

Stone wrote back: "See you then, and as long as you're buying, I'll pick the wine."

EVERYBODY WAS on time for dinner, and the waiter knew to bring Stone's bourbon and Dino's scotch. Viv had a martini.

They clinked glasses. "I hear you're talking only to me," Viv said.

"It's a relief, really," Stone replied. "Your husband never shuts up, and it's hard to get a word in edgewise."

"Tell me about it," Viv said. "Are you still mad at Meg?"

"No, she wrote me a very nice note today, and I've gotten over it."

"Good," Viv said, "because she's right around the corner at The Pierre, and she's joining us for dinner, and she says she has some very exciting news. Ah! Here she comes! What timing!"

Stone rose to greet Meg, who kissed him on the lips before she sat down. "May I have some of that bourbon you drink, please?" she said to Stone.

Stone ordered the Knob Creek and it arrived quickly. A small jazz group began to play up front.

"All right," Viv said, "what's this exciting news you have?"

"I found an apartment," Meg said.

"What, on your first day of looking?"

"First day, first apartment I looked at."

"Tell us about it," Viv said.

"Well, to begin with it's in your building."

"Oh, I know the one—it's two floors up from us. The old gentleman who lived there died a couple of weeks ago. His wife died last year."

"Sounds like the one," Meg said. "It wasn't even on the market yet, but Margo got a tip from one of the doormen, and he let us in to see it. It has big rooms, and lots of them. The gentleman's kids had cleared it of his personal things, but it's available furnished. Not everything is to my liking, but there are a couple of beautiful Persian carpets that were left, and I'll need some upholstering and a few pieces of furniture. It's even got a grand piano! It will need painting throughout and new window treatments, but it's fit to move into immediately."

"Well," Viv said, "maybe not immediately, exactly. Did Margo explain the application and board approval requirements? It took us nearly three months to get it done."

"Margo and I spent the afternoon filling out the documents. My accountant is sending my tax returns, so all I need is some personal references and a meeting with the board."

"We'd be delighted to give you a reference," Viv said.

"As will I," Stone echoed.

"As will Arthur Steele," said Meg. "And the board meets next Monday. Margo says that half of the members are on Wall Street, so they'll know who I am, and that will help." She glanced at Stone. "I do need a lawyer to close the sale. Margo recommended somebody, but I'd rather have you, Stone."

"I'll get you the best real estate attorney at Woodman & Weld, and I'll look over everything to be sure it's right."

"Margo took a contract over to the seller, who is the owner's son. I made it easy for him by offering the asking price. She expects to get the contract back tomorrow, and if we get board approval, we can probably close by the end of next week."

"You're lucky the son didn't want to move in, himself," Dino said.

"He'd just bought a house in Westchester, and the place is too big for a pied-à-terre."

They ordered dinner, and the women took the opportunity to go to the ladies'.

"I've got some news, too," Dino said.

"Shoot."

"We braced Stanislav Beria this afternoon, and, as expected, he clammed up and claimed diplomatic immunity."

"But . . . ?"

"But we nailed the gorilla off the reservation, and we have him locked up. Turns out he works for Selwyn Owaki, not for the mission, so he has no immunity. He's being pumped right now for information on his boss. With a murder charge hanging over him, we might be able to turn him."

"That is very good news."

"His name is Boris Ivanov, and he's a nasty piece of work— ex-GRU, military intelligence, but forget about the intelligence part, he's just muscle."

"I'd be delighted to testify against him," Stone said.

"Funny thing," Dino said.

"What's that?"

"He had a notebook in his pocket with your car's tag number written in it."

"Damn it, he must have made my car when we were following the mission Mercedes."

"That is not good news," Dino said. "If Ivanov has your

license plate number, then Beria has it, too, and if he has it, Owaki has it, and by this time he will have a lot more information about you. Frankly, I wouldn't want Owaki to know that much about me, and since you're the only witness against his guy, you're going to have to watch your ass—at least until we can turn him."

"Well," Stone said, "hurry the hell up, will you?"

The women returned, and they had dinner.

Meg looked at Stone closely. "Are you worried about something?"

"No, nothing at all," Stone said.

39

Tommy Chang landed the Beech Baron at Essex County Airport as darkness was coming on. He arranged for hangar space and called a car service to drive him into New York.

The car arrived very quickly, his luggage was loaded, and they started into the city. Tommy got out his iPhone and tapped on the locator app. The blue dot appeared on Fifth Avenue, at the corner of East Sixty-first Street. This was a surprise, as he was expecting her to be on East Forty-ninth Street. "Driver, what's your name?"

"Gene, sir."

"Gene, what's at the corner of Fifth Avenue and East Sixty-first Street?"

"The Pierre hotel," Gene replied. "You want to go there?"

"Let me make a call." He called American Express Travel and asked them to book him into The Pierre. In moments, he had an affirmative reply. "Okay," Tommy said, "take me to The Pierre."

"Right."

AT THE PIERRE, Tommy got out of the car and asked Gene for his card. "Gene, are you going to be available for the next few days?"

"Sure, you can call me directly on the cell number."

Tommy paid and tipped him generously, then followed the bellman with his luggage to the front desk and checked in.

The desk clerk's nameplate read "Gloria." "Gloria, I'm meeting a friend here. Her name is Meg Harmon. Has she checked in yet?"

Gloria checked her computer. "Yes, she has, but she's just left to go out to dinner. I saw her go out."

"I guess I didn't get here soon enough," Tommy said. "What's her room number? I'll give her a call later."

"I'm afraid our security precautions prevent me from giving you her room number, Mr. Edwards," she said. He had checked in and presented a Texas driver's license and a credit card in that name.

"I'll just leave her a note, then. May I have paper and an envelope?" She handed it to him. He wrote a note saying: "Carl, I'm in town. Call me on my cell." He tucked it into the envelope, sealed it, and handed it back to Gloria, then he completed the registration form.

"How many keys, sir?" Gloria asked.

"Two, please." She gave them to him in a small packet, and he turned to follow the bellman to his room. As he did, he saw Gloria put the envelope into a box with the number 212.

"You're on the third floor," the bellman said, as they boarded the elevator, "with a view of the park."

"Perfect," Tommy replied.

The room was large, with a king-sized bed and a comfortable seating area. He asked the bellman for some ice, then he went to the window and looked out at the park. "I'll bet you have the same view," he said. The bellman returned.

"Tell me, Frank," he said, reading the man's name tag, "I like to go for a run in the morning, and I noticed a stairway across the hall. Can I go down and come back that way, instead of taking the elevator?"

"Yes, sir, just use your key card," Frank replied.

Tommy overtipped him and he left. Tommy gave him a head start, then left the room, went down the stairs, and let himself out of the stairwell with his key card on the second floor. Room 212 was just across the hall. He examined the door and its lock carefully: just like his own room's. He walked down to the ground floor, found the bar, and ordered a drink and some dinner. He finished dinner a little after ten, charged his food and drink to his room, and left. With any luck, the shift would have changed at the front desk. He was right.

Tommy approached the front desk and took his spare key card from its packet and handed it to a young man on duty there. "My name is Harmon. I'm in room 212 and my key card isn't working. Can you give me a new one, please?"

The young man checked his computer for the name. "It says here 'Meg,'" he said.

"Michael Edward George Harmon," Tommy said. "Meg, for short."

"I see." He put a new card into a slot and tapped in a code and the room number. "There you are, Mr. Harmon," he said, handing Tommy a new packet. He thanked the young man, then went to his room. He opened his weapons case, chose a small 9mm pistol, and screwed a silencer into the barrel. Then he stretched out on the bed for a moment. He would wait until the middle of the night to visit Ms. Harmon. He dozed.

TOMMY WOKE UP with sunlight streaming into his room; he checked the bedside clock: 7:20 AM. "Shit," he said. He had been more tired after the long flight than he had thought. He ordered some breakfast from room service, then shaved and showered. There was a *New York Times* slid under his door, and he put on a robe and read it until breakfast came.

When he was done, he dressed in a business suit, went downstairs, and crossed the street, carrying the Arts section of the *Times*. He took up a position on a bench along the wall that separated Fifth Avenue from Central Park and had a good look at the hotel. Room 212, he calculated, was to the left of the front door and one floor up. He took a small monocular from a pocket, concealed it in his fist, and pointed it at the windows. The curtains were still drawn; she must be sleeping late.

He folded the paper open to the crossword puzzle, took out his pen, and began. Twenty minutes later he was halfway through the puzzle and the curtains were open in room 212. He took the folded page from the business magazine containing the article on Meg Harmon and studied the face in the two photographs, committing it to memory. She was a very good-looking woman, he thought.

He began the puzzle again, checking a clue, then checking the hotel's front door, then writing in the answer and checking the door again. More than an hour passed in this fashion, then finally the hotel door opened and a well-dressed blonde walked outside and was immediately shown into a waiting Town Car, which drove away. He couldn't find a cab quickly enough to follow her, but at least she was out of her room.

He went back into the hotel and went up to his room. He opened the weapons case and took out some miniature electronics equipment, then he left his room, went into the stairwell, and went down to the second floor, opening the door with his 212 key card. A maid's cart was a few doors down the hall, and a card saying Please make up my room was hanging on the doorknob of 212. He used his new key card to let himself inside, turning the door card over to read Privacy, please.

It was a large, handsome suite, sitting room and bedroom.

He went to work installing a tiny camera and a microphone in each room. He wished he'd had a third camera; it would have been nice to install it in the bathroom so he could see her naked. Well, time enough for that, he thought.

He opened the front door a crack, checked for the maid, who was closer now. He turned the card on the door handle over again, then closed the door and took the stairway down to the street.

Might as well do some shopping, he thought. He'd check on Ms. Harmon around six, when she might be changing to go out.

40

S tone was in his office the following day when Joan buzzed him. "Ms. Harmon, on one," she said.

He picked up the phone. "Good morning."

"Good morning. I enjoyed myself last evening."

"So did I."

"If you're free this evening, come and have dinner with me at The Pierre."

"Love to."

"Come to my room, 212, and we'll have a drink there."

"All right, see you then."

They both hung up.

TOMMY CHANG SLEPT LATE, then checked his cameras in 212 with his iPhone. The rooms were empty, and there was a room-service table there, bearing dirty dishes. She had gone out. He checked the locator app: the blue dot was a dozen blocks downtown and moving. He'd have to make tonight the night.

STONE'S NEXT CALL was from Dino. "Good morning," he said.

"Good morning," Stone replied.

"I've got some more news, and it isn't good."

"Break it to me."

"Remember Boris Ivanov?"

"The gorilla? How could I forget him?"

"He's out."

"What?"

"He lawyered up. A senior partner at Craig and Zanoff showed up and sprung him."

"That's a white-shoe firm," Stone said. "What's the lawyer's name?"

"Greg Zanoff."

"The guy with his name on the door comes down and springs a Russian gorilla? That doesn't make any sense."

"I guess Selwyn Owaki can buy anybody he likes."

"I don't know much about Owaki, just what I've read in the papers."

"Owaki specializes in not having anybody know anything about him," Dino said. "He does his deals at arm's length—always has a lawyer or two between him and his customers. He has eight or ten houses in world capitals, lives like a potentate, makes large donations to charities. He's handsome and charming."

"I've never even seen a photograph of him."

"We have one in our files, but it's of very poor quality," Dino said. "I couldn't make him on the street."

"Do I have anything to worry about?"

"You're the only witness who can put Ivanov in Bellini's apartment at the time of the murder."

"But not enough of a witness to convict him?"

"I would have thought so, but Ivanov is on the street now, and probably has left the country. Owaki has a fleet of private jets, three or four, plus a couple of helicopters. In New York he works out of the four top stories of a very expensive apartment building that he owns on East Fifty-seventh Street."

"Sorry, he owns the apartment or the building?"

"The building *and* the apartment."

"That's a new one on me," Stone said.

"Listen, if you've got an army you want equipped, Owaki is your guy—weapons, aircraft, missiles, tanks, you name it, he can assemble and deliver the order."

"Anything else?"

"Yeah, during the short time he was talking, Ivanov told us his excuse for being in Bellini's apartment."

"Which was?"

"A computer thumb drive that contains the plans for something that his pal Beria had bought from Bellini."

"I know about the thumb drive," Stone said.

"You don't have the thing, do you?"

"No, I gave it to Meg—the designs belong to her company. And Bellini rigged his computer so that Beria could open the files once, but the second time the data would be destroyed."

"So Meg has what Beria—which means Owaki—wants?"

"Yes, she does."

"Does Beria know that?"

"No, but he may think I have it. Bellini could have told him."

"Listen, pal, I think you better go armed for a while, and I mean day and night."

"But you think Ivanov has left the country."

"I think *maybe* he has, but Beria hasn't, and he could walk into your office, blow your brains out, and we couldn't touch him."

"Well, he did get a look at me in that elevator, and he saw me get into my car."

"And he saw you following him, too, and he got your tag number, remember?"

"I remember."

"Maybe you should go to England or to Paris, Stone. I mean, you have those houses, so pick one and get out of town."

"I already got out of town once, and it didn't do a lot for me."

"Then call Mike Freeman at Strategic Services and get him to put some people on you for a while."

"I'll think about it," Stone said.

"Listen, I've got another call to take, so I've gotta run. I'll call you later."

"See you," Stone said, then hung up.

41

Stone took a cab uptown and presented himself at room 212 at The Pierre. Meg answered the door, put her arms around his waist, pressed herself against him, and consented to be kissed. "How are you?" she asked finally.

"Better than I was before I rang the bell," Stone replied.

TOMMY CHANG had just turned on his computer and the cameras when he saw a man let into the room. Ms. Harmon greeted him very, very warmly, then she led him to the living room sofa, and he sat.

"KNOB CREEK, I presume," Meg said, "and I had better presume correctly or call room service."

"That will be just fine," Stone said, and she poured one for him, then a vodka for herself. She sat beside him on the sofa, and they drank.

TOMMY FIGURED they would be having their drink, then going out. He fiddled with the sound and finally could overhear their conversation.

"I'VE MISSED YOU," Meg said.

"I've missed you, too, and it's only been twenty-four hours."

"I have an overwhelming desire to fuck you," Meg said, "but I've ordered dinner for us here, and I don't want to be interrupted by a room service waiter."

"WHOA!" Tommy said to himself. "This could get good."

MEG UNZIPPED STONE'S TROUSERS, freed him, and buried her face in his lap.

TOMMY FELT that she was doing it to him; he couldn't believe his luck.

———

STONE LAID his head back and enjoyed himself while Meg continued. Shortly, he climaxed, and she relented. She tucked him back into his trousers and zipped him up. "There," she said.

"There, indeed," Stone replied. "Now what can I do for you?"

"Well, since I came at the same time you did, just talk to me. After dinner, we'll consider our options."

Stone took a deep breath and tried to restore his heartbeat to its pre-fellatio condition. A large swig of bourbon helped. They finished their drinks, and she poured them both another. The doorbell rang, and she called out, "Come in!"

Tommy calmed himself. A waiter had appeared, pushing a cart, and he set it up by the windows. After that terrific first act, he was going to have to watch them eat dinner. He hadn't expected a caller, he hadn't expected the sex, and he hadn't expected them to remain in the suite for dinner.

THE WAITER SERVED their first course of seared foie gras and said that he would return to serve their second course.

"How was your day?" Stone asked.

"Very good. Margo Goodale and I completed all the co-op forms, and my accountant faxed me three years of tax returns and my financial statement, and you, Dino, and Arthur sent over your letters of recommendation. I have to pay to have their

detective service do a background check on me, which is supposed to be happening tomorrow."

"That means a man will sit down at a computer and do a
search for a criminal record, both federal and state. Have you
committed any felonies or misdemeanors?"

"None."

"Any DUIs?"

"None."

"Any lawsuits against you active?"

"None."

"Then he will so notify your board and collect his outrageous fee."

"It certainly was outrageous, for so little effort."

"Well, he had to pay for his computer and the software. Everybody has to make a living."

"Sometimes I have to think that everybody has to make a
living off me."

"It's what happens when you become suddenly wealthy in
public. Everybody in the United States who reads the *New York
Times*, the *Wall Street Journal*, or any other newspaper subscrib-
ing to the Associated Press wire service now knows your ap-
proximate net worth, and a significant number of them are
trying to figure out how to separate you from a portion of it by
selling you some product or service. Another, hopefully smaller,
number are trying to figure a way to swindle you out of some
of it."

———

TOMMY WAS GETTING bored. He considered going down there, letting himself into the room, and shooting both of them at the table, but then the waiter returned, removed some of their dishes, and set new ones before them. Also, it would be unprofessional to make that sort of mess. He'd rather the bodies were discovered the following morning, when the maid entered to clean the suite.

"I'VE HAD FIFTEEN or twenty e-mails trying to sell me a private jet," Meg said.

"That's something you should consider," Stone replied. "You've already seen, flying with me, how convenient it is to have your own airplane at your disposal."

"I have indeed," she said. "What would your recommendation be?"

"Your first consideration should be how far you are likely to fly and how often. Will your work take you, say, to Europe or the Far East, or will you most often just fly between San Francisco and New York?"

"I don't anticipate flying to the Far East, but I would like to travel in Europe."

"Well, a Citation Latitude will get you to London or Paris from New York, or to Hawaii from San Francisco."

"And how much does it cost?"

"Between fifteen and twenty million, I should think, depending on the equipment you choose."

TOMMY WAS CONSIDERING shooting them again, but the waiter kept coming and going, and shooting him, too, seemed excessive. After all, he was being paid to shoot only one person.

THE WAITER TOOK the tray table away and put the DO NOT DISTURB sign on the door. Meg took Stone by the hand and led him into the bedroom, where she proceeded to undress him.

TOMMY HAD BEEN prepared to go downstairs as soon as the waiter was out of the picture, but now they were in the bedroom, and he thought he might as well watch the sex. As she undressed him, he caught sight of a shoulder-holstered pistol. He wasn't going into that room if the guy was armed.

SOON THEY were both naked and Meg led him to the bed and climbed on top of him. "Now," she said, "let's consider our options."

———

TOMMY SIGHED and settled down to watch the sex. He was not disappointed with what he saw.

"IF YOU LIKE, I can recommend a consultant who will, for a fee, help you choose what you need in terms of speed, range, and accommodations."

42

Tommy woke up a little after seven AM; the camera was still on in the bedroom, and Harmon and Barrington were just waking up, too. In a moment, they were at it again.

TOMMY WATCHED the performance and was again impressed. Then they phoned down for breakfast and did it again while they waited for room service. Tommy shaved, showered, and dressed and checked the camera again. They were finishing breakfast and talking about getting up. The man went to take a shower, and Ms. Harmon lay naked on the bed.

Tommy heard the newspapers slide under the door, and he picked up the *Daily News*. There was a picture of a girl in a bikini, but a headline caught his eye. SUSPECT IN BELLINI MURDER IS RELEASED. Bellini? Who Bellini? Tommy turned to the designated inside page and read the brief story.

> The chief suspect in the murders of Gino and Veron-ica Bellini was released from jail yesterday, after a judge ruled that there was insufficient evidence to hold him. It is feared that Boris Ivanov, a Russian in the employ of that country's UN mission, may have fled the country.

Tommy stopped reading. "Fucking Gino is *dead?*" he asked himself. He read the remainder of the short piece. Fucking Gino was, indeed, dead. He put down the paper and thought about things. Gino must have sent him the package shortly before he cashed in his chips; Tommy was working for a dead guy. He considered the ethics of his situation.

First of all, the guy in Ms. Harmon's suite was probably Stone Barrington, the man at whose house she had been staying. Tommy knew nothing about him, had nothing against him, and was not being paid to kill him. Also, with two murders being investigated, his chances of being caught increased.

Second, if he didn't kill the woman, there would be no inves-tigation at all; he could just go home, forget the whole thing, and spend the money. Fuck Gino. Maybe he would come back to haunt him, but he doubted it.

Then Tommy heard Barrington's voice. "What's that?" he asked.

Tommy looked at his iPhone; Barrington was pointing at Tommy, via the living room camera.

"I don't know," Harmon replied. "Smoke detector?"

"That's not a smoke detector," Barrington said, "and it's not a CO2 detector, either." He left the living room, and Tommy switched cameras. Barrington was looking up and pointing again. "There's another one," he said. "It's a camera."

"Oh, my God," Harmon said. "Somebody has been watching us?"

"No doubt about it," Barrington said. He got out his phone and called a number. "Bob, it's Stone. How quickly can you get over to The Pierre? Good, I'll be in room 212. Bring your tool kit. I'll explain when you get here." He hung up.

"Well," Harmon said, "that was quite an exhibition we gave for whoever was watching. Is this going to end up on the Internet?"

"I doubt it," Barrington replied, then he looked up at the camera and spoke to it. "Because then I'd have to find whoever did this and KILL the sonofabitch!"

Tommy's phone rang, and he answered it. "Hello?"

"Hey, it's Sheila."

"Did you get to the bank yesterday?"

"I did. Everything is just fine—the bills are paid, and so am I. There's other good news, too. A guy just walked in and wants to get his multi-engine rating, but you've got the twin. He's hot to trot, and we might be able to sell him an airplane, too. When are you coming home?"

"I'm leaving the hotel shortly," Tommy said. "Put him off until nine AM tomorrow."

"I think he'll buy that, and even with the ninety grand I deposited, we could use the money."

"See you this afternoon." He hung up and called Gene, his driver; Gene said he'd be out front in fifteen minutes. Tommy finished packing; he didn't bother calling for a bellman since he just had his one bag and the weapons case. He gave some more thought to killing them both, but then he unscrewed the silencer from the pistol and packed them both in the weapons case. That settled his ethics problem: he didn't have time to kill either of them.

He left the room with his luggage, went to the elevator and pressed the button. The car arrived and he pressed the lobby button. The door opened and another man started to get into the car, but backed up to let Tommy out. He was carrying a good-sized toolbox. I'll bet your name is Bob, Tommy said to himself.

He walked toward the front door, and the man got onto the elevator. Gene was waiting at the curb; Tommy gave him his luggage and got into the car.

"A successful trip?" Gene asked as he pulled away from the curb.

"Well, I made some money," Tommy replied.

"That's always a good idea," Gene said.

———

STONE ANSWERED the door and let in Bob Cantor, who was his genius tech guy. "Good morning, Bob."

"Morning, Stone."

Stone introduced Meg, who was sitting on the sofa.

"What have we got?" Bob asked.

Stone pointed up at the molding. "That's not a smoke detector, is it?"

"Nope, and it's not a CO_2 detector, either. It's a camera, and a good one."

"We've got another one in here," Stone said, leading him into the bedroom.

Bob looked up at the camera. "You sure have." He looked at the thoroughly unmade bed. "Were you here all night?"

"Yes," Stone said.

"Did you turn off the lights?"

"Not until we were ready to go to sleep."

"And I guess that wasn't right away."

"Good guess. Can you yank those things out?"

Bob dragged a chair over from the dressing table, stood on it, and pulled the camera off the wall. "I've used these things myself, although this is a newer model—beautiful color and high definition, you can see every pore."

"I was afraid you were going to say something like that," Stone said.

Bob hopped down. "The other one, too?"

"Yes, but just a minute, I've got a question."

"I bet I know what it is," Bob said. "Can I trace the camera to somebody?"

"That's the question," Stone said.

"The answer is no. However, as I was getting on the elevator, a guy was getting off, and two things about him struck me."

"What was that?"

"I thought it was funny that, in a classy hotel like this, he was carrying his own luggage. Unusual."

"What else?" Stone asked.

"In addition to a regular suitcase, he was towing a pretty big aluminum case, the kind that might contain guns or tools. Or both. And he was in a hurry, went right out to where a car was waiting for him."

"Did he introduce himself?"

"Unfortunately, no."

"I was afraid of that. Give me a description."

"About five-ten, a hundred and seventy, and he looked Asian—coal-black hair and slightly slanted eyes—maybe half-Asian. Very fit-looking, too, martial arts type."

"That's all you got?"

"No, I got a look at the luggage tag on the aluminum case. Joe Cross, Islamorada, Florida."

"You have just identified a dead person," Stone said.

"How do you know that?" Bob asked.

"Because I saw him shot dead, in Maine, a few days ago."

"Well," Bob said, "I guess somebody stole his tool kit."

They went back into the living room.

"Let me guess," Meg said. "You can't tell who put the cameras in, and you can't trace him."

"Not exactly," Stone said.

"What does that mean?"

"It means that, with a little luck, we might find the sonofabitch."

"Well, that's good news," Meg said. "Sort of. What do we do with him then?"

"I haven't gotten that far, yet," Stone replied. "Meg, I think we should move you back into my house."

"I'll start packing," she replied.

"Bob," Stone said, "have you got a plastic bag? Might be worth trying to get some prints off those cameras."

"Sure thing," Bob said, opening his toolbox. "I can do that for you, and since I know what my prints look like, there won't be any mix-ups."

43

Stone called Fred, who collected them and Meg's luggage and drove them home. All the way home, Stone thought about the cameras and the man who had installed them.

Fred took Meg's luggage upstairs to her dressing room. Stone buzzed Joan.

"Good morning," she said. "Sleep well?"

"What do you mean by that?" Stone asked.

"A simple inquiry into your health and well-being," she said.

"Thank you. You remember that time we used that private dick in Key West for that thing?"

"Sure."

"Have you got his name and number?"

"I'll need ten seconds," Joan replied, then put him on hold and came back. "Not Key West—Sugarloaf Key," she said.

"That's close enough."

"His name is Paul Toppino. Shall I get him for you?"

"Please," Stone said. He waited until she buzzed him.

"Paul on line one."

"Paul?"

"Stone?"

"How are you?"

"Just great. How 'bout you?"

"Not bad. I need to find a guy in the Keys, maybe Islamorada."

"I do that sort of thing. What's his name?"

"I don't know, but he has a friend in Islamorada."

"Okay, what's his friend's name?"

"Joe Cross."

"Dirty Joe? What do you want with him?"

"Just his friend."

"That's just as well, because Dirty Joe bought the farm up in Maine a few days ago. It made the *Key West Citizen*."

"Yeah, I was there at the time."

"Really? Did you shoot Dirty Joe?"

"No, but I was standing next to the guy who did. I'll tell you about it when I see you, but what about his friend?"

"The one whose name you don't know?"

"That one."

"You got a description?"

"Five-ten, a hundred and seventy, black hair, fit-looking. Might be Eurasian."

"Tommy Chang. That'll be fifteen hundred dollars."

"You know the guy?"

"Sure, he's Dirty Joe's business partner."

"Doing what?"

"The two of them own a little charter flight business and flying school at Marathon Airport. They've got a Baron and two or three Cessnas. Tommy does some avionics work, too, installing radios and GPSes, and the like. Tell me something, when Dirty Joe got shot by your friend, was he trying to shoot your friend?"

"No, he was trying to shoot a different friend, or at least, his girlfriend was."

"Jungle Jane? No shit?"

"None at all."

"There've been rumors around the Keys for years that Dirty Joe and Tommy were doing hits on the side. They were living too well for their business to support their lifestyle. And it doesn't surprise me much that Jungle Jane was helping out. They both got killed, didn't they?"

"With a single bullet."

"By accident?"

"No, on purpose."

"Jesus, nice shot."

"Yes, it was."

"So, you want me to do something to Tommy Chang?"

"No. I didn't know you did contract work, Paul."

"I don't, but I can get him arrested for you, if you've got a charge that'll stick. I'm not going to try and beat him up, either, because he's a martial arts nut. I saw him kick a guy's ass in a bar one time who was twice his size and mean as a snake. Did Tommy do something to you?"

"To a client of mine," Stone half-lied.

"Down here or up there?"

"Up here, last night."

"Well, the guy's got that Baron, I guess he can go wherever the work is."

"I guess so."

"What do you want me to do?"

"I haven't got a charge that will stick," Stone said, "so nothing, for the time being. I'll get back to you when I know more, and I'll send you a check."

"Just joking about the fifteen hundred. I wouldn't charge an old client for top-of-the-head info. Buy me a steak the next time you're in town."

"I'll do that," Stone said. "See you around." They both hung up.

Stone called Dino.

"Bacchetti."

"Dino, can you run a name for me? Criminal record, wanted list?"

"What's the name?"

"Tommy Chang—residence, Florida Keys, probably Isla-morada."

"Hang on," Dino said, and Stone could hear computer keys. "Here we go—juvie record in California, two arrests out there for burglary, charges dropped. Another for assault, no weapon. Then nothing."

"Nothing in Florida?"

"Nope. He must have kept his nose clean after he moved."

"Is it a crime to put cameras and microphones in a hotel room in New York?"

"Whose room?"

"Meg's, at The Pierre."

"That's what she gets for moving out on you."

"She's back now."

"Well, it's breaking and entering, if he got into her room. Also, if he made a recording of what he saw—without her per-mission, of course."

"He didn't have that."

"What did this character see in her room?"

"Meg."

"Naked?"

"Yes."

"Were you present at the time?"

"Yes."

"Naked?"

"Well, yes."

"We could pick him up, but he would probably plead down to a misdemeanor and get a suspended sentence. If he was trying to sell tapes, then it would be a bigger deal."

"I've no evidence of that, so far."

"Is he in New York?"

"Probably back in Florida."

"Well, the DA isn't going to extradite him for that—again, unless he's selling tapes."

"I'll let you know."

"Sure. If he is selling tapes, I'd like to buy one."

"Oh, fuck off." Stone hung up.

44

Stanislav Beria appeared at Selwyn Owaki's apartment building at noon, the appointed hour. He identified himself to a receptionist with his diplomatic passport, then submitted to a stroll through a metal detector and a body search so thorough that he was uncomfortable with it. His laptop computer was thoroughly checked, then he was allowed to board an elevator that swept him at high speed to the top floor, where he submitted to another search, and was admitted to the enormous living room of Selwyn Owaki's multistory penthouse.

A man in a white jacket settled him on a sofa and brought him a small bottle of San Pellegrino mineral water and a saucer containing half a dozen canapés. He had finished them all before Owaki finally made his appearance, walking down a curved staircase while his eyes swept the cavernous room. He was a tall, thickly built man of indeterminate national origin, wearing what Beria was certain was a $25,000 suit.

Beria stood to greet him. "Selwyn, how are you?"

Owaki motioned for him to sit down, and he did. "I thought I would ask *you* that," he said in mid-Atlantic English. "Do we have the material?"

Beria tapped the computer. "Right here."

Owaki picked up a telephone and murmured something. Shortly, a young man appeared. "Give him your laptop," Owaki said. "And the file name."

Beria did so, and the young man took the computer to a table, opened it, and switched it on.

"I understand you found it necessary to rid yourself of the source and his wife."

"Regrettably so. He was the only person who could connect us to the theft of the software."

The young man at the computer suddenly screamed, "Oh, shit!"

"What is it?" Owaki asked.

"The fucker planted a bomb in the software."

"Then why do you still have hands?"

"Not an explosive—a program that destroyed the files."

Owaki turned to Beria. "You have copies, of course."

"I do not," Beria replied, as firmly as he could manage. "I am not brilliant with computers, and I didn't try to view or copy the files."

Owaki turned back to his techie. "Is there any way to re-cover the files?"

"No way at all," the young man replied. "If there were, I would know it. Whoever set this up was a genius at software."

"Did the bomb destroy anything else on the computer?" Beria asked.

"No," the young man replied.

"Your money is on the table," Owaki said to him. "Now, go, and speak to no one about this."

The young man nodded, retrieved an envelope from the table, and departed.

"Now," Owaki said. "Two things. One, you owe me twenty million dollars that I paid Bellini."

Beria stammered, "I will repay you. I'll need some time, though."

"Two," Owaki said, "you get to decide who dies for this insult."

"I decide?"

"Only if you can't come up with the twenty million and you can't tell me who is responsible for this."

"Bellini is responsible, and he is already dead. And his wife."

"Is it possible that Bellini made a copy without a bomb?"

"Entirely possible—probable, even. It could fit on a large thumb drive."

"Who else would have known about this?"

"I believe there was another man in Bellini's apartment when Boris and I arrived," Beria said.

"And who would that be?"

"A lawyer named Barrington. When Boris and I got on the service elevator to leave, this man was already on it. He said he had come from upstairs, but I have come to think that was a lie, that he was in the apartment when Boris shot the Bellinis."

"I presume that you know where to find him?"

"I know where he lives in New York, but it is my understanding that he has half a dozen other residences in the U.S. and in Europe." Beria took a sip of the water because his mouth had become dry. "He also appears to be very well connected. His closest friend is the police commissioner for New York City, and he is also personally close to the President of the United States and her husband and to the secretary of state."

"Let me explain the situation to you," Owaki said. "In anticipation of receiving this software—entirely on your assurance—I have hired a genius automotive designer and engineer and purchased a bankrupt motorcar factory in England. I have ordered and paid for extensive equipment, as well. My investment amounts to well over a hundred and fifty million dollars. *So far.* Are you beginning to get the picture?"

"I understand," Beria replied, and clasped his hands together to keep them from trembling.

"There is more than your life at stake here, Stanislav," Owaki said smoothly. "There is also the character and quality of your life during the lengthy period before you would be put to death. Do you understand me?"

Beria was unable to speak, so he nodded rapidly.

"Good," Owaki said, rising. "I will give you seven days to place the software in my hands, and when you do, it had better not explode, so to speak."

"I will need Boris Ivanov," Beria said.

"He will be at your side during your every waking moment," Owaki replied. "He is waiting for you downstairs. Be here exactly one week from today, with the intact software. If you can do it sooner, you will be rewarded." Owaki turned toward the stairway and started up.

Beria managed to leave quickly without actually running. He retrieved his laptop and took the elevator down. When the doors opened, Ivanov was standing there, waiting.

"Your car is outside," he said.

"Thank you, Boris, but before we get into the car, let's take a little walk. I don't want my driver to overhear our conversation."

"As you wish," Ivanov replied, ushering Beria to the door.

When they had left the building, Beria motioned for his driver to follow them, and he began walking slowly up East Fifty-seventh Street. "I have some things to tell you," he said to Ivanov in Russian, "and it is most important that you understand me, because both my life and yours depend upon it. Do you understand?"

"Not yet," Ivanov said. "Perhaps you had better explain."

Beria began explaining. "The most important thing for you to know," he said, "is that whatever happens to me, happens to you." He could see that he had the man's full attention.

45

Stone was in his office when Joan buzzed him. "There is a Mr. Beria to see you, along with another gentleman," she said. "They do not have an appointment," she added pointedly.

"Are you on the handset?" he asked.

"Yes."

"Stall them while I call Mike Freeman."

JOAN HUNG UP the phone and addressed the two men before her. "Mr. Barrington will see you, but he must first conclude a telephone conference call," she said to them. "Please have a seat."

Beria pointed to the phone on her desk. "There are no lines lit up," he said.

"He is on a private line."

The two men sat down.

STONE USED his cell phone to call Mike Freeman at Strategic Services.

"Yes, Stone?"

"I need the protection we talked about yesterday. Specifically, I need four armed men here *now*. There are two men in my outer office that I do not wish to be alone with."

"I'll find people in your neighborhood," Mike said, then hung up.

Stone went to his safe and took out a Terry Tussey custom .45 pistol, which weighed only 19 ounces, and a light shoulder holster, put them on and donned his jacket. He had just resumed his seat when his office door opened and Beria and his gorilla entered the room.

"I see you have concluded your conference call," Beria said.

"Yes, I have." He motioned toward the sofa. "Please have a seat." They did so, and he sat in a chair opposite. "I believe we may have met before," he said, "but I can't remember where."

"It was in an elevator," Beria replied. "Do you recall?"

"Ah, yes."

"Let me come directly to the point," Beria said.

"Please do."

"I believe you are in possession of a computer device given to you by Gino Bellini."

"Is that the same Bellini who was murdered in an apartment in the building where we met?"

"It is, and I have reason to believe that you were in the apartment when the murder occurred."

"I was in an apartment upstairs," Stone replied, "and in the elevator, of course."

"Mr. Barrington, if you stick to that story things are going to become very uncomfortable for you very fast."

"That sounds very much like a threat, Mr. Beria."

"It most certainly is. Mr. Ivanov here is very accomplished at carrying out my threats."

Ivanov gave Stone a small smile.

Stone produced the .45. "How would Mr. Ivanov perform this duty with a bullet in his head?"

Beria looked very irritated. "Mr. Barrington, I possess the means to end your life before this day is out. I suggest you listen to my proposal before I take that step."

"Oh, you have a proposal? I thought you only made threats."

"I think a more businesslike conversation would be in both our interests."

"Does Mr. Ivanov speak English?"

"He does, and very well."

"Good. Mr. Ivanov, please remove the firearm from your person with your left hand and place it on the coffee table in front of you."

Ivanov looked at Beria and got a small nod. He placed the

pistol on the coffee table. Stone reached over and swept it onto the floor.

"Now you, Mr. Beria."

Beria opened his jacket to show that he was unarmed.

"All right, now proceed with your proposal, and take your time." He thought he would like it if Beria were still talking when the Strategic Services men came into the house.

"As I said earlier," Beria stated, "I wish to retrieve the computer device given to you by Mr. Bellini."

"I'm afraid you're not off to a very good start," Stone said, "because I don't know what you are talking about."

"Come now, Mr. Barrington," Beria said, "you are being obtuse."

Stone shrugged. "Please explain, and slowly, so that my dull wits may grasp your thought."

"The device, probably a thumb drive, contains software that I purchased from Mr. Bellini for twenty million dollars."

"And you paid that sum before receiving the software? You're not a very good businessman, Mr. Beria."

Beria was beginning to become agitated. "Mr. Barrington, my associate in this matter is a Mr. Selwyn Owaki. Is that name familiar to you?"

"I believe it is," Stone replied, "and you have my sympathy."

"Your sympathy?"

"For finding it necessary to associate yourself with such a thoroughly disreputable person."

"You are very fortunate that Mr. Owaki is not present," Beria said.

"I agree. I certainly would not seek the company of such a man."

"Mr. Barrington, you are wasting my time."

"You come into my office without an appointment and make silly threats, and *I* am wasting *your* time? You are confused, Mr. Beria."

Beria was now turning red. "Now, you listen to me," he began.

"No, you listen to me," Stone said. "I have the grounds to shoot you both right now, with no legal consequences."

"There would be consequences beyond your imagination," Beria said.

"All right, I'll play your inane game for a moment. Why do you think I possess this software?"

"Because you are associated with one Meg Harmon."

"Are you referring to the Harmon who is the rightful owner of the software of which you speak?"

"I am."

"Well, since she is the rightful owner and you are only a thief, we have nothing further to talk about," Stone said. "Except you can tell Mr. Owaki that if he wishes to speak to me not to send buffoons with messages. I'm in the Manhattan phone directory, if it still exists."

Stone's door suddenly opened, and four men filed into the room, each holding a handgun before him.

"Ah, gentlemen, welcome," Stone said. "There is a handgun on the floor over there. Please unload it, give it to the uglier of these two gentlemen, and then escort them both to the street. I expect they have a large black Mercedes waiting for them."

The four armed men followed Stone's instructions explicitly.

"You will be hearing from me, Mr. Barrington!" Beria shouted, as he was frog-marched from the room.

46

Joan came into Stone's office as he was inserting the little .45 back into its nest under his arm. "What the hell was that all about?" she asked. "You should excuse the expression."

"Should those two return," Stone said, "you have my permission to shoot them." Joan kept a .45 of her own in her desk drawer.

"It would be my pleasure," she replied. "I hate rudeness in a man."

"Should you decide to do so, shoot first and think about it later," Stone said. "And I wouldn't be shocked if we received another such visit from a man named Owaki."

"Selwyn Owaki?" Joan asked, as if he were someone she had met at a bar.

"How is it that you know that name?" Stone asked.

"I read the *New York Post*," she said. "On occasion."

"And from your deep research, what is your impression of Mr. Owaki?"

"That he has an enormous amount of money, none of it honestly earned, that he is personally responsible for roughly half of everyone on the planet who dies of a gunshot wound, that he eats innocent babies for breakfast." She thought about it. "Have I left out anything?"

"A great deal," Stone replied. "For instance, you failed to mention that he uses the Russians' UN mission as sort of a branch office, which is the rock from under which our two recent visitors crawled, and that he derives a great deal of personal pleasure from the deaths of those whom he considers to be his enemies, which is pretty much everybody."

"Why hasn't someone killed him?"

"Because he makes that work almost impossibly difficult. He dwells in an aerie of a building he owns, not all that far from here, that no one can enter without a full body scan and considerable goosing of the private areas."

"Doesn't anybody know how to kill with their hands anymore?" she asked.

"Apparently not."

"I don't know what the world is coming to," she said sadly. "In my day select people—secret agents, hired guns, Girl Scouts who expected to sell their cookies without getting raped—were taught to kill with a single thumb."

"Were you a Girl Scout?" Stone asked.

"Of course. How do you think I know this stuff?"

"Go bolt the front door and guard it with your life," Stone said, "and tell Fred to be on his guard." He picked up the phone and called Dino.

"Now what?" Dino asked, sounding exasperated.

"Well, for a start, the Russian gorilla Ivanov has definitely *not* left the country."

"And you know this how?"

"He just left my office in the company of Stanislav Beria and four of Mike Freeman's finest."

"Why was he in your office?"

"He was supposed to intimidate me into giving Beria what he wants."

"Which is what?"

"A computer thumb drive containing all of Meg Harmon's greatest hits."

"The car without a driver?"

"Indeed."

"And why does he think you have this thing?"

"Because I got it from Gino Bellini, shortly before he was dispatched by these same two gentlemen."

"I would get rid of it, if I were you."

"I have already returned it to its mother."

"Then I would get her out of town."

"I tried that once, remember?"

"I remember very well that your leaving town kept that awful thing from happening on my turf."

"That's your only concern, isn't it? Moving it off your turf?"

"You guessed it, pal."

"You're not concerned about my personal safety?"

"That's what Strategic Services is for. It's not my job to provide you with a personal police force, though you often seem to think it is."

"I'm hurt."

"Well, I hope you're ambulatory, so you can get your ass moving. You do remember who Beria works for, don't you?"

"If I had forgotten, Beria and Ivanov were anxious to remind me."

"Why didn't you have Joan shoot them?"

"I have already given her instructions to that effect, but a little late."

"Timing is everything," Dino replied. "That's why I'm telling you to take Ms. Harmon and visit one of your many residences."

"For how long?"

"Until somebody offs Selwyn Owaki, or you give him what he wants, whichever comes first."

"Joan says she could kill him with her thumb."

"I believe her," Dino said. "Viv could probably do that, too. She says the Girl Scouts taught her."

"That's what Joan says."

"Enough of this banter," Dino said. "Pick a house, pack a bag, grab your girl, and get your ass in gear."

"I'll think about it."

"Not for too long. I don't want to have to scrape you off a sidewalk somewhere in my fair city. Call me when you get wherever you're going." Dino hung up.

Stone called upstairs, and Meg answered.

"Are you all unpacked?" he asked.

"Pretty much."

"Well, start packing again, and bring your passport."

"Why?"

"We have to get out of town all over again."

"That didn't work out so well last time, did it?"

"I thought it worked out very well indeed," Stone said.

"People died."

"I don't mind that so much, as long as it isn't you and me."

"You have a point. How long do I have to pack, and what sort of climate have you chosen?"

"An hour, cool and damp, with occasional sunshine."

"I can handle that without major shopping."

"Oh, and do you still have that thumb drive of Bellini's?"

"Yes."

"Where is it?"

"In my purse."

"Don't you have any pockets?"

"Certainly not, I'm a girl."

"I forgot."

"After last night? You're not very observant, are you?"

"Ah . . ."

"Oh, all right. An hour." She hung up.

47

Stone completed his preflight checks and escorted Meg onto the airplane and into the right cockpit seat.

"Why can't I sit in the back, like before?" she asked.

"Because Viv isn't there to hold your hand, and I don't want you to be nervous."

"What if I'm nervous anyway?"

"I've put you in the cockpit next to me so that you can absorb what goes into piloting a jet airplane."

"Well, that's something I don't intend ever to do."

"One never knows, do one?" Stone handed her the checklist and commanded her to read it aloud to him, one item at a time. This took only about three times as long as if he had done it himself, but at least she was getting an idea of what was involved.

That completed, he called the tower and asked for a clearance. A company called Pat Frank, after a woman who was a client of his, had already sent him a detailed weather report and filed his flight plans for this day and the next.

Stone wrote down his clearance and entered his route into the flight computer, then he called ground control and was given permission to taxi to runway 1.

"When do I get to know where we're going?" Meg asked.

"Today we're flying to St. John's in Newfoundland," Stone replied. "Tomorrow will be a surprise."

"Newfoundland," she said. "Brrrrr."

"You'll find it pleasant this time of year," Stone said. He was cleared for takeoff, then taxied into position on runway 1 and pushed the throttles smoothly forward. "Here we go." A little longer than a moment later, he lifted the nose of the airplane and it flew off the runway.

"That was kind of fun," Meg said.

"Next thing you know, you'll be taking flying lessons," Stone said, raising the landing gear and the flaps.

"Why can't you teach me?"

"Because teaching you to fly would require reserves of patience and kindness that I do not possess. It's better if you learn from a professional."

"Like learning to drive?"

"Yes, but there are fewer things to bump into." At 450 feet, he pressed the autopilot button and took his hands off the yoke.

"What are you doing?" she asked, alarmed.

"I'm turning the airplane over to the autopilot, which does a better job than I." Stone received instructions to climb on course, and the airplane turned itself to the right.

"How long a flight?"

"A little over three hours. Would you like the *New York Times*?"

"I'd rather have a drink."

"We don't fly with alcoholic beverages aboard," Stone said. "The pilot might be tempted to have one, and we don't want that."

"Then I'll make do with the *Times*," she said.

He reached behind him, retrieved the newspaper, and handed it to her. "Remember to look out the window now and then. The views are nice."

"What will we do in St. John's?" she asked.

"We refuel and check into a hotel for the night. I want to land in daylight tomorrow."

"Why? Can't you land at night?"

"Yes, but in the daytime the views are better."

THEY LANDED on schedule at St. John's, refueled, checked into a hotel, made love a couple of times, had a good breakfast early the next morning, and lifted off at eight AM.

After a few minutes Meg looked out the window. "I don't see anything but ocean," she said.

"That's because we're crossing it."

"How long will it take?"

"About three and a half hours. We have a tailwind of more than a hundred knots, and that makes it fast."

"And where do we land?"

"That's the surprise." Stone leveled off at flight level 410, and the airplane began to pick up speed. Soon they were at a true airspeed of 425 knots, but the tailwind gave them a ground-speed of 650 knots. Stone selected some classical music on the satellite radio. "Eventually we'll run out of satellite and thus, music," he said.

"But it's calming my nerves."

"By that time you'll be as calm as you're going to get."

Nearly three hours later, he pointed into the distance. "Land, ho!" he said.

Meg peered into the distance. "I see it. Which land is it?"

"Ireland."

"Are we stopping there?"

"No."

"Well, the next country is England. Are we stopping there?"

"Yes."

"Where in England?"

"That's the surprise."

With Ireland behind them air traffic control gave them permission to descend, and soon the south coast of England was beneath them.

"You're right," Meg said, "the views are lovely."

"I'm usually right," Stone replied. "Not always, but usually."

They got lower and lower.

"Are we about to land?"

"Yes."

"Where? I don't see an airport."

"Look dead ahead. You'll see a long strip of pavement with trees on both sides. There's a fairly large house to your left."

"I see the runway, but there's no airport."

"It's a private runway. During World War Two it was a bomber base for the RAF."

"I see several large houses. Which is yours?"

Stone pointed. "The tour is over now. I have to concentrate on landing."

"But . . ."

"Shhhh."

Stone lined up for the runway, corrected for a slight cross-wind, dropped the landing gear, and progressively added flaps, until a woman's voice said, "Five hundred feet."

"Who was that?" Meg asked.

Stone didn't answer but slowed to 110 knots and smoothly set down the airplane. "We have arrived at Windward Hall," Stone said.

"Who are those people over there?" She pointed.

"The two gentlemen in uniforms are customs and immigration officials. The one in a suit is Major Bugg, the estate manager."

Stone taxied up to the two vehicles, stopped, and shut down the engines. Shortly, they were unloaded and were presenting their passports to officialdom.

"Welcome home, Mr. Barrington," one of them said. They got into their vehicle and drove away.

Stone introduced Meg to Major Bugg, who had already put their luggage into a Range Rover. "And the man driving the tug is George," Stone said, as George towed the aircraft into its hangar.

Shortly, they pulled up in front of Windward Hall, and help came to take their luggage to the master suite. Stone gave Meg a tour of the ground floor, and they were served drinks in the library. Major Bugg gave Stone the *Times* of London and the local paper and excused himself.

Something caught Stone's eye at the bottom of the front page of the local paper. "Oh, shit," he muttered.

"Really? My scotch is very good."

He showed her the story, which was about how a billionaire had bought a local car factory and saved the workers' jobs.

"Who is this man?" Meg asked.

"His name is Selwyn Owaki," Stone replied.

"And who is he?"

"He's the man we came all this way to get away from."

48

Meg stared at Stone. "Who is he, and why did we come all this way to avoid him?"

Stone handed her the newspaper, and she read the article, then put it down.

"Selwyn Owaki sells arms to whoever has the money, and he doesn't care where or how they got it."

"He sounds charming," Meg said wryly.

"Actually, he has that reputation, when he's not murdering his competition. All sorts of people—even people who are very rich themselves—are attracted to and deceived by people who have vast quantities of money."

"Why is that, do you suppose?"

"It is one of the great mysteries of human nature. Americans, particularly, seem to suffer from this affliction. Haven't you noticed differences in the way you are treated by others since you became very wealthy?"

"Well, now that you mention it . . ."

"You'll have to learn to distinguish between people who simply admire your industry and those who hope to take some of it away from you, in one way or another. Selwyn Owaki is one of the latter group."

"And what does he want from me?"

"The designs and specifications of your self-driving vehicles."

"You mean he's the one who bought the stolen files from Gino Bellini?"

"Yes, but he dealt through Stanislav Beria, an official at the Russians' UN mission. Owaki always deals through others when doing something illegal, immoral, or both."

"Ah, I think I see now why Mr. Owaki has bought an automobile factory."

"Yes, and one not five miles from this estate." Stone tapped out an e-mail to Mike Freeman, asking for protective measures to be taken for himself and Meg. "I'm afraid we're going to become prisoners in this house until the issue is resolved."

"Which issue is that?"

"Whether Owaki is able to lay his hands on your data, and whether he will try to kill us in the process."

"I would prefer not on either account."

"As would I. Don't worry, Mr. Owaki has no way of knowing

we're here, and even if he did, by tomorrow morning Strategic Services will have established a cordon around the house to keep out unwelcome visitors."

Meg rummaged in her purse and came up with a thumb drive. "So what he wants is this?"

"Yes."

She peered at it. "Sorry, wrong thumb drive." She went through her bag again and came up with another. "This thumb drive."

"Right. What's on the other one?"

"A draft copy of our quarterly report," she said. "Actually, it could be quite valuable to someone with knowledge of it, since it is very favorable, and the stock price will shoot up when it's released in a few days."

"I think we need to put the one containing the designs of the car in a safe place."

"Where would you suggest?"

"A safe," Stone replied. "Come with me." He walked across the room and swung out a picture the frame of which was hinged. Behind it lay a safe with a digital lock. Stone tapped in the code, asking Meg to memorize it as he did, then he opened the door, stepped back, and allowed her to place the thumb drive on a shelf. He locked it and returned the picture to its original position, then they returned to their sofa and their drinks.

"This is a very beautiful house," Meg said. "How did you come by it?"

"A friend of mine, Dame Felicity Devonshire, who lives just across the Beaulieu River—spelled the French way but pronounced 'Bewley.' I was in Rome on business and I got a call from her, asking me to come and visit her in England, that she had something to show me. That something turned out to be this estate.

"It was owned by Sir Charles Bourne, a delightful Englishman who was ill and slowly dying, and he wanted to sell the place to keep it from falling into the hands of either of his two children, both of whom he despised. Felicity brought me here to see the place, which was nearing the end of a complete renovation, paid for with money that would otherwise have gone to his heirs.

"She then arranged for Sir Charles and me to meet for dinner at the Royal Yacht Squadron, England's oldest yacht club, in Cowes, on the Isle of Wight, which lies a few miles from here across a body of water known as the Solent, an arm of the English Channel. Sir Charles and I got on famously, and at the end of our dinner I wrote him a check for his asking price, which I thought reasonable. The legal niceties were performed later. Sir Charles, who was living in a cottage on the estate during the renovations, died a few months later, sometime after I had moved in."

"Dame Felicity must know you very well to know that you would want the house on sight."

"Dame Felicity is director of the British Foreign Intelligence

Service, known as MI-6. She tends to know just about every-thing there is to know about everything."

"Nevertheless, it was kind of her to steer you to it."

"Her action was not entirely out of kindness—there was an element of self-service involved."

"How so?"

"She didn't want the place to be snapped up by some nouveau-riche hedge fund manager. She and her neighbors wanted someone who was the 'right sort of person' to buy it, so she chose a nouveau-riche American lawyer."

Meg laughed. "That means that she certainly did know you well."

"We have been friends for many years," Stone said.

"Why do I think that Dame Felicity is not a 'lady of a certain age' and is quite beautiful?"

"Because you are a perspicacious woman."

Meg laughed. "Will I meet Dame Felicity?"

"The moment she hears we are here she will invite us to dinner—or more likely, invite herself here for dinner—so that she can get a good look at you."

"And I at her."

"I warn you, Felicity is something of a carnal omnivore, so don't be surprised if you find her hand on your knee."

Meg laughed again. "It's been quite some time since another woman tried that—at Stanford, I think—and she didn't get lucky."

"Just giving you a heads-up," Stone said.

His phone rang. "Yes? Thank you so much. Goodbye." He hung up. "At some time during the night our guardians will be in place, so we may rest easily."

"I'll look forward to it," Meg said.

49

Stone showed Meg into the master suite and then, after she had oohed and aahed for a moment, into her dressing room and bath, where she repaired to unpack and undress. She was back sooner than he had expected, but he was glad to see her. He put aside his *Times*, and she shed her nightgown and dived into bed with him.

"Aren't you exhausted?" he asked.

"No, but I plan to be in just a few minutes," she replied, giving him a deep kiss and fondling him.

"By the way," Stone said, "before I forget—you have filed all the patent application paperwork for your designs, haven't you?"

"I expect so," she said, running a tongue in and out of his ear. "I gave the lawyers all that a long time ago."

"Remind me to remind you to check with them first thing tomorrow to see if everything is in order."

"Remind me to remind you," she said, and they gave themselves over to each other.

STONE WOKE to a peep of sunshine through the closed drapes and checked the clock. Ten AM. He had slept well, and Meg was still out. It was his turn to do the seduction, and he did so with relish.

BREAKFAST WAS served in bed, along with the papers, then the phone buzzed. "Yes?" Stone said into it.

"Good morning, Mr. Barrington. Major Bugg here."

"Good morning, Major."

"Have you, by chance, ordered a passel of security people to surround the house?"

"I have, last night. I take it they have arrived."

"They have. Shall I house and feed them in the cottage, as before?" This was not the first time this had happened.

"Please do, and give them every cooperation."

"Of course, sir." The major rang off.

"Are we surrounded?" Meg asked.

"We are."

"Will that prevent me from taking a walk around the grounds?"

"When I said last night that we would be prisoners in the house for a time, I meant exactly that. However, you may explore the interiors of the house, which will take you much of the day."

"Oh, all right," she said.

The phone rang. "Yes?" Stone said.

A young man's voice said, "I have Dame Felicity Devonshire for you. Will you accept the call?"

"Certainly," Stone said.

There was a click. "Stone, is that you?"

"It is. The word spreads quickly."

"My spies are everywhere," she said. "I thought we might have dinner tonight, if you and your lady friend are available."

"How do you know that I am in the company of a lady?"

"Oh, really, Stone!"

"Come to us at six-thirty," he said.

"That will work very nicely. I'm leaving the office a little early today. See you then." She hung up.

"I think I can guess who that was," Meg said.

"Good guess. She'll arrive at six-thirty, dressed to kill. Never mind that it's just the three of us."

"I'll do my best to rise to the occasion. Now," she said, leaping from the bed, "I'm going to put on my country tweeds and explore the innards of the house."

"How did you know to bring country tweeds?"

"A wild guess," she replied, and disappeared into her dressing room.

Stone read the *Times* fairly thoroughly, then gave up immediately on the crossword. He had never been any good at British crosswords; they were all riddles.

MEG WAS BACK at noon, while Stone was still dressing. "Wasn't I supposed to remind you of something?" she said.

"Yes, you were supposed to remind me to remind you to check on the status of your patent applications."

She looked at her watch. "Too early in California. I'll do it later."

"Remind me to remind you."

THEY LUNCHED in the small dining room, overlooking the rear gardens of the house.

"Lord," Meg said, gazing at the riot of color. "What does it take to run a place like this?"

"About fifteen people," Stone said, "and a bottomless bank account."

"What do fifteen people do?"

"Well, there's Major Bugg and his assistant, the cook and her assistant, four housemaids, a butler, and two of what used to be called 'footmen' but now prefer 'assistant butler.' On the outside a groom and his assistant, a gardener and his assistant, and six groundsmen, one of whom doubles as an aircraft handler and another as a dockmaster."

"That presumes a dock."

"Right over that way"—he pointed—"on the Beaulieu River."

"That comes to twenty-one," she said.

"Good God, as many as that?"

"You thought there were only fifteen."

"I would rather go on thinking that," Stone said. "Excuse me, I should check in with Joan." He called the New York house.

"Good morning, the Barrington Practice."

"Good morning. Is everything and everyone safe and sound?"

"Yes, but Bob is a little put out that you didn't take him with you."

"I didn't know, on short notice, whether the legal requirements for his entering Britain had been accomplished. Will you check into that?"

"Certainly."

"Anything at all odd going on?"

"Do you mean the two men lurking outside in the street and the phone calls from men who, when told you are unavailable, decline to identify themselves?"

"I believe I do."

"Do you want me to shoot anybody?"

"Not until their hands are at your bodice. What you could do, though, is to tell Fred to take the car out once or twice a day, so they'll think I'm in it. And tell him to watch his ass, in case they believe that too strongly and take a shot at him."

"I will do so."

"Call me if there are developments."

"Of course." They both hung up.

"Is all well?" Meg asked.

"As well as can be expected," Stone replied.

50

S tone and Meg had just finished lunch when the butler came into the room. "Excuse me, Mr. Barrington," he said, "but one of the security detail would like to speak with you at the front door."

"Please bring him in here," Stone replied.

A man Stone recognized came into the room. "Good afternoon, Mr. Barrington."

"It's Carl Atkins, isn't it?"

"Yes, sir. I have some rather unwelcome news for you, I'm afraid."

"And what is that?"

"The gentleman you're concerned about, Mr. Owaki?"

"Yes?"

"I'm very much afraid that he's a guest next door."

Stone turned to Meg. "Next door means a larger country house—much larger than this one—that the Arrington Group turned into a country hotel."

"And it's next door?"

"Yes."

"In the circumstances," Atkins said, "we feel strongly that you and Ms. Harmon should not appear outdoors on the front side of the house, as Mr. Owaki will certainly have his own security, and you might be spotted."

"How about the back side of the house?" Stone asked.

"That should be quite safe."

"Thank you, Carl, we'll heed your warning."

"Have a good afternoon, sir." Atkins departed.

"I suppose I was wrong about Owaki being five miles away," Stone said. "It's more like a quarter of a mile."

"Swell," Meg said.

"Would you like a walk in the garden? That's at the rear of the house." He pointed.

"Very much," she said.

They left the house through the rear entrance and walked into the garden, while Meg explained the species to Stone, who had no idea. Then they walked into the stable yard and had a look at the four horses there.

"May we ride?" Meg asked.

"Do you ride?"

"When I'm permitted to."

"I'm afraid our only trail passes within a few yards of the house next door."

"I should have known. In that case, I think I'll spend the afternoon in your library with a good book."

"What a good idea. Remember, drinks at six-thirty."

"I'll be there, suitably attired."

Stone was in the library at six, dressed in a blue suit and a tie, remembering that Dame Felicity was often early. At six-twenty, the butler announced her, and as soon as the door closed behind her she enveloped Stone in a hug and allowed herself to be kissed on both cheeks.

"I won't ask how you are," Stone said, "because it's perfectly obvious."

"You, too, darling," she said. She was dressed in a clinging cocktail dress of green, which set off her red hair.

"What would you like to drink?"

"A martini, please."

Stone went to the paneled bar and mixed the drink, then poured himself a bourbon. They settled into chairs beside the fireplace.

"I noted the presence of security at the dock and at the house," Felicity said. "May I know why?"

"You may," Stone said. He took five minutes to apprise her of the situation.

"Owaki is a nasty piece of work," Felicity said, "in spite of his oleaginous charm. I knew he was in the country, of course, and now I know why."

"I don't think he came in search of us."

"No, it's his factory, and now I know why he bought it."

"I don't suppose you could find an excuse to have him thrown out of the country," Stone said.

"I'll see what I can do," she replied.

Meg was ushered in by the butler, and Stone introduced her to Felicity, who looked her up and down appraisingly. She was wearing a red sheath dress, and Felicity obviously approved. He made Meg a martini and Felicity a second one, then they gathered at the fireplace.

"I understand you are in the intelligence trade," Meg said to her.

"I'm very much afraid that I can neither affirm nor deny that," Felicity replied. "I understand that you are receiving the attention of nefarious characters."

"I can affirm that," Meg replied. "Can you have people shot?"

"Not in my own neighborhood, I fear," Felicity replied. "I'm just across the river, you know."

"I have heard," Meg replied.

"I don't know why Stone couldn't handle something like that himself," Felicity said. "There's a very good deer rifle from Holland & Holland right over there in his gun cabinet." She nodded toward it.

"Not in my own neighborhood," Stone said.

"Perhaps I should do it myself," Meg said. "I'm a very good shot."

"I would certainly have no objection," Felicity said, "but I can't speak for Her Majesty's Government, who might take exception—in the nicest possible way, of course."

"Of course," Stone said.

"I could, perhaps, put in a word with the home secretary before your sentencing, though."

"How kind of you," Meg replied, and they all laughed.

DINNER WAS a country pâté and pheasant from the estate, accompanied by a bottle of outstanding old claret from Windward Hall's cellar, followed by Stilton and a vintage port.

Stone was pleased to see that the two women got on famously, and Felicity had been a perfect lady.

"Now then," Felicity said over her second glass of port, "we must do something about your situation. I think it's appalling that you can't even take a walk or go for a gallop."

"What can be done?" Stone asked.

"The insufferable Mr. Owaki believes himself to be untouchable," she said, "and I always enjoy upsetting the carts of the insufferable. Perhaps his new factory hasn't been subjected to the proper level of inspection by various departments of the county council."

"Since Owaki is a new employer in the district," Stone said, "I doubt if they would wish to make him uncomfortable."

"Still, he isn't actually building anything yet, is he?"

"The county newspaper says he is continuing to build the sports cars for which his factory is famous."

"And losing ten thousand pounds on every one," Felicity re-plied. "That's why he was able to buy the concern cheaply. I think you're already doing the thing that will hurt him most—depriving him of the designs of what he would really like to build."

"You know, my board has discussed the possibility of manu-facturing on this side of the pond," Meg said.

Stone smiled. "Perhaps they would vote to make Mr. Owaki an insultingly low offer for the place."

"That would be very satisfying," Meg said.

Felicity spoke up. "I could put you in touch with a British intermediary who would keep the source of the offer a dark secret."

"I'll make some calls tomorrow," Meg said.

51

Stone was taking a nap the following afternoon, paying the price for the good bourbon, claret, and port he had ingested the previous evening, when Meg came into the room and sat on the edge of the bed.

"Stone, wake up," she said.

"Mmmmf?" he replied.

"Open your eyes and ears. I have important news."

Stone opened one eye. "How much port did I drink last night?"

"Three glasses, just like Felicity and I. Now listen to me carefully."

"I'm listening carefully," Stone said, opening the other eye.

"I've just spoken with my attorneys in San Francisco, and they told me that they filed for all our patents on the date I asked them to. However, upon checking, they find that they have no acknowledgment of that fact from the U.S. Patent Office."

"That's all right, they will have confirmation of delivery from whatever shipping service they used."

"I'm afraid not," she said. "They sent it to the post office, along with all their other outgoing mail that day—their mail-room has a record of it going out—but it was sent by ordinary mail, not registered mail, so there is no record of a notice of receipt from the patent office, who say that they have no record of it being filed."

Stone sat up in bed. "Your attorneys should have received a notice that would allow you to use the designation 'Patent Applied For.'"

"I'm afraid they didn't."

"Then your attorneys need to begin an immediate investigation of what happened to the package, questioning every employee who could have handled it."

"They are doing that now. My question to you is, if they can't find a notice of receipt, what is my position?"

"Your position, in those circumstances, would be a person or a corporation who has not applied for a patent."

"I was afraid you were going to say that. How can I fix this?"

"First of all, it's necessary that you officially become my client."

"Stone, will you please represent me as my attorney in all matters relating to all my company's products?"

"Yes. Now I need Joan to e-mail us the correct paperwork,

but I don't want to wait until we receive it to start on this. May I proceed?"

"You may proceed."

Stone called Joan and requested the e-mailing of an exclusive client retainer document, then he called Bill Eggers, the managing partner of Woodman & Weld.

"Good morning, Stone," Eggers said.

"Good afternoon, Bill—at least it is in England."

"I see. What are you up to over there?"

"Well, I've just signed a new client—Harmony Software of Silicon Valley fame, and its CEO, Meg Harmon."

"It would be the firm's great pleasure to represent the company and Ms. Harmon. Has she signed a retainer agreement?"

"It's being e-mailed to me as we speak."

"Good. Well, I have a meeting to go to."

"Not yet," Stone said.

"Why not?"

"Because our new client's previous attorneys have fucked up royally, and unless we can sort this out in a hurry, the world may fall on both our new client and, by extension, us."

"Explain, please."

Stone explained.

"So, if this Owaki fellow can get his hands on the designs, he could file a patent application?"

"I am very much afraid that is correct."

"What is the name of the managing partner of her previous law firm?"

Stone put his hand over the phone. "Who are your San Francisco attorneys, and who is the top man there?"

"Coward, McMillan & Crane, and John Coward is the senior partner and my attorney."

Stone conveyed that information to Bill Eggers, then there was a knock on the door, and Major Bugg's assistant entered the room with a thick stack of papers.

"This was just received from your office, Mr. Barrington," she said, "and we printed it out for you."

"Hang on a minute, Bill," Stone said, and put the phone down. "Meg," he said, handing her the pages, "this is our standard agreement for new clients. Please read it, then sign the last page."

Meg skipped to the last page, signed it, and handed it to Stone.

"Bill," Stone said, "I have Ms. Harmon's signed representation agreement in my hand. I'll fax it to you." He handed it back to the woman and instructed her to fax it to Eggers.

"Good. Now I will call John Coward, whom I know, break the news to him, and make unreasonable demands about locating the notice of receipt from the patent office. I will also send two attorneys from our San Francisco office to their offices, to supervise the inquiry into what went wrong. Then I'll get back to you."

"Thank you, Bill." Stone hung up. "All right, Meg, you are no longer a client of Coward, McMillan & Crane, you are now represented by Woodman & Weld, under my direction."

"I feel better already," Meg replied.

"Not so fast. Don't feel better until we have fixed this problem. My managing partner, Bill Eggers, is sending two attorneys from our San Francisco office to your former law firm to find out what the hell happened. Then they will report to Bill, and he will advise us on how to proceed."

"All right," Meg said. "Now may I join you for a nap?"

"Of course," Stone replied, then the telephone buzzed. "Yes?"

"Mr. Barrington," Carl Atkins, the security man, said, "there is a Mr. Selwin Ozowi—oh, excuse me, sir—a Mr. Selwyn Owaki here to see you. He does not have an appointment."

"Is he armed or accompanied by anyone?"

"No, sir, neither."

"Please ask the butler to show him into the library, give him a drink, and tell him you will try to locate me."

"Oh, he wishes to see Ms. Harmon, as well."

"Tell him you will look for us both." Stone hung up.

"What's going on?" Meg asked.

Stone got out of bed. "Go and change into your riding clothes—tweeds, boots, et cetera. We are going to receive a visitor in the library, and we should look as though we have just come in from riding. If you have a perfume with a scent resembling horse sweat, spray a little of that on, too."

"And who are we receiving?"

"Selwyn Owaki. You have twenty minutes."

Meg ran for her dressing room and Stone for his.

52

I
t had been Stone's experience that important people who have been kept waiting become angry and say things they might otherwise not say, so he kept Owaki waiting for nearly half an hour before sauntering into the library with Meg, chatting about their ride.

Stone tried to look surprised to see the man. "Oh, are you the gentleman who requested to see me? *Without* an appointment?"

Owaki rose and tried to look pleasant. "My name is Selwyn Owaki. I am a guest at your hotel next door." He stuck out a hand, which Stone contrived not to notice.

"Please sit down, Mr. Ozaku, and tell me how I may help you."

"It's Owaki," the man replied, spelling it for him.

"Ah, yes, you're Japanese, are you?"

"I am not, sir. I am of mixed extraction."

"Something of a mutt, eh?"

A touch of pink appeared on Owaki's cheeks. "I have come to see you and Ms. Harmon on a business matter."

"Oh, you know Ms. Harmon?" Stone asked.

"Not until now."

"Meg, this is Mr. Owazu."

"It's Owaki. How do you do, Ms. Harmon?"

"I do very well, thank you," Meg replied.

"I should tell you, Mr. Owachi," Stone said, "that neither Ms. Harmon nor I are accustomed to doing business outside our offices, which are located on another continent."

"I am aware of that," Owaki said, "and I apologize for the inconvenience."

"Actually, it is less of an inconvenience than an intrusion. Do you normally call on those to whom you have not been introduced and with whom you do not have an appointment, to discuss business?"

"I *am* sorry," Owaki said, "but since the matter is one favorable to Ms. Harmon and rather time sensitive, I took a chance."

"And what did you hope to achieve by taking this chance?" Stone asked.

"I wish to buy something from Ms. Harmon, and if she is not willing to sell, then, perhaps sell her something."

"Well, what are you buying and selling, Mr. Onako? Encyclopedias? Pots and pans? Bibles, perhaps?"

Meg spoke up. "I haven't the faintest idea what he's talking about, Stone, do you?"

"Not a clue," Stone replied. "Mr. Tanaka, please enlighten us."

Owaki sighed. "I wish to buy Harmony Software," he said, "and I am prepared to pay a rich price."

"Perhaps you are unaware that a substantial minority of the shares of Harmony Software have already been purchased by the Steele Group, and they are not inclined to sell."

"But you have not heard my offer."

"That is so, but I am a member of the board of the Steele Group, and their attorney, and if you wish, I will convey your offer to its chairman, Mr. Steele."

"I do not wish to buy the Steele Group's shares," Owaki said. "I wish to buy Ms. Harmon's fifty-one percent."

"Did you have a figure in mind?" Stone asked.

Meg raised a hand. "Stone, will you please convey to this gentleman that my shares in Harmony Software are not for sale to him?"

"Mr. Oahu," Stone said, "Ms. Harmon's shares are not for sale—to you."

"Do you mean, specifically, not for sale, or not for sale to me?" Owaki asked.

"Not for sale to you," Meg replied.

"May I ask why not?" Owaki said.

"Because . . ."

Stone raised a hand. "Let me take this one, please, Meg."

"Of course, Stone."

"Ms. Harmon will not sell her shares to you, Mr. Opatu,

because you are a merchant of death, a murderer, and, generally speaking, devoid of any moral character."

Owaki was bright red now. "I do not understand," he said.

"I thought I was perfectly clear, Mr. Oleo. Now, you said you have something to sell?"

Owaki shifted in his seat and tried to recover his good humor. "I own, just a few miles from this house, twenty-five acres of land and on it, a factory building of some thirty thousand square feet, well equipped for the manufacturing of automobiles and with a highly trained staff of some three hundred people."

"Very well, Mr. Whatsyourname," Meg said, "I will offer you one hundred thousand pounds—no, make that dollars—for your land and factory." She smiled. "Take it or leave it."

Owaki's jaw dropped. *"What?"*

"Would you like me to repeat my offer?" Meg asked.

"Thank you, no. I had expected to have a business discussion with you people, and—"

"And you have done so," Stone replied. "So have we, and we are done now." He pressed a button on the table beside him.

Owaki stood up, and he was seething. "You are about to learn that it is unwise to deal with me in such a manner."

"Oh, we learned that several days ago," Stone said. "It was explained to me in great detail by your Mr. Beria."

There was a knock on the door, and the butler entered. "Mr. Olakoo has just had a telephone message," he said. "The county fire inspectors are at his factory and wish to speak with him there at once."

"Mr. Ozanna was just leaving," Stone said. "Please show him the door, and tell the security people to shoot him if he tarries."

Owaki stalked from the room and would have slammed the door behind him if the butler had not already closed it softly.

Stone and Meg burst into laughter.

"Oh, that was wonderful," Meg said, wiping tears away.

"I think he got the message," Stone replied, "and now he will send us a message, and in so doing, we can hope he makes a mistake. And we will do our best to be ready for him."

53

Stone walked out his front door in time to watch a black Mercedes-Maybach depart his house in a spray of gravel. Carl Atkins, the security man, was watching, too.

"I guess your idea was to have him go away mad," he said.

"Exactly, Carl, and now I think we must prepare for him to respond."

"From what I've heard of him in the security business, he loves revenge among all other things."

"Have you been in touch with the local constabulary?" Stone asked.

"Just once, when we arrived. That inspector you know

is now the chief constable, and he wants to be helpful, if he can."

"Then use him and his people to the hilt," Stone said, "and I will find a way to thank him later."

"Certainly, sir, and may I have your permission to request another six men to be sent down from London?"

"If you think we need them. And I think it would be a good idea to speak to the manager of our hotel and see what you can learn from him and his staff about Owaki's intentions."

"His car didn't head in that direction," Atkins said. "I think he may be visiting his car factory."

"I'm sure of it," Stone said. His cell phone rang, and he answered. "Hello?"

"Good afternoon, my dear," Felicity said. "I wanted to thank you for a delightful evening, though I was a little worse for the wear this morning."

"A condition I share," Stone replied. "I've just had a visit from Selwyn Owaki, who came to make a business proposal and left very, very unhappy, after a call to him requesting his attention to some county fire officials at his factory."

"I should think he might hear from more than one county department before the day is out," she said. "And tomorrow, with any luck at all, he may be summoned to the home secretary's office to explain why he should not be expelled from the country because of bad business practices and his indifference to the safety of his staff."

"You are a perfect angel," Stone said.

"We can discuss that on another occasion," Felicity said, "but in the meantime, I think you should prepare yourself for a further visit from Mr. Owaki or his associates."

"I have already taken steps," Stone said, "which reminds me, I must make a call to the hotel manager regarding his most infamous guest."

"Go, then. See you soon."

"Yes, indeed." Stone called the hotel and asked to speak to the manager.

"Yes, Mr. Barrington?" the man said.

"I hope business is good," Stone said.

"It is very good, sir. We are maintaining an occupancy rate in the region of ninety-five percent."

"I'm delighted to hear it. However, I'm calling to ask you to free up some space—that occupied by a Mr. Owaki and, perhaps, some of his associates."

"Ah, yes, a large suite and two smaller rooms. You would like them all to vacate?"

"I would."

"How soon?"

"With immediate effect."

"As you wish, sir. What reason shall I give Mr. Owaki?"

"Tell him that your headquarters have instructed you to evict him, and that he and his associates will oblige the management by leaving quietly."

"Certainly, sir. Would you like us to pack his luggage?"

"What a good idea! Neatly, of course, then set it on the front steps for collection on his return. How much is his bill?"

"They arrived only yesterday, sir, so it's right at three thousand five hundred pounds, so far."

"Hand him his bill, marked 'Paid,' and send a copy to my New York Office, which will reimburse you."

"As you wish, Mr. Barrington. I'll see to it immediately."

"Oh," Stone said, "if you should find any weapons when you are packing his things, retain them and turn them over to the chief of the local constabulary, and be sure to tell Mr. Owaki or his representative that you have done so."

"It will be done, sir. Is there anything else? Anything at all?"

"Thank you, that will do it," Stone said, "and I will favorably mention your cooperation to the main office at the first opportunity."

"How very kind of you, sir."

"Goodbye." Stone hung up.

Carl Atkins, who had overheard the conversation, was laughing quietly. "Good idea to disarm them, Mr. Barrington."

"We must try and keep the peace, Carl. By the way, I'm reliably informed that Mr. Owaki and his party will be told to leave the country tomorrow."

"I don't know how you arranged that, sir, but I admire your skills and your connections."

Stone turned to the butler, who had been present the whole time. "Would you please ask the head groom to saddle two of the horses for Ms. Harmon and me, and to bring them around front?"

"Yes, sir."

"And would you let Ms. Harmon know that we are going riding?"

"Immediately, sir."

"Anything else I can do for you, Mr. Barrington?" Atkins asked.

"Yes, you can loan me a compact firearm and a holster," Stone said.

"Right away, sir." Atkins left at a trot for the cottage where his crew were staying.

Stone's phone rang. "Hello?"

"It's Dino. Are you still alive?"

"Perfectly so," Stone replied.

"I mean, I heard that Owaki is in your neighborhood."

"Meg and I met with him only a few minutes ago, and, with the able assistance of Dame Felicity, we have rattled his cage sufficiently for him to be out of the country tomorrow."

"Which means he'll be coming back into my jurisdiction," Dino said. "Thanks a lot."

"I expect so. Can you think of any way to make his arrival memorable?"

"I expect so. I'll alert U.S. Customs at Teterboro, which is where he lands his Gulfstream. Might they be carrying any weapons?"

"Perhaps, but I have managed to put some of them beyond

his reach. Perhaps a strip search by customs might turn up anything he has left."

"I'll suggest a full cavity search, too," Dino said. "Those customs guys love that. When are you coming back?"

"I don't know—a day or two, I guess. Meg has to close on her new apartment."

"I spoke to the head of the committee," Dino said. "She's a shoo-in."

"I'll tell her, she'll like that." They said goodbye and hung up.

54

As Meg left the house, a stableman walked around the corner, leading two beautifully groomed horses.

"Yours is the mare, mine the gelding," Stone said.

"I hope I can tell which is which," she said, lifting a leg so that the groom could hoist her into the saddle.

Stone managed on his own. "We'll walk them for a couple of hundred yards, to let them loosen up," he said, and they did so. At the end of that Stone's gelding was champing at the bit, and a tap of the heel into his flank achieved a comfortable gallop. Meg pulled up alongside him. "Wall coming up," Stone said. "Are you up for that?"

"Sure I am," she said.

They took the stone wall that divided Windward Hall from the hotel's estate and galloped across the acreage of its front lawn.

"Magnificent house," Meg said. "You should have bought that one."

"I wasn't looking for a stately home," Stone said. "And there are at least sixty staff there, not counting the hotel keepers." He noted that two bellmen were piling up luggage at the bottom of the front steps. "Mr. Owaki appears to be checking out," he said, as the black Maybach pulled up to the front of the house.

He edged the gelding up into a full run, and Meg kept right up. They took another wall, then pulled up into some trees to rest the horses. Stone got down and took a small bag from its place behind the saddle. "Would you like a beer?"

"What a good idea!" They sat down with their backs against a tree and drank the cold lager.

"I would jump you," Meg said, "if riding clothes weren't so difficult to deal with."

"They'll come off easily enough when we get back," Stone said, kissing her lightly.

"I'll look forward to watching."

Stone gave her a leg up onto the mare, then got onto the gelding,

Then Meg pointed back to where they had come from. "Look!" she shouted.

Stone pulled his mount around to face Windward Hall.

From the rear of the house a column of black smoke was rising. He dug his heels into the gelding. "Come on, we'll run them the whole way!"

The horses sprang forward and hardly noticed the stone wall when they topped it. Stone could hear a siren in the distance, and as they drew up in front of the house, a fire truck drove around to the rear.

Stone and Meg jumped down and handed their horses to the waiting groom, then she followed him up the front steps, into the house and down a hall toward the kitchen. The fire was not inside but at the rear of the building. They ran out the kitchen door and found flames from some unidentifiable pile of material licking at the rear wall. The firemen were spooling out their hoses.

Stone and Meg watched anxiously from the rear as the firemen applied water to the burning pile, then, when that failed to stanch the flames, they produced extinguishers and sprayed it with foam. Gradually, the flames lessened and finally stopped, buried under a white mass of fire suppressant.

"Thank God," Stone muttered.

"Do you think this has something to do with Owaki?" Meg asked.

"Who else hates me enough to want to burn down my house?" Stone asked.

"Well, there must be a woman or two," Meg said, "even in England."

———

THE FIREMEN had removed their protective gear and were being fed sandwiches and tea by the kitchen staff.

"Do you know what the burning material was?" Stone asked their chief.

"Never seen anything like it," the man replied, between munches. "They had stuff like that during the war, you know, in the blitz. The devil to put out. Black stuff. Come to think of it, we were up at the motorcar factory earlier today, and I saw some black stuff piled up next to the trash-removal place. I'll have my investigator look into that."

Stone thanked them all, then he and Meg went upstairs and undressed, and she climbed into the shower with him, soaping his body and scrubbing him with a rough mitt, then he did the same for her. They toweled each other off and fell into bed.

HALF AN HOUR later, the phone buzzed. "Yes?"

"Mr. Barrington, it's Atkins. We had a call from the fire inspector, and he confirms arson, using some sort of tar-like substance as an accelerant. They're looking for Owaki."

"Tell them to try the home secretary's office in Whitehall," Stone replied. "I believe Owaki may be having a chat with that gentleman."

"Excuse me, sir, but how would you know that?"

"Like you, Carl, I have my intelligence sources."

"Of course, sir."

Stone hung up and called Dino.

"Bacchetti."

"It's Stone. Owaki set fire to my house earlier this afternoon."

"Did the bobbies catch the bastard?"

"He already had a date with the home secretary, set up by Felicity. My guess is he is, or will be soon, on his Gulfstream, winging his way west. Is there some opportunity for an international warrant?"

"I can look into that, but the evidence would have to be very strong for them to get an extradition warrant from the U.S."

"Oh, the hell with it," Stone said. "It will probably be easier to charge him with something in the States. That way he can be denied bail and will have to sit out the wait for trial in jail."

"That sounds just wonderful," Dino said. "Do you have a charge on the tip of your tongue?"

"Ah, not yet. Maybe they'll find something actionable on his airplane, when it gets to Teterboro."

"I'll give customs a call and ask them to be particularly thorough. I suppose I should give the U.S. attorney a heads-up, too, just in case."

"It couldn't hurt," Stone said. "Hang on." He covered the phone and turned to Meg. "Home tomorrow okay with you?"

"Yes. I had a call from Margo, and my board meeting is now on the day after and the closing the day after that, if they don't hate me on sight."

Stone turned back to the phone. "We'll fly tomorrow. Why

don't you and Viv come to dinner at my house, if she's back from wherever she is."

"She will be," Dino said. "Call me when you get in."

They both hung up.

"It seems we have an hour to spare before we have to dress for dinner," Stone said. "Is there something you'd like to do?"

"Oh, yes," she replied.

55

Carl Atkins called. "We have intruders on the estate," he said. "I have a party out searching for them now."

"Carl," Stone said, "please send somebody down to the airstrip and make sure the airplane is safe and fully fueled. Take the fuel caps off and look inside—they should be full right up to the top."

Atkins got on his radio and gave orders. Five minutes later he got a call back. "The airplane is secure and already fully fueled," he said, "and I've posted two men to guard it. Are you leaving immediately?"

"No, but we'll go at dawn tomorrow. We'll be there before first light to do a preflight and get the airplane positioned at the end of the runway."

"And what will be your destination?"

"Santa Maria in the Azores. We'll refuel there, then fly to St. John's, in Newfoundland, refuel, then to Teterboro. We'll be there late afternoon, eastern time."

"Got it. Everything will be ready before sunup."

Stone explained the plan to Meg.

"How far is it to the Azores?" she asked.

"Fifteen hundred nautical miles," he replied.

"Do we have that much range? It will be upwind, won't it?"

"We can always divert to Lisbon halfway if the range doesn't work. It will depend on the winds. I have at least two thousand miles of range, maybe considerably more, because of new winglets I had installed a couple of months ago."

"Okay, whatever you say."

THEY HAD a candlelit dinner in the library then packed and got to bed early. They were up at four AM and at the airstrip half an hour later. They stowed the luggage, then Stone did his preflight inspection by flashlight; they got aboard and were towed to the end of the runway, where Stone completed his checklists, then started the engines. As the first rays of the sun showed, he pushed the throttles forward and they began to roll down the runway.

Halfway down the strip, Stone saw some sort of commotion near the hangar, and there was the flash of gunfire. He gulped and kept rolling, his reasoning being that if he stopped, the airplane would surely be fired on, but if they took off he had a better chance of making it unscathed. If the airplane was hit and failed to pressurize, they could fly to Southampton, a short distance away, and land there.

Stone eased back on the yoke, and the nosewheel left the ground, followed shortly by the main landing gear. He flew southeast, checking the cabin pressure gauge until they were at ten thousand feet, along the way calling air traffic control for a clearance. They were cleared to flight level 400 and turned on course. Twenty minutes later, Stone leveled off, set the throttles for cruise, and let the airspeed climb. When they were at 400 knots, he checked the range ring, which showed they would reach Santa Maria with a 150-mile reserve of fuel.

"We're going to be fine on fuel," he said to Meg.

"Is there any way Owaki can find out where we're going?"

"Yes, but we'll be in Santa Maria, refueled, and off again before he could give chase."

"What about St. John's? Could he have us met there?"

"Half an hour out of St. John's I'll change our destination to Gander. We'll be in and out of there in half an hour, and he wouldn't dare try to pull anything at Teterboro. The police would be all over him. Fred and the Strategic Services people will meet us there, and escort us to the house."

"Good. My meeting with the co-op board is tomorrow morning."

THEY ROLLED into Stone's garage at five PM, tired and happy to be home. Bob was beside himself with joy to have Stone back, and Joan was pretty happy, too.

"I hear you had some aggravation across the pond," she said. "Don't worry, nobody's tried to burn down this house, yet."

"I'm glad to hear it."

"Dino called."

"Call him back and tell him we're still expecting him and Viv for dinner, and let Helene know they're coming."

Joan went to her work.

Stone pulled the drapes in the master bedroom and achieved something like darkness. They fell asleep without further ado—unusual, because they had become accustomed to further ado.

STONE HAD been asleep for an hour when the phone rang. Automatically, he picked up. "What?"

"It's Dino. I thought you'd like to know that Owaki's Gulfstream 650 landed at Teterboro about seven PM, and a squadron of customs people greeted them. They took the airplane apart, and in the rear luggage compartment, under the floor panels, they found half a dozen Kalashnikovs and a dozen handguns, plus ammo. They took Owaki in."

"How long before he's out?"

"That depends on you."

"On me?"

"Yeah, there'll be a bail hearing at eleven tomorrow morning at the federal courthouse, and we need you to testify to your knowledge of Owaki. If customs and the FBI can get the judge to deny bail, he'll spend the next few months on Rikers Island."

"I think that might be character-building for him," Stone said.

"In the big courtroom. Don't be late."

"I won't." He hung up and went back to sleep.

EARLY THE FOLLOWING MORNING he felt a hand creeping up his thigh. He glanced at the bedside clock: 9:30. "Hold it right there, missy," he said. "I'm due in federal court at eleven, so if you want to come, get dressed quickly." He freed himself, leaped out of bed, and thence into a shower. By ten-fifteen, munching on a muffin, he was in the rear seat of the Bentley with Meg and headed downtown.

At a quarter to eleven his phone rang.

"It's Dino. Where the fuck are you?"

"Enjoying the traffic in your fine city. Why didn't you give me a motorcycle escort?"

"Get your ass here, pronto!"

56

S tone got out of the Bentley, leaving Fred at the wheel and Meg, who didn't want to be present in the court-room, in the rear seat. He walked into the courtroom at the stroke of eleven on the big clock over the bench. Dino glared at him from the front row of spectator seats and waved him forward.

Stone took a seat. He saw Owaki's back ahead of him, next to a silver-haired attorney in a ten-thousand-dollar suit.

"It's about fucking time," Dino growled under his breath.

"What are you doing here anyway?" Stone asked. "You're not a fed."

"Once in a while I just like to enjoy myself, you know?"

The bailiff called for all to rise, and the judge entered the courtroom and sat down. "Call the first case," she said, and the clerk yelled, "Bail hearing for one Selwyn Owakow."

Stone suppressed a laugh, and the judge looked at him oddly. Stone had known her for a long time, but not for some years. He gave her a slight nod.

She turned toward the federal prosecutor. "Counsel?"

The prosecutor stood. "Your Honor, the defendant, one Selwyn Owaki—I believe I have the name right—last night arrived at Teterboro Airport in New Jersey aboard a Gulfstream 650, an aircraft valued at something on the order of sixty million dollars, upon which a search warrant, signed by Your Honor, was served by the United States Customs Service. Their search was fruitful, producing some two dozen illegal weapons, among them Russian automatic assault weapons. The defendant is an infamous weapons dealer, and extremely wealthy. He owns three jet aircraft with intercontinental range, the Gulfstream having a range of more than eight thousand nautical miles, and he has large quantities of cash in banks around the world. He has two passports, and thus is a monumental candidate for risk of flight, as well as being of poor character. We request that he be held without bail until trial."

"Do you have any witnesses to call on the question of risk of flight or character?"

"Indeed I do, Judge. I call Mr. Stone Barrington, who is a member of the New York State Bar and who has experience of Mr. Owaki's character and conduct."

"Swear the witness," the judge said.

Stone took the oath and had a seat.

The prosecutor consulted his notes. "Mr. Barrington, how long have you known Mr. Selwyn Owaki?"

"Too long," Stone replied, glancing at his watch. "Almost thirty-six hours."

The courtroom burst into laughter, and the judge smirked. "All right," she said, "get on with it."

"And how did you come to make Mr. Owaki's acquaintance?"

"I have a home in England, and I was there for a few days of relaxation when Mr. Owaki appeared at my door, uninvited. By way of context, I should explain that Mr. Owaki engineered the theft of some very valuable software belonging to a client of mine, and in the process, two murders were committed."

Owaki's attorney was on his feet. "Objection, facts not in evidence."

"Goes to character," the prosecutor said.

"This is not a trial, I'll allow it."

"The software was recovered, and I removed it and my client from the country after receiving threats from henchmen of Mr. Owaki's. To my surprise, he turned up there, in England, where he had already bought a factory to manufacture the product of the stolen software, which certainly goes to intent. He offered either to buy the software or sell the factory. When my client declined to sell the software and made a derisory offer for the factory, Mr. Owaki became incensed and began to make vile threats. I asked him to leave, and he did so angrily. Less than an hour later a fire was set at my home, which the local fire department declared to be arson. I made plans to depart England the following morning before dawn, and gunshots were fired at my airplane while it was still on the private runway."

"And you attribute these actions to Mr. Owaki?"

"I have no other enemies who would threaten my life and that of my client."

"Do you know whether Mr. Owaki had any interaction with the authorities during his stay in Britain?"

"I am reliably informed that he was deported from the United Kingdom yesterday by the home secretary, with immediate effect. He was escorted to the airport, put aboard his airplane, then he left for Teterboro, where U.S. Customs met him and served their warrant."

"I have no further evidence at this time," the prosecutor said.

"Mr. Kenneth Conway, I believe," the judge said to Owaki's attorney. "Do you have any questions for the witness?"

The lawyer rose. "None, Your Honor, but I have a statement."

"Proceed."

"Your Honor, Mr. Selwyn Owaki is widely known around the world as a distributor of defense materials to legitimately constituted governments. He holds a United States passport, has maintained a home in New York City for many years, and has been a model citizen. This is the first occasion on which he has been arrested. He is no risk of flight and will willingly surrender his passport while awaiting trial."

"All of them?" the judge asked, getting a laugh.

"He has only two."

"That we know of," the prosecutor interjected, gaining a warning glance from the judge.

"What's the other one?" she asked.

"Turkish, Your Honor."

"Is Mr. Owaki a native of either the United States or Turkey?"

"No, Your Honor. He is naturalized in both."

"Why does he have so many airplanes?" she asked.

"He does most of his business internationally and must always have an aircraft available."

"Do either of you wish to call Mr. Owaki to testify?"

"No, Your Honor," the prosecutor said.

"No," the defense attorney replied.

"Do either of you have any other evidence to submit in this matter?"

"No," the defense attorney said.

"Yes, Your Honor," the prosecutor said. He walked forward holding a thick file. "This contains facts about Mr. Owaki and his businesses from many sources. Your Honor might find it interesting reading. I have a copy for the defense." His assistant handed one to Conway.

The judge opened the file and leafed through it for a minute or two. "Very well," she said, "I'll rule."

Both attorneys and Owaki stood.

"The motion to deny bail until trial is granted. The defendant is remanded to the custody of the Federal Detention Center until trial." She leafed through her calendar. "I will set a date of three months from today at ten AM for trial," she said.

"The defense requests leave to file an appeal," the attorney said.

"File away," the judge said, banging her gavel. "This case is adjourned for the duration."

A court officer handcuffed Owaki and led him away. The prosecutor came over to Stone, shook his hand, and thanked him.

"How do you rate the chances of his appeal?" Stone asked.

"Not very good," the man replied.

"Let's get out of here," Dino said.

57

Stone and Dino walked out of the courthouse and down the long front steps. Stone's Bentley was idling at the curb, and Dino's official SUV pulled up behind it as they approached.

"I don't guess you need a lift," Dino said.

"No, Fred and Meg are waiting for me," Stone replied, then he stopped and looked at his car. Fred was slumped over the steering wheel, and the rear seat was empty. The driver's window was down; Fred liked his fresh air. "Hang on," Stone said. He opened the driver's door, and Fred fell into his arms.

"Do we need an ambulance?" Dino asked.

Stone examined Fred's head but found no wounds; then he saw a drop of blood trickle down his neck. "We're going to need an ambulance and a lot more," Stone said. "Meg has been taken."

Dino ran to his car and gave the driver a request for an ambulance, a description of Meg, and orders for an APB, then he returned to Stone. "An APB is out, and an ambulance is on its way."

Stone felt his cell phone vibrate in his pocket, and he looked at the phone. The caller was Fred Flicker. "We've got contact," Stone said, then answered the call. "Yes?"

"Do I have to tell you what we want?" a voice said.

"Yes, you do," Stone replied. He wanted to hear more of the voice.

"We want the thumb drive. As soon as we've verified the authenticity—and the efficacy—of the software we will return the lady unharmed. The time is now noon. We will expect a call from you by two PM stating that you are ready to turn over the drive. If it is not in our hands by two-thirty PM, you may locate pieces of the lady's body in the East River. Do you understand?"

"Yes," Stone said, and the man hung up.

"It was Stanislav Beria," Stone said. "You can add him to your APB—six-one, a hundred and seventy, dark hair."

"Are you sure?"

"I thought I recognized his voice, and as he continued talking, I was sure of it."

"What does he want?"

"A thumb drive containing the software of the designs and specifications of Meg's self-driving car."

"Where is it?"

"On a thumb drive in my office safe."

"How much time do we have?"

"He wants me to call him on Fred's phone by two PM. He says she'll be dead by two-thirty if we haven't handed over the thumb drive by then."

By the time the ambulance arrived, Fred was awake and standing up, though he appeared a bit woozy. He waved off medical attention. "I'll be all right in a few minutes," he said, "nothing wrong with me that fresh air won't fix."

"Come with me," Dino said. Dino ordered the detective in the front passenger seat of his car to drive Stone's car, which was still running, put Fred in the passenger seat, then he gave the detective Stone's address.

The car moved out, and Dino made a call, reinforcing the APB and adding Stanislav Beria to it. "Also, post a car and two men outside the Russian UN mission, in case Beria returns there."

Stone tugged at his sleeve.

"What?"

"Add the gorilla Ivanov to the APB—six-three or -four, two-fifty, black hair, deep five o'clock shadow."

Dino did so, then hung up. "Didn't we arrest that guy?"

"Yes, but he got released, and you couldn't hold Beria because he holds a diplomatic passport."

"What phone number did they give you?"

"They took Fred's phone."

"What's his number?"

Stone gave it to him.

Dino made another call and said to whoever answered, "This is Bacchetti I need a location on a cell phone number." He gave them the number. "How long? All right, I'll call it then." He hung up. "They need ten minutes to get set up, and I have to keep them on the line for two minutes."

They continued on toward Stone's house, occasionally using the siren to get through the traffic.

"Dino . . ." Stone said.

"Shut up, I'm thinking."

Stone shut up.

"Okay," Dino said finally. "Whaddaya want?"

Stone thought about it. "I forget."

"I've got a plan," Dino said, then told him what it was.

"That sounds great, Dino, but what if it doesn't work?"

"Then Meg is dead," Dino replied.

"I'm not willing to risk that."

"Where was the thumb drive before it got into your pocket?"

"In the library safe at my house in England."

"And you said, when you were testifying, that Owaki had been thrown out of the country?"

"Yes."

"What about Beria and Ivanov?"

"I don't know whether they were in England. I saw only Owaki, at my house and when his luggage was being loaded into his car."

"I don't understand," Dino said. "Luggage?"

"Owaki was staying at the Arrington hotel next door to my house, and I called the manager and had him thrown out. Meg and I were riding by on horseback, and I saw a couple of men loading bags into Owaki's car."

"Was either of them Beria or Ivanov?"

"I don't think so, I got only a glimpse of them."

"I wish you were more observant," Dino said with disgust.

"Gee, I'm sorry, I didn't know this was going to come up. What is it you want in England?"

"Somebody who can go to your house, open the safe, and get the thumb drive."

"But the thumb drive isn't there—it's in my safe."

"Not *that* thumb drive, dummy!"

"I don't get it."

Dino's phone rang. "Bacchetti. Okay, I'm calling the number in thirty seconds. He hung up, glanced at his watch, and tapped in Fred's number. At thirty seconds, he pressed the call button. "Here we go," he said. "It's ringing."

58

Stone watched Dino's face as the phone rang. It betrayed no emotion.

"Hello," Dino said. "I'm calling on behalf of Stone Barrington. What is it you want?" He listened carefully, nodding. "Is that all?" He listened again. "I'm afraid there'll be a delay. That item is not in this country." He listened. "The item is in a safe in the library of Mr. Barrington's house in England."

Stone could hear an angry voice replying.

Dino continued to listen. "Hold on, I'll find out how it can be opened." He left the phone near his lips as he talked to Stone. "Who knows how to get into that safe?"

"I do," Stone replied.

"No, I mean somebody else who can get into it—somebody in England."

"The manager of the estate, Major Bugg, has the combination. I will instruct him to open it on presentation of a password."

"And what is the password?"

"Let me think . . ."

"Not too long," Dino whispered, his hand over the phone.

"The password is Arrington."

"Did you get that?" Dino asked. He spelled the name carefully. "Now, when will you release Ms. Harmon?" He listened. "Surely Mr. Owaki has someone in England who can pop over to the house and see Major Bugg. Well, how long then? I would like to point out that Mr. Barrington has followed your instructions explicitly. You have no further reason to hold Ms. Harmon." He listened. "By the way, what is your name?"

Stone heard the click when they hung up.

"Well," Dino said, "that should be long enough for my people to get a location. By the way, Stone, you'd better call Major Bugg and ask him to put a thumb drive in your safe, and to open it for whoever gives him the password." Dino dialed a number on his own cell phone.

Stone called Major Bugg, who was probably having his tea interrupted, and told him what must be done.

"What is a thumb drive?" Bugg asked.

"It's a small computer device about the size of a thumb, hence the name."

"I don't have one. Where would I get it?"

"At a computer shop. Is there one in the village?"

"Yes, a small one."

"It's a small device. Could you send someone there immediately and buy one of the largest capacity available?"

"Yes, of course."

"I'll call you in a few minutes, and we'll do a data transfer from my computer to the thumb drive."

"Yes, my assistant knows how to do that, I believe."

"Thank you, Major Bugg."

Dino was still on the phone. "Keep that connection alive," he said to his officer. "Don't let it get away from you." He hung up.

"Did they get a location for Fred's cell phone?"

"Yes. It's a few feet from your house."

"What?"

"Apparently in a car, parked in front of your house. They'll track it, if it moves." He spoke to his driver. "You can keep the siren on, now. How long?"

"Ten minutes, if the traffic isn't too bad."

"Okay." Dino called his office and ordered a car situated at each end of Stone's block, then he sat back in his seat and appeared to relax.

"Why are you so relaxed?" Stone asked.

"I'm always relaxed when I've done all I can do. Can you think of anything else I should do, right this minute?"

"No, I guess not."

"Then I'm going to relax. I might even take a nap." He put his head against the back of the seat and closed his eyes.

"I wish I could relax like that," Stone said.

"It takes practice."

Dino's cell phone rang, and he answered it. "Bacchetti." He listened for a moment. "Well, shit," he said. "Call me back when you've reestablished— What? Okay." He hung up. "They lost the signal when the guy hung up. I'll call it again." He pressed the button and gazed out the window. "Hello? This is the same person who phoned a moment ago. Do you remember me? Yes, that's the one. Listen, Major Bugg has left his office for the day, and someone has been sent to his home to get him to return to the house. It's going to take about an hour, since he lives half an hour away from the house. Have you got that? Okay, then let's talk again in an hour, unless you'd just like to chat for a while— I've got plenty of time." Dino put down the phone. "Goodbye, Mr. Beria." He hung up.

"I'm not surprised they lost the connection," Stone said. "Were they able to get a fix again? Are they still sitting in front of my house?"

Dino's phone rang. "Bacchetti. Which way? Are you on it? Thanks." Dino sat back and relaxed again. "The car left your house and turned downtown on Second Avenue. We are in pursuit."

"But you've lost the connection again?"

"Yeah, but he said to call back in a couple of minutes so they can get a new location." Dino put his head back onto the head-rest and appeared to doze.

Stone waited impatiently, then jabbed Dino with an elbow.

Dino didn't open his eyes. "Yeah?"

"It's been a couple of minutes—make the call."

"It hasn't been more than half a minute," Dino said.

"I timed it with my watch," Stone lied.

"Oh, all right." Dino called the number. "Hi, Mr. Beria, how's everything going?" He held the phone away from his ear while the man on the other end shouted. "Why shouldn't I call you Mr. Beria?" Dino said. "That's your name, isn't it?" Another torrent of shouting. "I mean, have you sent somebody to the Barrington house in England to get the thumb drive? Well, he should be back at the house inside an hour. How's the weather where you are? Oh, good, I hear it's raining like hell in England, but then, it usually is. Tell your guy to drive carefully; those country roads can get slippery when they're wet." Dino put down his phone. "They hung up again. Some people just can't carry on a conversation, you know?"

"Yes, I know," Stone said.

Dino's phone rang. "Bacchetti. Did you get a new location? Why the hell would they do that? Okay, I'll call them again in a couple of minutes." He hung up.

"Now what?"

"Now they're on First Avenue, headed uptown. Every time they hang up we lose the connection. I'll call back in a couple of minutes, and this time I want to see you timing it."

Stone pressed the start button on his Rolex Daytona. "Okay, I'm timing it."

"Let me know when it's two minutes," he said.

"I'll do that," Stone said. "And we need to go to my house."

"Why?"

"I want to send Bugg some data from the thumb drive so when they check it out, it will appear to work."

59

Meg woke up slowly, realizing that she was in the luggage compartment of an SUV, with a pull-out cover closed over her head, cutting out much of the light. Her hands were secured behind her, her handbag chain around her neck, and her ankles were taped together. Her handbag lay about an inch from her nose. There were two things she immediately wanted from the handbag: a little sewing kit, and a small .380 pistol that Stone had given her from his safe when she had complained about feeling in danger. She would get some satisfaction from telling Stone that she had been right.

She heard a cell phone ring and one end of a conversation; she supposed Stone was on the other end. The talker hung up and said angrily, "He keeps calling me Mr. Beria."

"Why not?" another male voice asked. "It's your name."

"Yes, but he's not supposed to know it." Then for reasons unknown to her, they switched to Russian.

Meg managed to get her small handbag between her teeth and drag it to a spot near her head, in the center of the compartment that contained her.

WHEN THEY REACHED the house, Stone told Fred to put the Bentley in the garage, just to give him something to do. Then he took Dino into his office.

"What's going on?" Joan asked as they passed her desk.

"Beria has taken Meg," he replied, and continued into his office. He sat at his desk and turned to his computer, then glanced at his watch. "Time's up," he said to Dino. "Call Fred's number again."

Dino pressed the button and waited for an answer, which came quickly. "All right, Mr. Beria, we're making progress. Major Bugg has been summoned and is on the way to Mr. Barrington's house. He should be there in about half an hour. It's still raining hard over there, by the way, so let's hope he doesn't drive into a ditch. Okay, okay, I'll call you in half an hour." He hung up. "Beria doesn't like chatting with me."

"How do you know it's raining in England?"

"It's always raining in England," Dino said. "Also, I needed something to talk about to keep him on the line long enough for my people to get another fix."

Stone called Major Bugg's cell phone. "Mr. Barrington? I have obtained a thumb drive from the computer shop in the village. What shall I do with it?"

"Please plug it into your computer's USB receptacle," Stone said. "I want to send you some files." He took the thumb drive from his office safe, plugged it into his computer, and established contact with Bugg's machine. He chose the first file from each of four sections of the files on his computer and transmitted them to Bugg's computer as different documents. "There," he said, "all done. Now please take the thumb drive to the safe and lock it inside. Someone will come for it, then you can open the safe and hand it over."

"Of course, sir," Bugg said. "Will you be calling again?"

"When the transaction is complete and the person has left, follow him out and get a description of his car and the number plate before he drives away."

"Yes, sir. Are you sure you don't wish me to capture the man?"

"Not necessary, just call me back with the car's description and the number plate."

"Yes, sir."

MEG MANAGED to maneuver into a sitting position, with her back against the rear of the SUV's backseat, and her handbag near her hands. She managed to unzip it and find the sewing kit, then unzip that and find a small pair of scissors. Cutting the duct tape that held her hands was harder than she had expected, but she managed to free her hands, then her feet. She then opened the handbag, found the small pistol, pumped a round into the chamber, and set the safety. Now she examined the latch of the rear door of the vehicle and decided she could open it from the inside. She tried to relax while she waited for the car to stop for a traffic light.

"WHERE WAS the last fix on Fred's cell phone?" Stone asked.

"While you were talking to Bugg they seemed to be heading for the FDR Drive," Dino said. That highway ran along the East River, north and south.

"All right, time to call them again," Stone said.

Dino made the call. "Hi, Mr. Beria," he said. "It's me again, remember? Well, sure I'm hard to forget. I just wanted you to know that Major Bugg has arrived at Mr. Barrington's house and is waiting there for your man to come and get the thumb drive. No, no, he's unarmed. He's happy to give your man the drive. He won't be a problem. How are you doing? Are you making progress toward where you're going to let Ms. Harmon out of the car? Thanks, I appreciate that." Dino hung up.

"He hung up again, but that should have been long enough for a fix. He says he'll let Meg go as soon as his man in England calls and says the drive checks out." Dino's phone rang again. "Bacchetti. No shit? All right, I want every unmarked vehicle you can muster there as soon as possible. No sirens or lights, and don't bunch up in a pack. Go!" He hung up.

"Where is Meg?" Stone asked.

"Apparently Beria left the FDR Drive and drove onto Randall's Island, in the East River, and now he's on Wards Island, where the garbage collectors' school is."

"The garbage collectors have a school?"

"Well, sure, they've got to learn to make the truck work and how to load it properly and how to empty it, and all that."

"Who knew?" Stone said.

THE SUV had not stopped, but it had slowed down a lot. Meg decided not to wait for it to come to a halt; she would just roll out onto the ground and hope for the best. She reached for the door latch and struggled with it, but it didn't work. She tried to retract the cover over her head so she would have access to the rear seat, but that didn't work, either. She would have to wait until someone unlocked the rear hatch from the outside.

The SUV had made a turn and was now on a rougher road with lots of potholes. Where the hell could she be? Then she heard brush scraping along the sides of the vehicle.

The car stopped, and she could hear the two men arguing, still in Russian. She wished she knew what the hell they were talking about.

She heard the two front doors open, then slam shut. The two men continued to shout at each other as they walked along the two sides of the vehicle toward the rear hatch.

Meg scrunched down with her feet against the hatch and her head against the back of the rear seat, then flipped the safety with her thumb and held the weapon in both hands, pointed at the hatch.

Then the hatch opened and daylight flooded in.

60

The rear hatch swung up, and two men stood there, staring at the gun in her hand.

"Kill her," the slim one said to the gorilla. He took a step toward the car.

Meg recalled something Stone had said: "Shoot first, think later." She aimed between his eyes and very deliberately squeezed the trigger. Her aim was off; a hole appeared over his left eyebrow, and his legs seemed to collapse. He fell below the tailgate, out of sight. Meg swung left to fire at the other man, but he was not there. She heard a scrambling in the bushes beside the car. Still holding the gun, she got herself out the rear door of the SUV. The gorilla was lying on his back, blood pooling in his left eye socket. The other eye stared straight ahead, looking surprised. She thought about putting another bullet in his head, but thought better of it. He seemed dead enough.

———

BERIA RAN STRAIGHT through a thick line of tall shrubs and heard vehicles coming closer. He plunged into more bushes on the other side of the road and kept going, flailing at the brush to keep from putting his eyes out. He kept on and on, then, exhausted, collapsed and fell, still in thick brush.

MEG PATTED the big man's pockets, looking for a phone, then found it on the ground near his body. She picked it up and dialed Stone's number.

"BERIA?" Stone said.

"Hardly," Meg replied. "How did you confuse him with me?"

"Meg?" he cried. "You've got Fred's phone—did they let you go?"

"Hardly," she replied. "I freed myself and got out the gun you gave me, and when they opened the rear hatch, I shot the big one in the head. The other one moved too quickly for me, so he's out in the bushes somewhere. I could hear him thrashing about. I'm on a rough road with large, thick bushes on both sides. Apart from that, I've no idea where I am."

She could hear Dino say, "I've got another fix, on Wards Island."

"Meg," Stone said, "we know where you are. It's a place called

Wards Island, in the East River. A whole lot of police are coming for you now, so just stand in the road and flag them down."

"All right."

"Oh, and put the gun away. They'll be pretty wired, and you can give it to them later, when it won't cause them to shoot you."

"Okay, done. It's in my handbag. Oh, here comes a car!"

"You're safe, kiddo. Tell them to bring you home."

Dino got on the phone and issued instructions to secure the scene and to bring the woman to him. He hung up and slapped Stone on the back. "We got her back, didn't we?"

"I guess we did," Stone said. He phoned Major Bugg. "You can stand down, now. Everything has been resolved here."

"Actually," the major said, "everything's been resolved here, too. Your man arrived, and he took a swing at me with a large pistol, so I took it away from him and gave him a stern rap on the head. He's bleeding on the carpet, I'm afraid, but we'll deal with that. I've already called an ambulance."

"Good work, Major," Stone said.

STANISLAV BERIA managed to get across the bridge to Randall's Island and hail a cab. He gave the driver an address two blocks from his mission, a building occupied by the Russian intelligence service. He knew the mission would be watched.

"Jeez, mister," the cabbie said, "what happened to you? Your face is all scratched up."

"I got lost," Beria said. "Now get me out of here."

———————

"DID YOUR MEN find Beria?" Stone asked Dino, as he hung up his phone.

"Not yet," Dino said. "He hasn't returned to the mission."

Stone picked up his phone and dialed a number in Washington, D.C.

"Hello," Holly Barker said. Holly was the current secretary of state, under President Katharine Lee.

"Hello, it's Stone."

"What a surprise! How long has it been, a month?"

"Oh, not as long as that."

"Hang on a minute, I just got in from the office. Let me pee and pour myself a drink, and I'll be right back." She put him on hold.

Stone put a hand over the phone. "I'm on hold," he said to Dino. "Holly is peeing."

Finally, she came back online. "There, that's better. I'm in a comfortable chair in my study, with my shoes off, my feet up, and a stiff Knob Creek in my fist. How the hell are you? What's going on?"

"We've had quite a day up here. A client of mine was kidnapped by some Russian thugs, but we got her back."

"Any Russian thugs I know?"

"A guy named Stanislav Beria and his thug, name of Ivanov."

"Beria? That piece of shit? He's nothing but diplomatically protected trouble. I've been looking for an excuse to deport him."

"Maybe I can help out there. He and his thug disabled Fred and took my client, trying to steal plans for a driverless car her company has built."

"I've read about that. Is she all right?"

"The police have her now. They're bringing her to my office. Is what I just told you enough to get Beria deported? Oh, I forgot to mention that Beria and Ivanov murdered two American citizens a few days ago."

"Consider it done. I'll have him declared persona non grata inside an hour. You want Ivanov gone, too?"

"He's already gone—bullet to the head."

"Well, that saves us some trouble, doesn't it?"

"Certainly does."

"Better let me hang up and get the paperwork started before everybody leaves the office. I came home early with a headache, but it's gone, now. I'll call you back tomorrow morning?"

"Okay."

Holly hung up.

Meg rushed into Stone's office. He rose to greet her, and she flung her arms around him. "God, I'm glad to see you." She hugged Dino. "You, too."

"Are you at all hurt?"

"I've got a headache—they drugged me—but I woke up sooner than they planned."

"Did you really shoot Ivanov?"

"I shot the first guy I saw. He didn't have time to introduce himself. Did you catch the other one?"

"Beria?" Dino asked. "Not yet, but he'll seek diplomatic shelter, and Stone just got him declared persona non grata by the State Department. He'll be out of the country tomorrow for good."

Meg fished her pistol out of her purse and handed it to Dino. "I guess I should give this to the cops."

Dino pocketed the weapon.

"What about Owaki?" Meg asked Stone. "How did the hearing go?"

"Couldn't have gone better," Stone said. "He's in jail pending trial, and that will be months. They've got him cold on a weapons charge, and the U.S. attorney will get him twenty years on that."

"He'll probably plead out and serve ten," Dino said, "but the feds have grounds to get his citizenship revoked, and they'll kick him out of the country permanently."

BERIA ENTERED a key code to the front door of an anonymous East Side town house a couple of blocks from the Russian mission and let himself in. A guard was waiting and he was shown in immediately to see the duty officer.

Beria presented his diplomatic passport. "The ambassador called," the officer said, dropping the passport into a drawer and closing it firmly. "The State Department has declared you persona non grata. You will be driven to your flat, where you will pack your bags, then to JFK Airport. You're on an eleven PM flight to Moscow, where you will answer to a personnel board for your actions."

"Owaki will take care of all that. I'll be living in London or Paris in a week."

"Mr. Owaki is in the Federal Detention Center, without bail, awaiting trial on certain weapons charges. I think you are more likely to be residing in some small town in Siberia, rather than London or Paris, for the remainder of your career." He motioned to an aide. "Put him in a car and get him out of here."

"I'M HUNGRY," Meg said. "I never got lunch, and I'm dying for a drink."

"I can do that," Stone replied.

AUTHOR'S NOTE

I am happy to hear from readers, but you should know that if you write to me in care of my publisher, three to six months will pass before I receive your letter, and when it finally arrives it will be one among many, and I will not be able to reply.

However, if you have access to the Internet, you may visit my website at www.stuartwoods.com, where there is a button for sending me e-mail. So far, I have been able to reply to all my e-mail, and I will continue to try to do so.

If you send me an e-mail and do not receive a reply, it is probably because you are among an alarming number of people who have entered their e-mail address incorrectly in their mail software. I have many of my replies returned as undeliverable.

Remember: e-mail, reply; snail mail, no reply.

When you e-mail, please do not send attachments, as I never

open them. They can take twenty minutes to download, and they often contain viruses.

Please do not place me on your mailing lists for funny stories, prayers, political causes, charitable fund-raising, petitions, or sentimental claptrap. I get enough of that from people I already know. Generally speaking, when I get e-mail addressed to a large number of people, I immediately delete it without reading it.

Please do not send me your ideas for a book, as I have a policy of writing only what I myself invent. If you send me story ideas, I will immediately delete them without reading them. If you have a good idea for a book, write it yourself, but I will not be able to advise you on how to get it published. Buy a copy of *Writer's Market* at any bookstore; that will tell you how.

Anyone with a request concerning events or appearances may e-mail it to me or send it to: Publicity Department, Penguin Random House LLC, 375 Hudson Street, New York, NY 10014.

Those ambitious folk who wish to buy film, dramatic, or television rights to my books should contact Matthew Snyder, Creative Artists Agency, 9830 Wilshire Boulevard, Beverly Hills, CA 98212-1825.

Those who wish to make offers for rights of a literary nature should contact Anne Sibbald, Janklow & Nesbit, 445 Park Avenue, New York, NY 10022. (Note: This is not an invitation for you to send her your manuscript or to solicit her to be your agent.)

If you want to know if I will be signing books in your city, please visit my website, www.stuartwoods.com, where the tour schedule will be published a month or so in advance. If you wish me to do a book signing in your locality, ask your favorite bookseller to contact his Penguin representative or the Penguin publicity department with the request.

If you find typographical or editorial errors in my book and feel an irresistible urge to tell someone, please write to Sara Minnich at Penguin's address above. Do not e-mail your discoveries to me, as I will already have learned about them from others.

A list of my published works appears in the front of this book and on my website. All the novels are still in print in paperback and can be found at or ordered from any bookstore. If you wish to obtain hardcover copies of earlier novels or of the two nonfiction books, a good used-book store or one of the online bookstores can help you find them. Otherwise, you will have to go to a great many garage sales.